**REMO WAS NOW OFF█████ ████████ ████
OF SINANJU.**

Since Chiun was still a█████ ████████ ██████
of assassin, he had assumed the seldom-used
honorary title of Reigning Master of Sinanju
Emeritus. As such, he retained in all but the
most formal circumstances the title of "Master
of Sinanju."

"Won't that get confusing?" Remo asked. "Two
Masters of Sinanju at one time?"

"You will actually be Master of Sinanju," Chiun
explained. "I will merely hold the title of Master
of Sinanju. Or do you wish to deny a dying old
man the respect he has earned? Especially
given all he has to endure training a certain
title-grubbing white lump who shall remain
nameless."

"You don't look like you're dying."

"Says nameless you."

"Okay I give. You're Master of Sinanju. You
happy? Now get off my case."

Created by Murphy & Sapir

THE Destroyer™

UNNATURAL SELECTION

A GOLD EAGLE BOOK FROM
W🦅RLDWIDE.

TORONTO • NEW YORK • LONDON
AMSTERDAM • PARIS • SYDNEY • HAMBURG
STOCKHOLM • ATHENS • TOKYO • MILAN
MADRID • WARSAW • BUDAPEST • AUCKLAND

First edition April 2003

ISBN 0-373-63246-0

Special thanks and acknowledgment to
James Mullaney for his contribution to this work.

UNNATURAL SELECTION

Again, for www.sinanju.com and www.sinanju.net—
unofficial, but fun just the same; as well as for
www.sinanju.ca and Cam Bailey, proprietor of same

And for the Glorious House of Sinanju which, regrettably,
for the last time recognizes the e-mail address
housinan@aol.com.

Many thanks for five fun-filled years. Happy trails to you...

1

In the last hour Burt Solare's intestines still worked; while his heart still pumped blood, his lungs and other organs toiled in concert—while all that comprised the inner workings of Burt Solare remained hidden inside his delicate flesh shell, as nature had intended—Burt Solare found he had a problem somewhere along the miles of compressed tubing that was his intestinal tract.

"Dammit, this ulcer's gonna kill me."

Check that. Make it two problems.

"Helen? Dammit, Helen, where the hell's the Maalox?"

At 220 pounds, five foot six inches and standing on tiptoes on a fragile rattan chair, Burt was a looming figure pawing through the cabinets in the upstairs bathroom of his Lubec, Maine, home. Given his size and disposition, he looked like a hungry bear rummaging for food in an abandoned vacation cabin.

"What's with all the hollering?" Helen Solare said as she stomped into the big room, the pink fur fringe of her satin dressing gown swirling around her thick ankles. She stopped dead near the Jacuzzi.

A mouth surrounded by too much Purple Sunset

lipstick dropped open in horror the instant her eyes, decorated with Mediterranean Midnight Blue, saw the boxes of spare toothpaste and Gold Bond powder that had been dumped on the floor near the buckling legs of Burt's chair. A flung box of cotton swabs nearly struck her midpermanent.

"What the hell are you looking for, you maniac?" Helen demanded, ducking below the box. It struck the aqua ceramic tile behind her, exploding on impact. Q-tips flew everywhere.

"The Maalox! The goddamn Maalox, Helen. Where the hell did you hide it this time?"

Burt flung a fistful of unused toothbrushes over his shoulder. They clattered into the porcelain basin.

"Stop it!" Helen screeched, flinging up her hands. "Just stop where you are!"

On his chair Burt wheeled on his wife. His eyes were bloodshot and black-rimmed. In his right hand was a jar of blemish cream. In his left, a can of hairspray—one of dozens Helen went through every month.

"Where?" he barked.

Sandals flapping angrily against her pumiced heels, Helen marched over to the medicine cabinet. Ripping open the door, she stuck a handful of Lee Press-Ons inside. They reappeared clutching a familiar blue bottle.

"Next time try looking under your nose," she snapped.

"Give it here." Burt scurried down to the floor, snatching the bottle from Helen's hand.

He popped the lid and dumped the Maalox down

his throat. His Adam's apple bobbed gratefully as the chalky liquid rolled down into his burning belly.

"You could ask before you throw one of your fits," Helen complained as she surveyed the bathroom. It looked as if a hurricane had blown through the cupboards.

"I wouldn't have to ask if you left the damn stuff where it belonged," Burt panted between swigs.

As he gulped, Helen stooped to pick up a toothbrush. Halfway to the floor, she changed her mind. Straightening, she planted two fists on her ample hips.

"No. I am *not* picking this up."

"Big surprise," Burt grunted. Burping, he capped the bottle. Wiping blue gunk from his lips with the sleeve of his shirt, he headed out the door.

"I'm not kidding," Helen warned, storming into their bedroom after him. "*You* made that mess. *You* can pick it up."

"Have Mrs. Parkasian do it."

Burt dropped onto the edge of their queen-size bed. He began pulling on a pair of white athletic socks.

"Oh, no. I'm not letting that old bat see that mess. She'll tell everyone in town I'm a slob. That's all I need. They already look at me like I'm goddamned Zsa-Zsa."

"What do you care, Helen?" Burt said as he stuffed his feet into his sneakers. The antacid wasn't working. His belly still burned. "In a month you'll never see anyone in this town again."

Helen dropped into the chair at her dressing table. "You're still going through with this?" she asked morosely.

"Yes," Burt said firmly.

"Only an idiot runs away from a million-dollar business," she suggested.

"Then sue me, Helen. I'm an idiot."

Burt pushed himself from the bed. On heavy feet he trudged across the room. At the door he stopped. One hand rested on the doorknob as the other gripped his potbelly.

"Geez, it feels like something's eating my guts for lunch."

"Why don't you get medication for that thing?" Helen said impatiently. "They've got stuff that'll get rid of ulcers now."

"They'd put me on pills or something." Burt winced. "It's not natural."

"Oh, and I suppose it's natural to bail out of a million-dollar business?" Helen hollered as he headed out the door. "Is that natural, Burt? Tell me, because I'm *dying* to know."

And rather than argue with the cause of fifty percent of his ulcer, Burt Solare quietly shut the door.

ALTHOUGH BRISK, there was finally a tiny hint of warmer weather in the Northeast. Burt left his jacket unzipped as he headed down his front walk. Damp pine needles stained the slate.

He was on his way to visit the cause of the other fifty percent of his ulcer for what would be the last time.

The air was refreshing. Beyond the gate he took a few deep breaths into the pit of his ailing stomach.

A sudden cold breeze tipped the tall pine trees.

Burt cut across the driveway and struck off down the rutted dirt road.

The surrounding forest made him feel as if he were the only man on Earth. As he walked along, he concentrated on the solitude, trying to will his flaming ulcer to heal. After all, that was part of the reason he had moved here in the first place.

Burt hated cities. Despised crowds. Detested the thought of those teeming masses of humanity pressing against him, smothering him. It was a phobia that had nearly paralyzed him in his younger days. The worst thing back then was how his own life had trapped him. His living was made off those same teeming masses he so abhorred.

Burt had run a successful ad agency in New York for more than ten years. In those days he had been driven. His goal was to make enough money by the time he was forty to leave the squalid city of his misspent youth forever. The greatest day of his life was when he finally achieved his goal.

When he came home to his humble Bronx apartment with the news more than ten years before, Helen had been livid.

"Are you out of your mind!" she snapped.

"Helen, I've been talking about this for fifteen years."

"Talking, shmalking. I figured that was all it was with you. Talk. I'm not going."

"Fine. Stay."

Helen was surprised by his indifference.

Although she pretended nothing was changing the entire time he was selling his agency and transferring funds to Maine, three weeks after his announcement she could stand it no more. She finally asked a question.

"So where are we moving? Not that I don't think you should be moving to the rubber room, you're acting so crazy."

"A beautiful small town called Lubec."

"I hate it."

"Did you ever hear of it?"

"No, but I hate it."

"Don't come."

There it was again. Such firm indifference. Burt had never acted that way toward her before. Not only that, he *looked* different.

"Are you feeling okay?" Helen asked, a hint of genuine wifely concern in her shrill voice.

"Never better," Burt insisted.

"You look funny. Not as pale. And you're standing different. Straighter."

"My ulcer's almost gone. A month in Maine and I'll be a new man."

"I'll say. You'll be a schmuck who gave away a million-dollar business."

But Burt wouldn't be dissuaded. He dumped all of his New York business interests and moved everything he owned to Maine. A year after, he sold his last stock, severing his ties to New York forever.

With the clarity afforded by hindsight, Burt realized that his life hadn't truly started until his big move. And in spite of the fact that Helen had accompanied him to Maine, his ulcer nearly healed. Everything was going along swimmingly until the day the well ran dry. Literally.

"You've got two hundred acres here," Burt's neighbor, Owen Grude, had drawled. Among other things, Grude drilled wells for a living. "Lubec's known for our water. Shouldn't be a problem finding another source around here."

It turned out his neighbor was right. Owen found water on the first try. Not only that, it was the sweetest water either of them had ever tasted.

Owen sent a sample away for testing. The lab confirmed that it was purest water in a state filled with pure water.

"You should bottle this," Owen Grude suggested when he brought the test results to Burt Solare's rural home.

"Why?" Burt asked. "In case of drought?"

"To sell," Owen had replied. "City folks'd pay a pretty penny for water this pure."

"You mean like a business," Burt said levelly.

Owen nodded. "Could be good for us both. I see you wandering around here, nothing to do. A man should do *something*."

"I'm not sure, Owen," Burt said warily. "How big are we talking?"

"Small operation. Couple of fellas. You won't even have to do much, unless you want to. But like I said, you don't have much to do now. Aren't you bored?"

Like many people in that part of the country, Owen Grude was a lot more savvy than he let on. In his quiet, backwoods way he had cut to Burt Solare's heart.

The truth was, Burt *was* bored. He was more fit than he had ever been in his life, but with nothing to occupy his days he was beginning to feel as if he were stagnating.

Owen's suggestion came at a time of perfect weakness. It didn't take much convincing. That very afternoon, Burt Solare accepted his new partner's proposal. After that, everything happened in a blur.

There were trucks and buildings—at Burt's insistence, confined to the woods on the other side of his land. Owen had underestimated the number of people they would need to hire. The employees numbered in the dozens at the Lubec plant alone. Soon the cacophony of the outer world began to intrude on Burt's rural life.

Within two years, Lubec Springs water blanketed the East Coast. In five it had exploded nationally. The next year the tidal wave spilled into the international market.

By the time his fiftieth birthday rolled around, the solitary existence Burt had longed for was long gone.

Rather than remain the silent partner he had hoped, Burt had taken an active role in the growth of the business. The success of Lubec Springs was largely due to the advertising skills he had developed in New York. But, as had happened in New York, Burt's health suffered in inverse proportion to the health of his business.

He was fifty-five now. Rich several times over.

And with a gnawing wound in his gut that refused to surrender to all the medications he poured into it.

For Burt it was finally enough.

For the second time in his life, he was going to chuck it all. He'd sell his home, his land and his interest in Lubec Springs. He would move farther up into the wilds of Maine, and if success came sniffing at his door this time, he'd shoot it, bury it and move to Canada. Hell, he'd take a dogsled to the North Pole if he had to. This time enough was absolutely, unequivocally enough.

The decision had been made a few days before. It was now just a matter of summoning the strength to tell Owen.

When he had first moved up to Lubec more than a decade earlier, the only twisting path through these woods was his own long driveway. Now a half mile from his house was an electronically controlled gate. On the other side was another road, this one paved.

During the week, trucks drove back and forth along that isolated path. Fortunately it was Saturday. The sounds of wretched civilization would not return until Monday.

Burt slipped around the gate that separated his private property from that of his business.

Someone had sneaked in during the night again. Green-and-pink paper from the local copy center had been nailed to dozens of the trees. A picture of a curled blob that looked like a bumpy comma was in the center of each page. Below were the letters *S.O.L.* The papers rattled in the breeze.

When Burt saw the papers, he shook his head in disgust. His hand searched for his burning belly.

Amid all the fluttering papers beside the paved road was a small sign. It read simply *Lubec Springs*.

"May you burn to the ground and your ashes scatter to the four winds," Burt grumbled at the sign.

Feeling the fire in his belly, he headed up the road to the bottling plant.

SINCE ITS FOUNDING a decade before, the single-story Lubec Springs bottling plant had expanded from a small wooden shed to a sprawling complex nestled amid the lonely pines.

The main plant was a cinder-block affair that had been erected hurriedly several years previously. Tucked around back, barely visible from the road, a few Lubec Springs trucks sat idle near concrete loading platforms.

Jutting from the front of the larger building was a clapboard addition that housed the main offices.

A car was parked out front. With a frown, Burt noted the out-of-state license plate. He had told Owen this meeting was business-related. Burt hoped his partner had sense enough not to bring guests to the plant. The last thing he wanted was to wait another day to tell Owen he was calling it quits.

Wearily he climbed the three wide steps and pushed open the front door. Walking down to the offices from the reception area, he found Owen behind his desk. The cofounder of Lubec Springs was not alone.

"Oh," Burt said, irritated. One hand gripped the door frame. "Owen, we had a meeting, remember?"

Burt glanced at the three strangers in the room. Two were men in their late thirties or early forties. The third was a woman. When he saw her, Burt's irritation bled away.

She was gorgeous. The woman's hair was as black as a raven's wings. Her eyes were quick and sharp. Her skin was cream. She stood with a confident grace that announced to the world she owned whatever room she was in.

As the woman fixed him with a cold stare, Burt gulped.

"I, uh… Sorry. We can do this later, Owen."

"No," Owen insisted. "You said you had something important to tell me." His voice was a deep growl. It sounded strange. Stronger than normal.

Burt tore his eyes away from the woman.

Owen was stepping out from around his desk. He was even walking differently. Owen Grude was forty pounds overweight. He usually stomped and wheezed when he walked. But this day he seemed to glide. The other two men fell in behind him.

"No," Burt insisted, suddenly clenching his molars with fresh pain. His ulcer was flaring again. "It can wait. You have company. We can talk tomorrow. Nice to meet you," he said, nodding to the woman.

Silent until now, the woman seemed distracted by the men. A hint of disapproval creased her brow.

"Please wait, Mr. Solare," she said to Burt.

In the doorway Burt paused. "Yes?"

"This is so awkward," she said with a cool smile

that indicated it was anything but awkward. "Mr. Grude wasn't sure how to tell you this himself, so I'm just going to tell you. He has signed his fifty percent of Lubec Springs over to me. I'm your new partner."

For a moment Burt didn't know what to say. The pain in his belly was forgotten. "Owen?" he asked, confused.

His partner just stood there, brow hanging low over sharp eyes. Burt had eaten supper at Owen's house enough over the past ten years to know that look. Owen got that same look when he was drooling over a plate of pork chops.

"Your water is very pure," the woman announced.

Owen and the other two men snorted softly—pulling in soft, inquisitive breaths. Like animals sniffing prey.

"That's true," Burt Solare said slowly. "Okay, Owen, what is all this?"

"Business, Burt," Owen said. "Thanks to you, we're in every convenience store and supermarket in the country."

As he spoke, his nostrils flared, sniffing the air. He circled around Burt.

"Down," the woman snarled suddenly. She sounded like an obedience trainer scolding a bad dog.

"Helen already called to tell me you were quitting, Burt," Owen said from behind, his voice a quiet growl. "It came as quite a shock. I've got one for you, too."

"No," the woman commanded, taking a step for Owen.

Too late.

Burt felt someone grab him from behind.

Owen. Owen had gone crazy. Selling the business without telling Burt, dragging strangers in off the street and now assaulting Burt in his own offices. That was it. To hell with it all. Burt was going to quit already, but now he'd do it with a song in his heart and not look back.

Burt had played high-school and college football. He still outweighed Owen. He'd flip his demented ex-partner to the floor and then leave Lubec Springs for good.

Burt intended to tell Owen all this. But then a funny thing happened. He suddenly couldn't speak.

He felt pressure on his throat. Felt a sudden jerk and twist of sharp pain. Pain far worse than his ulcer. Pain more excruciating than anything he had ever felt before.

Burt gasped. Bubbles came. Red and frothy.

Burt staggered back, grabbing at his throat. His hands clutched a glistening hole. And then Burt Solare saw the ragged remnants of his torn-out throat. They were dangling from the blood-streaked mouth of Owen Grude.

Burt tried to run. The other two men were on him.

With hands and teeth they attacked Burt's soft belly. Screaming silently, he hit the wall and fell to the floor. They came in a pack. He tried to knock them off. His weak blows scarcely registered.

When he glanced up in horror, he found that one man's face had disappeared inside his abdomen. He reappeared an instant later, sharp teeth dragging a bundle of glistening viscera.

With a tip of his head and a few quick gulps, the

man slurped up the ulcerous part of Burt's intestine like a string of bloody spaghetti.

Another shadow. A face frowning deep disapproval.

The woman. Burt saw her through his pinwheeling gaze. Pouncing, she fell in among the men, grabbing shoulders and arms, flinging them away. For someone so small and graceful, she was inordinately strong. When she gripped Owen by the back of the neck and yanked, Owen became airborne. He soared across the office, slamming hard against the wall. The particleboard buckled beneath him.

With uncharacteristic delicacy, Owen righted himself as he dropped to the floor. Flipping, he landed silently on the rug. His face was enraged, yet he made no move on the woman. The other men prowled near him.

"Stay," she commanded firmly to all three. Although they clearly didn't want to obey, the three men stayed back. Blood and saliva drooled from their open mouths.

Burt lay in a bloody heap, weak hands clutching belly and throat. The rug was stained red. Every thready heartbeat sent more blood gurgling from his open wounds.

The woman crouched beside him. Her nose crinkled unhappily as she studied his wounds.

She had stopped them. Maybe she could save him. If she called the police, the hospital. Burt pleaded with his eyes.

Her mouth thinned. "He's too far gone," she announced.

No! Burt wanted to shout. *Call 911! Help me!*

Did she hear his unspoken plea? The woman turned her attention back to his gaping stomach wound.

Yes, I'm alive. I'm fighting to live. Save me!

She reached for him. Did she know first aid?

And then the horror returned full-blown.

Hands thrust inside his ripped-open belly. Grabbing either side of his rib cage, the woman twisted.

Burt heard his sternum crack.

Baring fangs, the woman proceeded to stuff her face deep into his exposed chest cavity. With a lick and a snap, fangs pierced the left ventricle of his feebly beating heart.

And in that instant of horrific pain, Burt Solare had an epiphany. The blinding realization came clear as glass in that last moment of his weak, frail mortality.

Maybe I should have stayed in advertising.

WHEN SHE WAS THROUGH feeding, she allowed the males to eat. They chewed greedily, Owen more than the others. This was his first. The hunger was strongest the first time.

When the males finally finished, she was lying on Owen Grude's desk, her rough pink tongue licking gently at the last hints of sticky blood on her long fingers.

They padded over to her, faces smeared red from their feast. The two males yawned contentedly. Owen Grude mewled apologetically. She continued to lick her fingers.

"You behaved recklessly," she said, not looking up.

"I couldn't resist."

She turned her eyes lazily, fixing him with a glare. "A word from the wise. Next time? Resist."

The threat was clear. Owen nodded obediently.

Pulling herself to a squatting position, she looked at the other two. "He has a mate," she said, nodding to the half-eaten carcass of Burt Solare. "Kill her."

No more instruction was needed. With barely a sound, they slipped from the office.

Pushing from her haunches, she bounded to the floor. Her bare soles touched silently.

"Show me the bottling plant," she commanded, prowling past Owen.

He hesitated. "What about him?" he asked, lingering near the desk. He nodded to the body of his partner. Burt's glassy eyes stared up vacantly in death.

She paused. "Oh, do you want a human funeral for your dear, dear friend?" she asked with mock sympathy.

"No, of course not," Owen said. "I don't see him as I did. He used to be important to me. Now he's just—"

"A meal?"

Owen nodded. "I'm just afraid someone might find him."

She padded up to Owen, pressing a firm hand on his shoulder. She growled. Flecks of red gristle clung to the spaces between her flawless white teeth.

"Don't try to think too hard. Now, we have a lot of work to do. The fun is just beginning."

With catlike grace, Dr. Judith White prowled out the office door.

2

His name was Remo and it wasn't that he didn't want to squash a few more cockroaches. His only problem was the wrong man was asking him to do the squashing.

"Let me talk to Smith," Remo said.

"Dr. Smith isn't here," Mark Howard explained.

Howard was assistant director of CURE, the supersecret organization for which Remo worked as enforcement arm. That is, on those days Remo was actually working. At the moment, as Remo stood on the sidewalk in Little Rock cradling the pay phone between ear and shoulder, it wasn't one of those days.

"No offense, Junior," Remo said to Howard, "but I don't scrunch cockroaches for you. Put Daddy on the phone."

A few students from nearby Philander Smith College strolled down the sidewalk chatting loudly. Like most college students of the past forty years, these seemed to have an abundance of loud opinions and a lack of actual textbooks. Remo watched them as they walked through the historic Quapaw Quarter of the city's downtown.

On the phone there came an exasperated exhale.

"Remo, you know Dr. Smith leaves the office at five on Tuesdays and Thursdays now," Mark Howard replied, his youthful voice straining to be patient. "He said you can talk to me."

"Talk to, yes. Take orders from, no. You want to talk about the weather?"

"No."

"See you in the funny papers." Remo hung up the phone.

The receiver rang the instant he broke the connection. Remo had to hand it to Mark Howard; the young man was quick on the ol' keyboard. He picked up the phone.

"Joe's Porn Palace. You can't spell coitus without us."

Howard's voice was growing irked. "Remo, please."

"Sorry," Remo said sweetly. "Still not the right guy for me." He hung up once more.

This time the pay phone fell silent.

While he waited, Remo whiled away the minutes counting the birds that flew overhead. He was up to thirty-one when the phone finally rang again. He scooped up the receiver.

"Hi, Smitty," he announced.

The lemony voice on the other end of the line was not that of Mark Howard. Where Howard's voice was young, this voice was older, more tired and infinitely more irritated.

"What is the problem?" announced Dr. Harold W. Smith, the director of CURE.

"No problem," Remo said. "Except that I don't

take orders from your helper monkey. Why are you whispering?''

"I am in my bedroom on my briefcase phone. My wife is downstairs and I don't want her to overhear. What's wrong? Mark says you are having trouble with the assignment.''

"No trouble. I don't even know what it is. You know the rule, Smitty. I'm Sinanju. Sinanju gets hired by an emperor. You're my emperor. I work for you.''

He could almost see Smith wincing on the other end of the line. "Please don't you start calling me that, too.''

Remo was the Reigning Master of Sinanju, the original martial art. Born in blood on the rocky shores of North Korea, Sinanju was the sun source of all the other, lesser martial arts. For millennia the Masters of Sinanju had rented their services as assassins to rulers throughout the world. Remo's teacher, who had been Reigning Master until Remo's ascension to that position a few months before, had refused to admit to working for anything less than a true tyrant king, and so had long before dubbed Harold W. Smith "emperor.'' It was an honorific Smith didn't embrace. And it was definitely something he didn't wish to see carried through into Remo's fledgling Masterhood.

"Whatever you call it, you're the boss,'' Remo said. "Tradition says I can't start taking orders from the kid. And I happen to agree with tradition here. What if Smitty Junior goes nuts and starts giving me whacko assignments, like maybe I should make him President or pope or something? Or he tells me to start assassinating petunias 'cause they give him the sniffles? Or what if he orders me to kill you?''

"At the moment I would consider that a blessing," Smith said tightly.

"You're not out of it that easy, Smitty," Remo grumbled. "If I'm stuck with Howard, you are, too."

"Yes," Smith said dryly. "Just so you know, Remo, I do not consider myself stuck at all. Mark has helped lighten my load considerably. Two nights a week now I am able to have dinner with my wife. And might I remind you, Mark has also saved both our lives."

Remo's face darkened at the memory. There had been a terrible battle back in the village of Sinanju. On that dark day months before, it was Mark Howard's timely intervention that had provided insight that might have turned the tide.

"Maybe," Remo admitted. "The jury's still out on what would have happened back then if he'd butted out." He frowned with a sudden thought. "What do you mean both? You weren't in the line of fire back then."

Smith cleared his throat. "Er, yes. Can we get on with this? My wife nearly has dinner ready."

"Fine. Sue me for wanting to hear your dulcet tones," Remo said. He drummed his fingertips on the steel phone-book tray. "What's the deal? More cockroaches, right?"

As Smith quickly sketched out the details of that night's assignment, Remo's fingers continued to drum a hollow staccato on the pay phone's metal tray.

After a few moments, Smith stopped suddenly. Bored, Remo was back to counting birds.

"What is that noise?" the CURE director asked abruptly.

"What noise?" Remo asked.

"I don't know. It sounds like a jackhammer."

Remo glanced around. He didn't see any jackhammer. In fact, he saw no road construction whatsoever. He did see a few more college students. They were staring at him as they walked past. More accurately, they were staring at his hand.

Remo glanced down.

Four deep hollows in the shape of drumming fingers pitted the otherwise smooth surface of the stainless-steel phone-book tray. It looked as if the metal had superheated and melted into four neat pockets.

"It stopped," Smith said over the phone.

"Yeah," Remo grunted, stuffing his hand in his pocket. "Can we just finish this up?"

Smith seemed to sense something was wrong. "Were you even listening?"

"Sort of listening, mostly bored." He sighed. "Sorry, Smitty. I've got a lot of stuff on my mind lately."

It was true. He had been preparing nearly all of his adult life to take over as Reigning Master of Sinanju. He thought it would be a snap once he finally accepted the position. He had come to find out that there was no way to be completely ready for so awesome a responsibility. All the training in the world had not prepared him for the new reality of his life. Once he actually became Reigning Master, it just *felt* different than he had expected.

Remo was surprised by the CURE director's sympathetic tone.

"I understand," Smith said. "Even when one knows it is coming, it still takes time to come to grips psychologically with the burden of great responsibility. There has been some research into the subject. If it would be helpful, I could send some published papers on the topic."

"Pass. But feel free to quiz me on the state capitals. Better yet, ask me the boons granted to past Masters of Sinanju. For instance, did you know Master Cung managed to bamboozle three hundred armfuls of silk, a skepful of Sui dynasty myrrh, twenty golden flagons of rice wine, forty she goats and thirty pheasants from the Chinese? Chiun says they were *peasants,* but I think he's misreading the scrolls."

"Yes," Smith said thinly. "In any event, the target is across the Arkansas River and up Route 161 near Furlow. Did you get enough of the rest?"

"Enough. I've already got my squashing shoes on."

"Good. Please report back to Mark when you are finished. Sinanju rules do allow that, don't they?" There was a hint of thin sarcasm in his voice.

"Yes, that's kosher," Remo sighed.

"I don't understand why you've become so prickly lately in regard to Mark. I thought you had worked through your difficulties with him."

"I've got nothing against the kid, Smitty. I just

liked it better when it was you, me and Chiun. Although right now Chiun isn't that much of a help.''

''Is there something wrong with Master Chiun?''

''Nah. He's just being Chiun again. He came with me to Little Rock, but now he's sitting in a hotel room. He said he was contemplating his place in the cosmos or something. As if being the pain in my neck wasn't full-time job enough.''

''Very well,'' Smith said. ''Just remember, Remo. Nothing stays the same forever. Things change. Sometimes for the better, sometimes not, but change is inevitable.''

He was interrupted by a distant voice.

''Harold,'' Smith's wife called. ''Dinner's ready.''

''I have to go,'' the CURE director said. ''Good luck.''

With a soft beep, the line went dead.

Remo held the cold phone loosely in his hand. He stared down at the permanent marks imprinted in the steel tray.

''Preaching to the choir, Smitty,'' he said softly.

He hung up the pay phone.

THE TWIN-ENGINE CESSNA had flown up through the Gulf of Mexico. Staying low to avoid radar, the small aircraft hugged much of the shared border of Louisiana and Texas, finally breaking out across the Ouachita Mountains in southwestern Arkansas. It hummed into the Arkansas River Valley on the way to its evening rendezvous.

When it first appeared out of the cool, late spring

night, it was as a sound rather than something visible to the eye.

The lone man waiting at Furlow's small airport heard the noise. Behind him, a red, white and blue banner slung from the side of a tin hangar advertised the *Happy Apple Pie American Patriotic Flight School And Good-Time Hotdog Stand.*

The man on the ground had come up with that name himself. The secret world in which he lived had become far more treacherous of late. Everything was about being inconspicuous now. Faysal al-Shahir was as proud of the very inconspicuous, very American-sounding name of his business as he was of his own false identity.

Faysal al-Shahir had cleverly picked his American cover name at random from a telephone book. He was now known as John Smith. That was much better than the first name he had cleverly picked at random out of the phone book. His contact in the radical al-Khobar Martyrdom Brigade had read him the riot act when Faysal al-Shahir had requested a false driver's license and credit cards under the name Jiffy Lube.

But that teeny mistake had been months ago. Faysal had learned much about fitting in since then.

He had been forced to shave his beard. His dark hair had been colored with blond highlights. Gone were his midnight-black eyes, disguised with blue contact lenses. His forearms had five-o'clock shadow from daily shaving.

Even Shahir's clothing had been Americanized. His first week in the hated den of vipers that was the devil West, Faysal had been delighted to find a store that sold typical American clothes at a price that would not break his allowance. His first trip there he had bought a garbage bag full of beautiful clothes. Now, months later, decked out in his Salvation Army Thrift Store finery, Faysal al-Shahir was as wholly inconspicuous as the next puke-green leisure-suited, bell-bottomed American flight-school instructor.

Although day had bled away, the rim of the twilight sky was still colored in shades of pinkish gray. It was out of the gloaming that the plane finally appeared.

"They are here," Faysal announced in Arabic.

Three other men had been sitting on wooden crates inside the door of the hangar. Like Faysal, they were dressed in decadent Western garb. With fat lapels on ghastly colored polyesters, they looked like a 1970s prom band.

At Faysal's announcement, the men hurried outside.

It took several more minutes for the plane to reach the airport. By the time the Cessna came in for a landing, shades of gray had seeped into enveloping blackness. In darkness, guided only by soft runway lights, the plane touched down with a shriek of rubber. It sped toward them.

Faysal offered a wicked grin. "It begins," he said.

He was turning to roll the hangar doors wide when one of his companions spoke.

"What is that?" the man hissed.

Faysal glanced back. The man who had spoken was pointing a wholly inconspicuous, mood-ring-disguised finger down the runway.

The Cessna was rolling toward them, slowing as it came.

When Faysal saw what his associate was pointing at, his eyes grew so wide he nearly popped his blue contacts.

A man had appeared from the dark woods next to the plane. He loped along in the wake of the small aircraft.

Faysal felt his stomach tighten.

"Who is that?" he demanded, wheeling on the others.

"I do not know," his men replied in chorus.

Faysal looked from the men to the runway. The stranger was gaining on the Cessna.

"Should we shoot him?" one man asked.

Rifles and handguns were already being raised.

"No!" Faysal snapped. "We cannot risk hitting the plane. Besides, are you forgetting there are houses beyond the woods? We cannot draw the authorities to us. Not now."

Light from the plane and runway enabled Faysal to glimpse the stranger's face. It was cast in cruel shades. Above high cheekbones, the eyes were black-smeared sockets. It was more a vengeful skull than a human face.

He ran with a gliding ease that seemed slow, but which propelled him forward ever faster. As Faysal watched, the stranger caught up to the left wing. Hands attached to abnormally thick wrists reached out for the shuddering tip.

"What is he doing?" asked a fearful voice in Arabic.

"It does not matter," Faysal hissed.

Faysal's mind was finding focus. All was not lost. After all, this was just one man. He was certainly not from the American government. The United States came at you as polite agents in suits who worried about search warrants and due process and extending civil liberties to terrorist noncitizens. They fretted over how their behavior would look to Amnesty International, the CBS evening news and the editorial board of the *New York Times*. Real U.S. government agents were so panicked about doing what all these groups considered to be the right thing that they forgot that the right thing first and foremost was protecting their fellow countrymen from maniacs who would blow up buildings and murder innocent Americans.

No, Faysal knew with growing certainty, this man running toward them up the runway and about to touch the tip of the Cessna's wing—heaven knew what he intended to do once he reached it—was not with the United States government. He was just an average American. And in this holy war, *all* Americans were targets.

"He is just some harmless fool," Faysal said. "When he gets close enough that there is no risk of hitting the plane, shoot him. Use a silencer. We will dispose of the body in the woods."

Faysal tightened his jaw, which, despite a morning ritual of Nair and painful home-hair-removal strips, was still speckled with the dark stubble of a Riyadh street beggar.

Faysal was certain all would still go exactly according to plan. He was certain of this straight up until the moment the running stranger ripped the wing off the Cessna.

The cluster of Arabs near the hangar blinked, stunned.

It was true. Their eyes had not lied.

The stranger's fingers had seemed to barely brush the surface of the wing. With a shriek of metal, it tore away from the main body, leaving ragged strips on the fuselage.

As the gathered men watched in growing shock, the wing and its suddenly dead engine fell back on the runway. The Cessna, coasting forward with one wing engine, began to spin away from Faysal and the rest.

''What manner of man is this who can tear a plane apart with bare hands?'' one of the men near the hangar breathed.

Faysal barely heard. He was listening to a new sound.

Over the crashing of the tumbling wing and the spluttering of the Cessna's one dying engine, Faysal al-Shahir heard a terrible sound that froze his very marrow. It was the sound of a man whistling. Strong and confident, it carried across the small airport.

During his time in America, Faysal had deliberately stayed out of the sun to keep his skin as light as possible. But at this moment, that particular precaution proved unnecessary. As he watched the plane roll out of control and heard the first strains of that sweet, terrifying song, the color drained from the face of

Faysal al-Shahir, leaving behind a sheet of ghostly white.

"That is no man," Faysal whispered with certainty, his voice laced with doom.

Faysal al-Shahir knew well of Heaven. For their coming sacrifice on Earth, he and his fellows in the Martyrdom Brigade had been promised an eternity of palaces and plentiful concubines in the next life. And Faysal knew equally of Hell, home of torment for the unworthy. For its wealth and power in this world, America had made a pact with Satan. And before Faysal was the proof.

For many months, throughout the al-Khobar movement there had been rumors of an agent from Satan's realm who had come to Earth. America's unholy bargain with the prince of the underworld had come with a protector, a creature in the shape of a man who struck without warning and slaughtered without mercy. On the soil of Asia and Europe and America had this creature trodden. And death had followed.

While the troops grew fearful, the al-Khobar leadership tried to squelch these tales of the unstoppable devil who wielded an invisible sword in the name of the hated West. Faysal had never believed the stories. Until this night.

When the awful melody started—the whistling song described by witnesses to horrors beyond human comprehension—Faysal knew with certainty that it was all true. And if rumor could be trusted, no force of man could stop this creature. Death was coming for them all.

Helpless in the chilly Arkansas night, Faysal al-

Shahir could only stand and listen to the approaching song of America's Hell-summoned demon.

As HE TORE the left wing off the speeding Cessna, Remo Williams continued to whistle a peppy version of "La Cucaracha." He was still whistling as he let the wing slip from his fingertips.

As the wing banged and spiraled away behind him, Remo was already ducking under the belly of the plane.

The crippled Cessna whipped around in a 180-degree arc.

Remo came up on the other side. A sharp hand caught the leading edge of the second wing. The momentum of the plane sliced around his stationary hand.

The second wing plopped off into his upturned palms. He caught it with a tidy flourish and a click of his heels.

"La-la-la-la-la-la-la! Olé!" Remo sang as he flung the wing with its dead engine deep into the dark woods.

The Cessna rolled to a dead stop. As it did, the small door popped open and two furious men sprang to the tarmac. With shouts of angry Arabic, they aimed rifles at Remo.

"U.S. health inspector," Remo announced to the men, ignoring the guns leveled at his chest. "We had a tip at HQ there'd be a cockroach incursion tonight. And what do you know? Here you are. Prepare for fumigation."

The two new arrivals sized up the thin young

American in his black T-shirt and matching chinos. They seemed to regard him more as an annoyance than a threat. They shouted to the men over at the hangar.

The men who had been awaiting the plane were already racing over. Only Faysal al-Shahir remained rooted in place.

All five men surrounded the thin young man who had torn the Cessna to shreds, seemingly with his bare hands.

"Who do you work for, American?" asked one of the new arrivals, a higher-up in the al-Khobar organization.

"Funny you should ask," Remo said. "I've just spent half the day sorting that one out. But I think Upstairs has gotten the message now. Technically I'm a free agent who hires out to one guy at a time. One boss, one set of orders. Simplifies the chain of command, don't you think?"

"Who is, as you say, 'Upstairs'?" asked one of the al-Khobar agents, prodding Remo with a rifle barrel. "Is this American slang for CIA?"

"Didn't you hear? We decided we didn't need the CIA anymore. That is, until we got attacked and needed something to give the politicians a fig leaf for blowing our spy budget on daffodil stuff like measuring cow farts and making sure little Timmy gets a free lunch at school. And what's with that anyway? In my day parents were able to master the complexity of smearing peanut butter and jelly on two slices of bread."

Obviously the terrorist wasn't satisfied with this response. His gun barrel jammed harder into Remo's ribs. Or at least it tried to. To the terrorist it felt as if Remo's rib was hinged. It swung out of the way of the barrel.

"What are you doing here?" the al-Khobar leader asked.

"I told you, I was sent to crunch cockroaches. My boss is wired in to this stuff. Don't ask me how he does it. But he figured out what your plan was. How next week you were going to blow up a couple of little bridges out in the middle of nowhere. Then with the authorities distracted in the heartland, how a few hours later you were going to fly planes loaded with explosives into commodities exchange buildings in big cities. Chicago, Atlanta, wherever the hell they are around the country. He even found out that you'd gotten smart this time and bought your own flight school here, rather than run the risk of taking lessons somewhere else. And he knew a couple of big shots were coming in to oversee the final stages of everything. That's you. I've already taken out the rest of your teams. You fellas are the last."

As Remo spoke, the two new arrivals glanced at each another with growing shock. Their latest scheme was only supposed to be known to the upper echelon of the al-Khobar terrorist organization. Yet this American had just recited all of the broad details.

To insure secrecy, the various al-Khobar cells around the country operated independently of one another. It would take hours to track them through channels to find out if they had indeed been dismantled.

In the meantime, there was one thing that could be done.

The time for questions was over. Exchanging tight nods, the two newest men promptly opened fire on the American agent. The other terrorists fumbled with their guns and followed suit. Barrels flashed and bullets screamed through the night.

Remo danced around the volley of lead. "Now, you've probably noticed that I don't have any cans of pesticide," he said as the men continued to fire. "That is because I am an environmentally friendly, completely organic exterminator. Spraying is for sissies. For dealing with the really big cockroaches like yourselves, we enviro-organo-exterminators adhere almost exclusively to the bang-crunch method." He held up a finger. "Observe."

He vanished.

The stunned terrorists stopped firing.

When they twirled around to look for Remo, they found that he had somehow reappeared ten feet from where he had been standing, directly behind one of the baffled terrorists. The man had only an instant to wonder why all of his companions were suddenly staring directly at him.

Remo grabbed him by the scruff of his neck.

"Abra cadaver," he announced.

And with that, the terrorist was airborne. A human missile, he zoomed at the crippled Cessna. When he hit the fuselage, the plane went bang and the head went crunch.

As the dead man crumpled to the runway, the remaining terrorists wheeled back on Remo.

"Of course, if you don't like bang-crunch, we've got other options," he said.

"Kill him!" an al-Khobar leader screamed.

The men opened fire once more. Stray bullets peppered the tail of the plane, somehow missing the thin American who was even now advancing on the group of desperate terrorists.

"There's pop-splat," Remo said.

Blurry hands found the sides of a terrified terrorist's bleached head. A single squeeze and the dome of his skull went pop. The splat came a few seconds later when his cannon-launched brain hit the roof of the distant hangar.

"Or maybe crack-crack-whomp."

A twirling toe took out the kneecaps of one man with successive cracks. A nudge as Remo darted by sent the tumbling terrorist to the ground with a whomp so powerful it shook the near runway and collapsed the man's skeleton to a formless lump encased in a shroud of purple polyester.

"Or thump-bong."

A thump from an unseen heel sent a head sailing from a set of shoulders. The decapitated head landed in a trash barrel near the closed hotdog stand with a rattling bong.

All told, it took no more than ten seconds. When Remo was through, there was only one al-Khobar terrorist left alive on the runway. The man stood in shock, gun hanging slack from his shaking hands, as he stared down at the dismembered, flattened corpses that had been the pride of the al-Khobar Martyrdom Brigade. He dropped his gun.

"I surrender," he cried in English, falling to his knees. "See, I love America, in all her sinful decadence." To prove it, he pressed his lips to the ground.

As he gave the ground a sloppy, wet kiss, a shadow cut between the al-Khobar leader and the nearer runway lights.

Remo loomed above, his face now grave. "But you know," he said, not listening to the terrorist leader's words, "if you want to know my personal preference for cockroaches like yourself, there's nothing in my book that beats just plain old squashing."

He put his heel on the al-Khobar leader's head, just behind the ear. Very slowly, so that the man could feel every fused section in his skull separate, Remo proceeded to squash the man's skull. The terrorist screeched and howled in what was the most excruciating minute of his life, but which was only prelude to his eternal punishment.

When he was done, Remo cleaned the sole of his leather loafer on the dead terrorist leader's shirt.

He turned his cold eyes toward the hangar.

Faysal al-Shahir was on his knees. Rooted in place, he had watched the horror from afar.

Remo walked over to him.

"You heard of me?" Remo asked.

Faysal nodded. "You are the devil's minion."

"No," Remo said coldly. "I'm the soul of America. I'm every crippled tourist you bastards push off a cruise liner in the name of religion. I'm every Marine you blow up while he's sleeping. I'm every stockbroker with two kids and a mortgage who just sat down at his desk to eat a jelly doughnut only to have the building blown out from underneath him. I'm America. And I'm pissed.'' He fixed his dead eyes on Faysal, boring through to the terrorist's dark soul. ''Today is your lucky day. You get to live. Tell all your brother cockroaches America is coming for them. And we will show them no mercy, for they have earned none.''

And Remo was gone.

Faysal didn't try to track the dark stranger with his eyes. A ghost of vengeance could not be followed.

He was alone once more. And in the suddenly chill night air, Faysal heard a voice in the wind, but it was not the voice of one, but the voice of millions united. And he knew in his heart that the end would come and that when it finally did, it would not be the end that had been promised.

On his knees at the small airport, surrounded by dark woods, Faysal al-Shahir buried his face in the ground of the nation he had been taught to hate. And wept.

3

In social situations whenever anyone asked Elizabeth Tiflis what she did for a living, her response was always the same. She'd vaguely say she was in publishing and then would promptly change the subject.

On those occasions when the hint wasn't taken and she was pressed for details, she would put a hand to her forehead, feign a headache and quickly excuse herself. After that it was the street, her car and home. One time she had even climbed out a bathroom window in order to avoid a particularly stubborn interrogator.

The truth was, Elizabeth liked talking about work about as much she liked having a tooth drilled. To Elizabeth, her job was a necessary evil. It was just something embarrassing she had to do to pay the bills. If she could find other work, she would. It was just that the industry had gotten so cutthroat in the past decade. It was hard to get a break, especially with her background.

It was her own fault. Fresh out of college, she had taken the first offer that had come her way. How was she supposed to know that it would poison the well for future employment? But it had, and so she was stuck as copy editor at a New York publishing house.

Her mother had told her time and time again it wasn't like she had anything to be ashamed of. After all, she didn't exactly work for *Hustler*.

"It's worse than porno, Mom," Elizabeth would lament. "I work for Vaunted Press."

"I know, dear," her mother would reply. "And I'm very proud of you. They're famous. I see their ads in the backs of all my favorite magazines."

Elizabeth had long ago stopped trying to explain to her mother that legitimate publishing houses don't advertise for clients alongside astrologers, at-home tanning beds and term-paper 800 numbers.

Vaunted Press was what was known as a vanity press. One of many self-publishing houses around the country, Vaunted would, for a fee, publish anything that came its way.

It was a lucrative market. Everyone with a word processor and fingers fancied themselves a writer. They couldn't wait to send their manuscripts to Vaunted for a "professional critique."

Although she held the title of copy editor, Elizabeth mostly just read over-the-transom manuscripts. In that she was little more than a rubber stamp. Unless it came in on a wet Kleenex, very little was rejected by Vaunted.

Elizabeth would scan a few grimy pages that spilled out of each ratty manila envelope. A little pen tick in the corner of the cover letter signified Vaunted's interest in the book.

Those whose books were greenlighted would be

sent back an enthusiastic form letter stating Vaunted's interest. In a few short months after acceptance, men and women whose work had been previously unpublishable would be allowed the giddy thrill of seeing their words in print.

"As well as the thrill of being bilked seven grand," Elizabeth muttered as she walked down the main hallway of Vaunted's Manhattan offices.

"What?"

Elizabeth blinked. She'd been daydreaming again. She glanced over at the young woman walking alongside her.

"Sorry," Elizabeth said. "My mind's gone. What were you saying?"

Her companion shook her head. "Is your job bugging you again?" asked Candi Bengal. Candi was twenty-five, a secretary and had a body that was equal parts boobs, bleach and Botox. "If you ask me, you shouldn't be so bothered by it. You're doing something that makes people happy."

"And poor."

"There you go again. You think too much, Lizzie. You shouldn't think so much about work. Take me. I dance nights and weekends at that club I told you about. You think I care what people think? Hell, no. My boyfriend—the bouncer I told you about? With the snakes?" She patted her stomach.

Elizabeth didn't need to be reminded about Candi's boyfriend's snake tattoos. Candi told her anyway. She was talking about body art and weird skin rashes when the two of them reached the break room.

A delivery man was just leaving, wheeling a cart

filled with empty plastic jugs. The clear blue containers bore the same waterfall logo as the man's jacket and cap.

"Morning," he said, holding the door open with his heel.

"Thanks," Elizabeth said, grabbing the door.

Humming, the man pulled his cart down the hallway and out of sight.

"See, that's just the kind of guy I can't stand," Candi proclaimed as she stepped over to the small fridge. "Treating us like a couple of grandmas. You want a Loco?"

Elizabeth was barely listening. Rather than trail Candi to the fridge, she made a beeline for the opposite corner.

"No, I'm all set," she said, taking her Powerpuff Girls coffee mug from the shelf.

"I thought you didn't do morning coffee," Candi said.

"I don't. My mom lost nine pounds cutting out soda. Thought I'd give it a try."

Candi scrunched up her nose. A few men and women were filtering into the room. Most headed for the coffee machine.

"You're not gonna stop at just nine pounds?" Candi asked, tipping to get a look at Elizabeth's thighs.

"We can't all be exotic dancers," Elizabeth said thinly.

She took her mug to the watercooler and thumbed the blue tab. The tank burped as she filled the coffee mug.

"I suppose," Candi conceded. She held up her soda can. "But this *is* diet."

And because she was in a malicious mood, Elizabeth shook her head. "That stuff's poison in a can," she insisted. "This—" she held up her mug "—is one hundred percent natural."

A young man was waiting behind her at the cooler. She sidestepped him, joining Candi at their usual table.

"Is it really that bad?" Candi asked, concerned. "It's practically all I drink."

"Mmm," Elizabeth said, sipping from her mug. The water was just what the ads claimed. Cold and clean.

She almost wouldn't have cared if the soda was poisoned. Elizabeth cared about as much about Candi, her choice of soft drink and her biker boyfriend as she did about her own job. At thirty-five, Elizabeth Tiflis was suffering a major bout of career stagnation.

Depressed, Elizabeth took another sip of water. It was good. Powerfully so. It seemed to quench some primordial thirst she never knew was there.

"Phosphoric acid," Candi said. She hadn't drunk her soda yet. She was studying the label. "Acid? Isn't that, like, the stuff from chemistry class?"

She looked up worriedly.

Elizabeth had finished her water. She had slurped the rest down as if her throat was on fire. The empty mug was lying on its side on the table. Elizabeth gripped the table's edge. She stared at the wall, eyes blank.

Candi looked back at the label.

"'Phen-yl-ket-on-nur-ics,'" she read with deepening concern. "Ooo, that sounds even worse."

When she looked up this time, she found Elizabeth was no longer looking off into space.

Elizabeth was staring directly at Candi. A strange expression had come over her face. Her eyes were wide. It seemed as if the irises were bigger. And they were now brown. Candi always thought they were pale blue.

"Elizabeth?" Candi asked cautiously.

Elizabeth continued to stare. She was looking at Candi in the same way as her strip club's patrons.

Candi shifted uncomfortably. "Well, *I* don't think they'd sell it if it was bad for you," she said, picking up her soda can. She tipped it to sip, exposing her long neck.

When Candi looked over again, she thought there was a bit of drool at the corner of Elizabeth's mouth. She wasn't quite sure, distracted as she was by the low, inhuman growl that suddenly rumbled up from deep in the pit of Elizabeth's stomach.

Candi frowned. "Rude much?" she complained.

She lifted her soda can. Elizabeth slapped it from her hand. It splattered against the break-room wall.

"Hey—" Candi began. It was the last word she would ever speak.

Before Candi knew what was happening, Elizabeth had leaped up on the table. Without a word, she lunged.

As Candi screamed, Elizabeth buried sharp fangs deep into her soft neck. The scream became a wet gurgle.

Candi tried to struggle. Elizabeth swatted her to the floor with a single paw swipe. She threw herself on the young woman, pinning her to the floor.

By now more screams filled the break room.

Others had followed Elizabeth. Animal roars filled the room as bodies fell. A woman managed to run screaming into the hall for help. Elizabeth didn't care. For the first time in a long time, she didn't have a care in the world.

She tore a mouthful of stringy flesh from Candi's throat. The young woman had long since stopped fighting. Her legs twitched feebly as death overtook her.

Lifting her head once, Elizabeth sniffed the break-room air. She was more aware of everything than ever before. Nostrils twitched experimentally as she absorbed all the new scents floating around her.

Around the room, those like her were gnawing at bodies. One of the males raised his head. Instinct told him he was being watched. Elizabeth smiled at him, face slick with blood.

"I've been wondering for a year how to shut her up."

Jaws wide, she stuffed her face back into Candi's throat, tearing off a huge chunk of flesh.

And in the corner of the room, the Lubec Springs watercooler burped quiet approval.

4

With the eye of memory he watched the heavens begin to burn. The fire started there, to the left. In the ink-black sky a white star flashed yellow. Another followed, then, quickly, another and another.

The blaze raced through the sky, connecting the dots of the flaring night stars.

The ring formed as star after star ignited. When it was complete it began to descend, trailing fiery streams.

On the ground he watched with upturned face. The bleak landscape around him glowed with eerily flickering light.

As fast as it appeared, it was on him. Enveloping him.

The fire touched skin, but it did not burn. And then the fire became the skin, as well as bone and heart and brain. Then it was thought. A coursing consciousness that flowed through his veins and into his soul. And he was one with the fire and the fire was him.

And then came the knowledge. It came to him in a flash, but it was too much to understand, even for him. As the fire flared bright, he strained to grasp fully the truth.

But he wasn't ready. Not yet.

The fire flashed and burned away. And he was left with the memory and a hint of what would be.

Chiun, former Reigning Master of the House of Sinanju—until recently main guardian and benefactor of the small fishing village that bore the same name as his discipline, and custodian of the five-thousand-year tradition that was the glory of Sinanju—was alone once more.

The hotel room was sliced by deep shadow. The morning light that rose over Little Rock slipped through the open blinds. Though dust danced in eddies of air around the room, not a single speck alighted on the solitary figure.

Feeling the memory of the warmth of fire on his skin, the elderly Asian puckered his lips in mild irritation.

In the gloom of the unlit room, Chiun gave the appearance of a frustrated mummy.

If not for the fact that he breathed, it would have been easy enough to mistake the old Korean for a mummified corpse. His dry skin was like wrinkled parchment. Twin tufts of yellowing-white hair sprouted above shell-like ears. A thread of beard found root at his sharp chin. Hands like knots of bone rested atop folded knees. He didn't move.

The old Korean wore a simple robe of black. He sat on a woven tatami mat, his rigid spine at a perfect ninety-degree angle to the floor. Before him a bowl of incense glowed dull orange. Arranged around it were five fat white candles.

He had sat this way through day and night in a

vain attempt to force answers. Dawn had broken beyond the dirty blinds, and still he sat.

It was a foolish thing to do, he knew. The universe unfolded on its own time, not man's. Yet he had been granted a gift, and he wanted so much to understand it.

It had happened months ago back in his native Korea, in the wasteland far outside the desolate village of Sinanju.

The ring of fire had come to Chiun from the heavens. Though shocking, it wasn't unprecedented.

The same event had transpired one time before in the history of Sinanju, the original martial art. The first time had been to the greatest Sinanju master of all, the Great Wang himself. The fire had bestowed the essence of Sinanju on Wang, but—as legend had it—understanding of what Wang had been given had taken a lifetime to fully grasp.

Chiun was more than one hundred years of age. He had turned over his awesome responsibilities to a suitable heir.

Remo was now officially Reigning Master of Sinanju. But these were unprecedented times.

Since Chiun was still actively plying the trade of assassin, he had assumed the seldom-used honorary title of Reigning Master of Sinanju Emeritus. As such, he retained in all but the most formal circumstances the title of Master of Sinanju.

"Won't that get confusing?" Remo had asked months earlier. "Two Reigning Masters of Sinanju at one time?"

"You will actually be Master of Sinanju," Chiun

had explained. "I will merely hold the title of Master of Sinanju. Or do you wish to deny a dying old man the respect he has earned? Especially given all he has had to endure training a certain title-grubbing white lump who shall remain nameless."

"You don't look like you're dying."

"Says nameless you."

"I don't know, Chiun. I thought the passing of title was part of the job. Can we do this?"

"Ah, I see the truth. You wish to keep the title all to yourself. I understand. I have heard on the television broadcasts, Remo, how some very small men need big titles to prove to themselves that they are worthy." Thus spoke Chiun, wise former Master of Sinanju.

"Stop watching *Oprah*," suggested Remo, peeved current Master of Sinanju.

"We can call me something else. Something easy for inadequate you to remember. How about 'Old Nuisance Who Has Given Me Everything, But Who I Continue To Not Appreciate And Treat Like Something The Cat Buries In The Sandbox'?"

"Nah. For one thing it'd spill off the mailbox."

"Then I will simplify it for you. Henceforth I shall be known as 'Hey You.'"

"Okay, I give. You're Master of Sinanju. That's fine. You happy? Now get off my case."

"Good."

"Good."

"Good."

"Chiun?"

"Master Chiun to you."

''What am I going to be called?''

''Whatever it is you want to be called,'' Chiun had said. ''Numskull works for me.''

The retention of title had been necessary for the old man who had been chosen to break with tradition. This should have been Chiun's time of retirement and ritual isolation.

Fate had chosen a different, new course for the last Master of the pure Korean bloodline. Chiun understood some, but the rest was still a mystery to be discovered.

In his mind's eye, Chiun had brought himself back to that moment in the wilderness many times. He had hoped to catch a glimpse of something unseen until now. But it was no use. He would have to wait for full understanding to come. He had journeyed to the memory of that day for the last time.

Eyes closed, Chiun had just come to his reluctant decision when he heard the elevator bell down the hall. His hypersensitive ears detected the familiar, confident glide approaching down the long hotel hallway.

When the door opened and the room lights came on a moment later, the Master of Sinanju was still motionless. Ancient eyelids were pressed tightly shut when the ill-mannered braying began.

''Pee-yew. What are you, burning cats again? And why is it so dark in here?''

Chiun's vellum lids fluttered open over youthful hazel eyes. Remo was kicking the door shut with his heel.

The ring of fire was forgotten. It would be under-

stood in its own time and not before. The Master of
Sinanju set it aside.

"Finally he returns," Chiun said, his voice a
squeaky singsong. "I am starving. Or is that your
plan? Did you want me to starve? Is that why you
abandoned me all night?"

The Master of Sinanju leaned forward, drawing a
sharp hand over the tops of the burning candles. The
vacuum of his sweeping hand doused the five flames.

"I didn't abandon you. You were the one who said
you didn't want to come with me this time. In fact,
your exact words were—and I quote—'I have killed
enough Arabs for that madman Smith in recent
months to populate a New Baluchistan. I'm staying
here. You do it.' End quote."

"That does not sound like me," Chiun said.

"You also said your robes reeked of camel's milk
cheese and bread flaps and that you were sending
Smith and Saudi Prince ibn bin al-Gaspot Mc-
Something the cleaning bill."

"Perhaps it sounds a little like me," Chiun conceded.

"And you could've eaten without me," Remo said.
With a frown, he noted the old man's clothes.
"What's with the celebration outfit?"

"None of your business, O breaker of tradition."

"Fair enough. I've got to report back to Smith."
Remo headed for the phone. "I'm going to be order-
ing trout for breakfast. Trout okay for you?"

"Of course, when I say it is none of your business,
I am only being polite. It is entirely your business.
Which is to say your *fault*."

"Well ring-a-ding-ding, it's my fault you're celebrating," Remo said. "Hey, when I'm done checking in with Upstairs, you want me to order brown rice or white? Won't matter. Kitchen will screw up both."

Chiun's face became a displeased pucker. He had put up with many things from his pupil over the years. Disrespect, clumsiness, stubbornness and that abusive tongue—oh, how Chiun had withstood that. But worse than anything was lack of interest. It was for the Master to not care what the pupil had to say, not the other way around. But, of course, Remo did care. How could he not care what Chiun had to say? This was just a trick, this feigned indifference.

"Stop pretending you don't care," Chiun accused Remo's back.

"I do care," Remo called over his shoulder. "Just not enough to do some verbal dance to beg you to tell me what you *want* to tell me and probably *will* tell me anyway."

"Stop talking about this," Chiun insisted.

"I've already stopped." Remo picked up the phone.

"Fine," the old man said, quickly throwing up his hands before his pupil could dial. "I was not going to tell you, but since you refuse to drop the subject…"

With a sigh, Remo replaced the phone in the cradle.

"Okay, what's the story?" he asked, turning.

Across the room, Chiun rose from the floor in a single, fluid motion. His hands were spread out to either side, extending ten daggerlike talons, the better to display his outfit.

The black robes were shorter than normal, hanging down to just above the ankle. A pair of black trousers—tight at the ankle—peeked out from below. The cloth was far more plain than the Master of Sinanju's usual brocade kimonos. Gone were the shimmering colors of embroidered peacocks and fire-breathing dragons. This was simple black cotton.

"If you must know, Nosy One, I wear the garments of celebration because a new day has dawned for the House of Sinanju. Thanks to your ascension to full Reigning Masterhood and my retention of title, we have entered a new, unprecedented age." He brushed imaginary wrinkles from the skirts of his simple black robes.

"That doesn't sound so bad to me. Where does 'it's all my fault' come in?"

"Since you stubbornly refuse to wear the proper attire of an assassin, I must do so for both of us during this ritual. Thanks to you, my time in these garments is doubled. I have been forced to pack away my robes for the duration of this time of celebration."

Remo looked the old Korean up and down. "I am not wearing an outfit like that one, Little Father," he warned.

"Of course you are not, Remo. Why would you? After all, I want you to. Why would you do anything I want? Why break a perfect thirty-year record now?"

"Chiun, they look like Broom Hilda's pajamas."

"And when I sleep in them, I will dream I have a son who treats me and the traditions of his village with respect."

Remo felt his resolve weaken for just a moment.

After all, he was the Master of Sinanju now. Maybe if it was just for a couple of days he could do it. Stay in the hotel. Order room service. Yeah, it was doable. And it would maybe be nice to give in to Chiun on the kimono thing this time. Maybe it would buy the old codger out of nagging him about his clothes for a few more years.

"How long would I have to dress like that?" Remo sighed.

Chiun's face brightened. "Six months."

"So you want trout, or what?" Remo said, turning away. He dropped his hand back on the phone.

No sooner had he touched the receiver than the phone rang. He quickly answered.

"Perfect timing, Smitty," he said.

"Remo?" the tart voice of Harold W. Smith asked. "Is everything all right? You were supposed to check in with Mark last night after your assignment."

"I walked back to the hotel," Remo said. "I've got a lot on my mind these days."

"Do not listen to his lies, Emperor Smith," the Master of Sinanju called. "His mind is as empty as his promises."

"I never promised anything," Remo said.

"See?" Chiun shouted triumphantly. "More lies."

Robes swirling, he marched from the room. He slammed the door with such ferocity that balcony windows cracked four floors in either direction.

"Is something wrong?" asked Smith, who had heard the slamming door over the phone.

"The usual," Remo replied, exhaling. "Everything is my fault, even the stuff that isn't. Anyway, last night went fine, Smitty. I left one cockroach alive to carry the message back to his pals and squashed the rest."

"Good. The way they operate, it is difficult to track all these cells. Our best hope beyond simply eliminating the ones we find is to make the rest fear attack."

"In that case, consider it mission accomplished."

"Very well. You and Chiun may return home."

Home for Remo these days was a town house in a new development in southern Connecticut. He had spent the past two weeks breaking up small al-Khobar cells. Remo was looking forward to getting back to his condominium.

"Okey-doke. Talk to you soon."

"One moment, Remo." There was the sound of fingers drumming as the CURE director accessed his computer. "Hmm. I know this is soon after last night's assignment, but when you land in New York there is something I'd like you to look into. There have been a few strange incidents in Manhattan this morning. They started about forty-five minutes ago."

"Al-Khobar?" Remo asked.

"No, not terrorists. At least I do not think so. The first was at some kind of publishing house. I might have ignored it if the computers hadn't found five more incidents since then. The people involved have been reduced to some sort of feral state, snarling and biting like animals."

"Sounds like New Yorkers fighting over a cab."

"This goes well beyond the norm, Remo. I suspect there might be some new form of drug at the center.

People are being mauled. Some reports even suggest there is cannibalism involved, although that obviously seems ludicrous.''

"Cannibalism? Smitty, you've got to stop getting your intelligence reports from the *Weekly World News.*"

"As I've suggested, things are still sketchy at the moment. But— Oh my.'' Smith paused. "There is a report here of a senior credit analyst at a bank suddenly going berserk and tearing out his supervisor's throat. Please check this out, Remo. I'll arrange a flight. Call me for the information when you reach the airport.''

"Can do, Smitty.''

He hung up the phone.

"Smitty wants us back home, so we're going to have to eat breakfast fast,'' he called to the Master of Sinanju's closed bedroom door. "You want trout?''

"Carp,'' the old Korean's voice replied.

"*I'm* still getting trout,'' Remo warned. "Don't go getting all pissy saying you wanted trout, too, when it comes.''

"Carp,'' Chiun said. "And I'm not talking to you.''

"I should be so lucky,'' Remo grumbled as he reached for the phone.

5

The plump, middle-aged woman on the flight from Little Rock thought that it was ghastly, just *ghastly*, that the old Asian gentleman's son had forced his elderly father to travel to New York in his pajamas. When Chiun explained that the black robes were mourning garments, she grew puzzled. The sad little man had insisted his garments were his murderous son's doing. She asked who died.

"My dreams. My hopes. My eternal, burning desire that a son to whom I have given the world would show me a mere ounce of gratitude for all he has had bestowed upon him."

"Knock it off, Chiun. Those robes are celebration. White is mourning."

The moon-faced woman turned her quivering jowls toward Remo. Green eyeshade rose haughtily on her broad forehead.

"You, sir, are a monster."

"Said Swamp Thing's grandmother," Remo said as he looked out the plane's window. He usually found the clouds pretty. They didn't seem very pretty today.

The woman's face became a mask of jiggling horror.

"You're right," she said to Chiun. "He's a brute. I'm going to report him the instant we land."

"Others have tried," Chiun said pitifully. "But he is as wily as he is cruel. He has escaped punishment for the many crimes he has committed against me and others. Even now he travels in luxury at the expense of your government."

"I know a thing or two about government," the woman insisted. "My cousin is a United States senator." She unclamped her handbag and rummaged inside, producing a small pad and a gold pen. "Give me your name," she demanded of Remo.

"Alfonse D'Amato. I'll let you figure out where you can shove the apostrophe."

The appalled woman immediately summoned a flight attendant, who in turn called the pilot.

The pilot was a pleasant-faced man in his late forties. He was muscular with a shock of black hair that was turning gray at the temples. In his shirtsleeves, shoulders marked with civilian captain's insignia, he picked his way through the cabin to the source of the commotion.

"Is there a problem?" he asked the woman who sat clucking like an angry hen between Remo and Chiun.

"I want police on the ground when we land," the woman insisted. She aimed a sausage-thick finger at Remo. "This man is guilty of elder abuse. I want him arrested and thrown in jail for what he has done to this poor, sweet man."

The pilot glanced from Remo to Chiun. "Sir, is this man mistreating you?" he asked the Master of Sinanju.

"He is wicked in both thought and deed," Chiun responded fearfully. "Just recently he locked me in a cell while he went off gallivanting for days on end."

"I was only gone a couple hours," Remo said.

"He shouldn't be left alone for one *minute* at his age," the matronly woman snapped.

"He locked you in a cell?" the pilot demanded.

"That cell had cable TV and a door that locked from the inside. He could have escaped a hundred times."

"My hands were too feeble to work the door handles," Chiun said weakly. "He even forced me to eat carp when I wanted trout."

"You poor, poor dear," the woman said. She patted Chiun's hand. The Master of Sinanju nodded morose appreciation at the small kindness.

"Quit it, will you, Chiun?" Remo snapped.

"Leave him alone, you tyrant," the woman barked.

"I've seen enough," the pilot said. "The authorities are going to want to question you when we land, sir."

"Oh, come on," Remo said. "I didn't *do* anything."

"Then you have nothing to worry about."

"Look what you did," Remo groused at Chiun.

"Can't you lock him away somewhere for the rest of the flight?" the plump woman whispered loudly to the pilot. "He seems unbalanced."

"I'll give you unbalanced, Aunt Bee," Remo snapped.

Quick as a flash, two hard fingers shot into the woman's doughy wattle, pressing into her throat. False eyelashes flickered, and the woman suddenly could not refuse the urge to sleep. Her head slumped forward.

"Peace and quiet. All I ever want," Remo complained.

As the woman began snoring, the pilot tried to flee. Remo grabbed him by his dangling tie and reeled him in.

"They need you to land this thing?"

The pilot shook his head.

"In that case, nighty-night."

Remo sent the pilot to slumberland. He dumped the pilot's face in the lap of the sleeping woman, then called over a flight attendant.

"Oh, my God!" the woman exclaimed. "What happened?"

"Beats me," Remo said.

"He did it," Chiun said.

"Put a sock in it, will you?" Remo said. "When's the in-flight movie start?" he asked the stewardess.

The bodies were quickly cleared away. While the cleanup was going on, there was a lot of whispering Remo didn't like the sound of.

When the plane reached La Guardia twenty minutes later and was immediately cleared for landing, Remo knew he was in trouble. There were police on the ground. Remo saw them out the window.

"This is all your fault," he groused, unbuckling his seat belt.

"Of course," Chiun said. "Blame the innocent, defend the guilty. The very underpinnings of white culture."

"Shake a leg, Johnnie Cochran," Remo insisted. He hurried up the aisle. The Master of Sinanju followed.

They found the flight crew hiding out in the galley. The crew was dismayed at Remo's appearance through the curtain.

"Please return to your seats," a flight attendant commanded.

"Believe me, I'd like to. No rest for the weary."

Remo stuffed the man in the rest room. When others protested, he stuffed them in, too.

"You missed one," Chiun pointed out blandly as the navigator tried to flee.

"Thanks a heap," Remo said, collaring the man. There was no room left in the bathroom. He jammed the man in a cupboard.

By the time the plane rolled to a stop, Remo had locked away pretty much everyone but the copilot.

"Great thinking for you to start this stuff up again now," Remo complained as he shoved a few loose arms and legs into a particularly cramped closet. "Calling attention to us on a plane flying in to New York. Smitty's gonna love this."

"I did nothing but make a friend," Chiun sniffed. "You introduced violence. That is your way. Violent and hostile. You should enroll in one of those classes that teaches people like you how to manage your anger.''

''Take my word for it, I'm managing it.''

All potential witnesses were now safely locked away. The passengers were still oblivious.

The plane had reached a dead stop by now. The police would rush inside the instant the door was opened.

In the middle of the galley, Remo banged the floor with the heel of his shoe. When he found the sweet spot, he hopped into the air, landing hard on both heels. The welded steel plate beneath the carpet broke loose, rising like a teeter-totter and tearing up a long strip of rug.

''You coming?'' Remo asked as he slipped down into the newly made trapdoor.

Chiun frowned. ''Will the indignities never cease?''

The two Masters of Sinanju disappeared through the narrow opening. Through the belly of the plane, they made their way to the aft cargo hold.

As SWAT teams stormed the plane above, Remo was standing on an American Tourister suitcase and kicking open the big cargo door. The two men jumped to the ground.

''Welcome to New York,'' Remo muttered.

A moment later they had vanished amid the growing confusion.

6

By midmorning word of the bizarre murders had spread like prairie fire through lower Manhattan. In a city now conditioned for particular types of attack, this was something new.

New York was a target of terror and the home of murder, rape, drive-by shootings, gang wars, pimps, whores, drug dealers and all of the seven deadly sins, plus a million more unknown to theologians. But the one fear New Yorkers had never been prepared for was wholesale cannibalism in Manhattan's steel-and-glass canyons.

So far, more than two hundred people had been affected. As many as that and more were dead. Since the killers seemed to not be in control of their own actions, police had been ordered to use guns as a last resort. The NYPD was armed with Tasers and animal tranquilizers.

Bronx Zoo officials had been brought in as advisers on the capture of the most dangerous of prey: animals with the capacity of human thought.

Although civilian authorities were doing their best to deal with the situation, there was no clue yet as to the cause. By late morning the number of attacks continued to increase with no explanation in sight.

By the time Remo and Chiun arrived by taxi at the Second Avenue home of Vaunted Press they could sense the fear hanging heavy in the air.

The streets were virtually empty. A dozen cruisers had converged on the building six hours earlier. Only two remained. Since early that morning, the isolated incident at Vaunted Press had become epidemic.

The two Masters of Sinanju met not a living soul as they crossed the sidewalk and entered the lobby. They took the elevator to the fourth floor.

"I guess we should have seen this coming," Remo said as the car rose. "Cannibal chic. Probably started in the Village."

Chiun was watching the floor lights. "Do not drag Sinanju into this perversity," he sniffed.

"Different village, Little Father," Remo explained. "And from where I stand, tongue studs and navel piercings are a hop, skip and a jump to rampant workday cannibalism."

"The lesser races have a history of playing at the edge of anarchy," Chiun agreed. "It has always been the yellow man's burden to keep the savages in line. Still, when I pass from this life and join my ancestors in the Great Void, I will now owe my grandfather a gold coin. He always said you Americans would be the first to start eating one another."

"You bet against us?" Remo asked, surprised.

"Of course. There are still French in the world."

The elevator doors opened on the lobby of Vaunted Press.

The police officers whose patrol cars were parked downstairs were nowhere to be seen. Sensing a cluster of heartbeats far down the hall, Remo and Chiun struck off in that direction.

They found a group of eight men and women hiding out in a small office. Tense, black-rimmed eyes looked up fearfully when Remo and Chiun entered the room.

"Who are you?" one trembling man asked.

"FBI," Remo said, flashing false ID. "Why are you people still here?"

The man exhaled. "We were witnesses. Most everyone went home, but we had to stay. Then it got worse out there and they advised us to stay put."

Remo stabbed a thumb over his shoulder. "You know where it happened?" he asked.

The man nodded. "I was there," he said sickly.

"How about giving us the nickel tour?"

Reluctantly the man pushed himself out of his chair. The rest remained behind as he followed Remo and Chiun out into the hallway.

"So what exactly happened here?" Remo asked as they walked down the long hall. The lights were on in all the silent offices they passed.

"I don't really know," the man said. "Four people went crazy this morning. They were like animals. I was lucky to get out alive. Then the police arrived, and we found out it was going on all over town."

"Where are the police now?" Remo asked. "We saw the cruisers downstairs."

"They're around here somewhere. Some of them had to leave on other calls. It's crazy." They had reached a short hall. "Down there," the office worker said, pointing.

Yellow police tape hung at the dead end of the corridor. A few rooms opened onto the hall. Remo and Chiun smelled the heavy scent of human blood in the recirculated air.

Remo lifted the tape for Chiun and the office worker to pass. The man waited outside the first door, averting his eyes. "In there." He pointed.

Remo thought he'd be prepared. After all, he had seen much in his life. But the gruesome scene inside the Vaunted Press break room was far worse than he had expected.

The floor was painted in sticky, drying blood. There were only a few clear spots here and there. Police and morgue attendants had barely been able to navigate across the mess. Dried blood clung to the walls, splattering the refrigerator, coffee area and watercooler.

"Where are the bodies?" Remo called out the door.

"They took them," a voice replied from outside.

"We'll have to take a trip to the morgue, Little Father. The victims might be able to give us a clue."

The Master of Sinanju nodded. He was standing in a clear patch, examining the floor with an experimental toe of his sandal. When Remo looked, he saw that Chiun was tracing deep furrows in the linoleum. They looked almost like claw marks.

"What are those?"

"It appears to be the work of an animal," Chiun said. "See the depth of scarring. There was strength behind this blow. You are certain the things that did this were human?''

"People did this, right?" Remo shouted out the door.

"Yes," the Vaunted employee said. "Well, they *were* people. I don't know what came over them."

"You know if they were hepped up on goofballs? Snorting Liquid Plumr? Anything like that?"

"I don't think so. You could ask them."

Frowning, Remo stepped back into the hallway. "I thought they were dead."

The office worker shook his head. "Two of them are. The police had to shoot them. They were like animals. But they captured the others."

"Beats questioning a corpse. I guess our next stop is the police lockup, Chiun."

The Master of Sinanju had just padded out into the hall, a troubled look on his leathery face.

The three men were heading back to the police tape when a low sound caught Remo's attention.

He stopped dead, listening. The Master of Sinanju paused at his side.

"What is it?" the old Korean asked.

After a silent moment, Remo shook his head. "I thought I heard something."

Shrugging, he started up the hall when the soft noise floated to him once more. This time the Master of Sinanju heard it, too. They shared a tight glance.

"What's wrong?" the nervous office worker asked when the two men turned abruptly away from the yellow tape.

"Don't know," Remo said, pitching his voice low.

"But, hey, I've got a fun idea. Why don't you run back as fast as you can and hide with the others?"

The man blinked. "Um…"

"Lock the door," the Master of Sinanju added darkly, his button nose upturned and sniffing the air.

The office worker did not need to be told again. He turned and ran, snapping into two neat halves the thin plastic police tape. He was out of sight before the yellow ends had fluttered to the floor.

Remo and Chiun headed in the opposite direction. Senses tuned to the soft vibrations of the building around them, they swept stealthily down toward the end of the hall.

They felt it now. It had been far and weak. So weak that even their highly tuned senses had failed to detect it.

A dying heartbeat.

No matter what Chiun thought about the marks in the break-room floor, the sound was distinctly human. The thready thump came from the last office.

Like sharks honing in on a single droplet of blood in an ocean of water, they tracked the noise.

The door was slightly ajar; the room beyond was dark. Dusty blinds had been twisted shut on the late-morning light.

Gently Remo nudged the door open. Eyes trained to see in darkness drew in enough ambient light to illuminate the room.

The body was sprawled on the floor, head propped at a painful angle against the wall. The stomach was ripped open, exposing curved bones of a broken rib cage. The man wore the tattered uniform of a New York City police officer.

As Remo and Chiun watched, the exposed heart of the dying cop offered a feeble beat.

Wincing, Remo began to step toward the dying man. A strong hand held him fast.

"Look," Chiun whispered. With a long nail, the Master of Sinanju pointed at the shadows.

A second uniformed policeman had been dragged behind a desk. Craning his neck, Remo saw the other man had suffered the same fate as the first. He was luckier than his companion. The second man was dead.

Remo shook his head, confused.

"I thought they rounded them all up," he whispered. "What the hell is loose in here?"

Chiun's face was a troubled mask. "Whatever it is, my son, walk with care."

Stepping across the room, Remo knelt next to the living man. To his right beside the desk, a door was open to an adjacent room.

The police officer was too far gone. There was no way to revive him even for a moment of questioning. Cruel face darkening in disgust, Remo used a sharp temple blow to kill the officer swiftly and mercifully.

When he turned, he found the Master of Sinanju standing at the second body. Chiun was examining the man's injuries.

Remo was surprised to see a strange look on his teacher's parchment features. If Remo didn't know better, he would almost say it was fear.

"Chiun?" he asked, taking a step toward the old

Korean. And in the fraction of slivered time it took him to speak his teacher's name, there came a soft growl at Remo's back.

It shouldn't have been there. It was too close. His senses should have detected anything living. Yet there *was* something alive. Breathing warm down his neck.

Shocked, Remo had barely time to twist around.

The creatures sprang. Like shadowy lightning they launched from the murky recesses of the adjacent office.

. With fangs bared and a jungle roar, the two remaining New York police officers flew at the exposed throats of the two Masters of Sinanju.

7

Though they had the outward appearance of men, the two leaping creatures seemed possessed with the strength and speed of wild beasts. They moved on instinct and rage. Animals, not humans.

At the last moment, one soared past Remo in a blur, head tipped to one side. Sharp teeth sought the scrawny neck of the Master of Sinanju.

Strong arms extended, the second attacker flew for Remo's chest.

A primitive urge compelled him to knock his prey down. Ease the kill.

But while these animals that wore the flesh of men attacked on primal instinct, their prey were much more than mere men. They were Sinanju—beings trained to the very peak of mental and physical perfection.

Behind Remo, Chiun's right hand lashed out. A sure stroke behind the ear separated bone from bone. Flesh and muscle split apart before the old Asian's slicing nails.

Chiun did a little pirouette and the creature flew past, wind whistling through the empty space where a moment before his jaw had been. The severed jaw dropped to the floor.

The shocked animal tumbled to the floor, scrambling to right himself near one of the dead police officers. A long tongue flapped in empty air. The creature whimpered in pain and confusion.

Chiun sent a hard heel into the animal's forehead.

The creature that was a grotesque mockery of man collapsed onto the gutted corpse that had been his last meal.

In the split second Chiun was removing his attacker, Remo was dealing death to his own.

When the hurtling beast was an inch away from ramming Remo's chest, Remo moved. He fell with the blow, lower spine bending at an impossible angle until his back was parallel to the floor. His startled attacker flew over.

The creature slammed against the nearby wall, snarling confusion.

He was back up in an instant. Twisting with remarkable speed, he launched himself on powerful legs back at Remo.

But this time, the instant before he could make contact with his prey, the creature suddenly stopped. He landed in an alert crouch, sniffing the air suspiciously.

A new scent wafted to his nose, carried on eddies of fetid office air. Fresh blood.

Sharp eyes located the source.

Two yards away, Remo held up one hand. A single drop of crimson glistened on the index fingernail. Remo flicked it off. Slowly lowering his hand, he used the same finger to point at the animal's stomach.

At the same instant, the man-beast felt a strange yawning sensation in his belly.

The creature glanced down just in time to see the meaty sacks of his own internal organs spilling from a razor slit in his abdomen. He was still staring down in utter incomprehension as Remo sunk a loafer toe in his downturned forehead. The beast dropped to the floor.

As dust began to settle on the body, Chiun was swirling to Remo's side.

"Proof again that I don't need to grow all my nails longer," Remo said tightly. He cleaned his index fingernail—trimmed slightly longer than the rest for scoring glass and metal—on the uniform shirt of his dead attacker.

"Human opponents rarely offer themselves up for slaughter," the Master of Sinanju replied, his voice cold and still. "These things were not men."

Remo was studying the bodies. A memory had already begun to stir in his troubled mind, like an old fear awakened from a long hibernation.

"They have to be," he insisted, more to himself than to Chiun.

But the old Korean was adamant. "You saw with your own eyes," he said. "Men have not the strength or speed of these brutes. And witness their intent, the animal glint in their eyes. I have seen things like these only twice before."

Remo shook his head firmly. "I know what you're thinking, Chiun, but that's impossible." His eyes alighted on the empty stomach cavity of one of the cannibalized victims. "Isn't it?"

Chiun wasn't listening. The old man was examining the nearer creature.

"Okay, I didn't think it was possible the second time," Remo admitted. "But she's dead."

"You are positive?"

"You were there," Remo argued. "You saw her die."

"I saw that creature injured. I did not see it dead. Or perhaps another has taken up that one's unholy cause. In either case, we obviously were too quick to lay the evil to rest."

As Remo studied the hollowed-out body on the floor, he felt the certainty draining from him. The scene in the Vaunted Press office was too eerily reminiscent of something they had encountered before. Something horrible. But his logical mind told him it could not possibly be.

"We should contact Smith," Chiun announced abruptly.

Remo tore his eyes from the body. "Maybe," he said reluctantly. "Still, I don't want to send him into cardiac arrest until we're absolutely one hundred percent sure. The cops have some of these locked up. Let's check them out first."

"These constables were infected," Chiun pointed out. "Others might be, as well."

"Maybe a few," Remo said, "but not all. The two they chowed down on here were cops. We'll be okay."

"Said the mouse to the cat," the old man sniffed. Hems of his black robes twirling near his bony ankles, he swept past Remo out into the hall.

Alone in the office, Remo bit his lip thoughtfully as he glanced at the bodies one last time.

''It can't be,'' he insisted.

But even he could hear the soft strain of doubt in his own whispered voice.

8

The PCP craze back in the seventies had been bad. Back then they'd had to peel angel dusters off the ceiling. Bones in hands and wrists were shattered as fists that could not feel pain pounded over and over against cinder-block walls. One junkie had broken all his teeth trying to chew his way through the iron bars of the lockup.

That was bad.

The rest of the time was regular assorted hopheads, winos and psychos. Some of those were real humdingers. The Bellevue Express hummed night and day from the station filled with your general order of whacko. They were bad, too.

But in his more than twenty years on the force, Sergeant Jimmy Simon had never seen anything like this.

The creatures that had been brought in that morning were not human. Whatever they had sniffed, smoked, shot up or swallowed had turned them into ranting, snarling, growling, snapping animals. *Cannibals.* Honest-to-God New York City cannibals. These fruitcakes hadn't been arrested; they'd been *caged.*

Booking them in the traditional sense proved impossible. Simon already had two men in the hospital with severe chest and neck lacerations. They had made the mistake of trying to fingerprint one of the original Vaunted Press pair.

They'd all been Mirandized through cell bars. There was no way to mug shot them. A Polaroid was brought to the cells with special instructions to the photographer not to get within an arm's length of the cages.

Sergeant Jimmy Simon had been relieved at the main desk of the South Precinct Midtown station more than half an hour before, but had yet to leave. As the day wore on and the crisis worsened, the order came for everyone to stay put until further notice. Men were being called in from home.

Jimmy Simon had always thought the place was a zoo. But now it was...well, a *zoo*.

"A zoo. A goddamn zoo," Simon muttered to himself.

Simon sat in a wobbly chair behind the on-duty desk sergeant, filling out paperwork. As he spoke, a terrible roar rolled up from the depths of the station.

The new desk sergeant wheeled, startled at the sound.

"What the hell was that?" Sergeant Jeff Malloy asked.

Jimmy didn't look up from his paperwork. "Must be feeding time," he replied. "They been doing that all day."

The noise came again. A tiger's roar.

Sergeant Malloy felt the short hair on the back of his neck stand on end. "Jesus," he swore.

"Tell me about it," Simon grunted.

Simon doubted he'd ever get used to the sounds that had been coming from downstairs all morning.

Every time someone went to check on the more than two dozen prisoners, the commotion got worse. It was twelve-thirty in the afternoon and Sergeant Simon still got chills from the roars and snarls that had been rolling up from downstairs for the past three hours.

"A freaking goddamn zoo," he muttered to himself.

Another roar. So loud Jimmy Simon jumped, dropping his Bic disposable.

He couldn't take it any longer. Simon spun in his chair. "O'Reilly, go see what the hell's going on down there," he hollered across the room.

A young officer looked up from where he had been filling out a report. "I told you an hour ago," O'Reilly complained. "They're mostly just sniffing and stretching. They looked at me like I was a T-bone or somethin'."

"Just go," Simon barked. "And watch your Irish ass."

Grumbling, the patrolman got to his feet. O'Reilly was disappearing down the back squad-room staircase when Simon caught sight of a pair of new arrivals coming up the main stairs from the street.

"What now?" he muttered.

One was young, the other ancient.

The Asian looked to be a hundred years old and moved with a gliding shuffle that barely stirred his black robes. The young one wore a black T-shirt and chinos. Wrists as thick as small trees rotated absently as the two of them approached the desk.

The young one was about to speak when the old one bullied his way in front.

"We would see the beasts caged in your menagerie," the Master of Sinanju demanded of Sergeant Malloy.

Jimmy Simon was relieved these two hadn't come in during his desk shift. "Gotta be a full moon tonight," he grumbled.

"Tend your own affairs or invoke the Master's wrath, doughnut gobbler," Chiun spit at the seated man. "Show us the beasts," he ordered Malloy.

Behind the Master of Sinanju, Remo could see the color rise in Simon's flabby cheeks. Before the sergeant could say something he would have plenty of time to regret as a team of surgeons worked to unplug his badge from his sinuses, Remo hastily interceded.

"FBI," he said, waving his phony ID. "We want to see the people you brought in today."

"They are not people," Chiun corrected.

"Yeah? Well, you got that right," Jimmy Simon said from his chair. "But no dice."

"We're just going to take a quick look," Remo said.

"No, you're not," Sergeant Simon replied, standing. He hitched up his belt under his sagging gut. "I've got a city-wide panic going on out there, and those nutcases downstairs are in on it. They're already wired up from missing breakfast. Listen to the roaring down there. You get your ass too close to a cage, and they'll have both of you for lunch. And I'm not mopping up the mess.''

He tugged at his belt again. It felt good to throw his weight around. Especially after a day like today. He waited for this FBI agent to argue.

But the Fed didn't argue. He just got a funny look on his face. So did the old coot in the black pajamas.

''What roaring?'' Remo said.

Sergeant Simon's broad face grew confused. ''Huh?''

''That's funny,'' Sergeant Malloy said. ''They stopped.'' He glanced beyond Simon to the stairs at the rear of the squad room. Silence rose up from below.

Jimmy Simon listened. He heard only the normal bustle of the busy station house.

''That's weird,'' Simon said.

Remo and Chiun were no longer listening to the police officers. Hearing more acute than any other human ears on the face of the planet was trained on the building's lower floors, filtering out the noise, absorbing the soft sounds. All at once, both men snapped alert.

''They are attacking,'' the Master of Sinanju snapped.

A sudden blur of movement, faster than the naked eye could perceive.

One moment they were standing in place; the next, both Remo and Chiun had vaulted over the desk. Sergeants Simon and Malloy spun a stunned dance around them as they flew past. Before Sergeant Simon could voice a protest, a fresh sound erupted from beneath his feet.

Gunfire.

"Oh, God," Simon said.

Remo and Chiun were moving swiftly across the squad room toward the rear stairs. Belly jiggling madly, Sergeant Simon sprinted to catch up. His gun was out of its holster.

"I just sent a man down to check on them," he huffed.

All objections to Remo and Chiun's presence were gone. Other officers were running for the narrow stairway.

"How many are there?" Remo demanded.

"Twenty-seven," Simon replied.

More muffled gunshots. Firing wildly. The kind of crazed shooting that indicated panic.

When they reached the basement level, they followed a short, gloomy corridor to a closed steel door. Remo, Chiun and the crush of officers massed outside the door. One man was already there when they arrived. His face was ashen.

The gunfire had stopped.

"What's the situation?" Simon demanded, panting.

"Two men inside," the uniformed officer at the door volunteered breathlessly. "The shooting started once they were locked inside. I don't know what's going on."

A small Plexiglas window sat at eye level in the door. The young officer jumped when a hand abruptly slapped against the glass.

"It's O'Reilly," Sergeant Simon said, exhaling relief. "That's his high-school football ring. Let him out."

"No," Remo snapped, snatching the keys that had been heading for the lock.

"What?" Jimmy Simon growled angrily. "What the hell—" He stopped dead. "Oh, my God," he breathed.

Sick eyes were trained on the door. The red flush of his cheeks paled.

O'Reilly's hand continued to tap against the window. But on closer scrutiny Simon saw now that the fingers were pale and lifeless. And then he saw the other hand holding it aloft, and saw the ragged flesh where O'Reilly's hand had been severed from his forearm. And then Sergeant Jimmy Simon—eighteen years on the force, immune to everything this crummy job could throw at him—was vomiting up his lunch onto the Midtown station cell-block floor.

The face of the man who had been pressing O'Reilly's hand to the window appeared briefly. Eyes wild, fangs bared, the creature took a vicious bite out the patrolman's severed hand before disappearing from view.

"Shit," Simon said, wiping puke on his sleeve. "Sweet Jesus, they're out of their cells." He slumped against the cold wall.

"Can they escape this?" Chiun demanded, waving at the door.

"I don't know. Maybe. There's this door and one way on the other side. They were built pretty tough."

Chiun turned to Remo. "Even now they look for

weaknesses in this dungeon's fortifications," the old Korean said. "They must be contained."

"Why is it always us?" Remo sighed. He turned to Simon. "Okay, stand back, Pop 'n Fresh. We're going in."

"Are you nuts?" Jimmy Simon asked. "Did you see what they did? They'll eat you alive."

"Fine with me," Remo grumbled. "Dead is the only way I'm ever gonna get a rest in this life. All the time it's work, work, work."

The police could see by the look of angry resolve on the strange FBI man's face that there would be no arguing.

"At least take my gun," Sergeant Simon pleaded.

Chiun swatted gun and sergeant away. The police fell back from the door, weapons leveled should anything try to escape when it opened.

"There's no way you two guys are going to get them back in their cells," Simon called, perspiring on the far end of his Smith & Wesson. "And if they charge out of there, you're getting mowed down, too."

"Go deep throat a cruller and let me work in peace," Remo suggested, jamming the key in the lock.

Before he could give it a turn, Chiun touched Remo's wrist. "My son," the Master of Sinanju whispered, "there is something I did not mention to you when last we encountered these creatures." His parchment face was drawn tight.

"I don't think now's a good time, Little Father."

"Listen," the old Korean snapped. "It is impor-

tant.'' There was a gleam of furious concern in his hazel eyes.

Remo felt the shudder of urgency pass from the frail little man who had taught him all he knew. He grew still.

''When we encountered the first of these beasts, I told you of the Sinanju legend. Do you remember?''

''That was over twenty years ago. And that time is still kind of fuzzy to me,'' Remo admitted. ''I had the wind knocked out of my sails.''

Chiun pitched his voice low. ''You are avatar of Shiva—'' He paused, waiting for the argument that always came after making this assertion.

But this time—for the first time—Remo remained silent. A shadow of acceptance crossed his brow.

The wizened Asian could not take joy in the fact that his pupil had finally accepted destiny.

''While now is not the time to discuss what it is the gods have in store for you, there is more than mere glory with which you must contend. The legend that speaks of Shiva also speaks a warning. You who have been through death before can only be sent to death by your kind or my kind.''

''I think I remember that,'' said Remo, who had been sentenced to die in an electric chair that did not work as part of the elaborate frame-up that had brought him into CURE. He scrunched up his face. ''I didn't know what it meant then, and crap if I know what it means now.''

''What's going on?'' Sergeant Simon called nervously.

''Silence, gaspot!'' Chiun shot back.

He spun to Remo. "You are the dead night tiger made whole by the Master of Sinanju," he said urgently. "Your kind are other night tigers. My kind—now *our* kind—are Masters of Sinanju. Since you need not fear death from me, if the legend speaks truth, it can come from but one other source."

"Night tigers," Remo supplied.

"Precisely. The legend states that even Shiva must walk with care when he passes the jungle where lurk other night tigers."

Remo considered his words for a long moment. Finally he looked down into the intent hazel eyes of the Master of Sinanju.

"Lucky for me this isn't a jungle," Remo said. And before the old Korean could stop him, he opened the door and passed like a shadow inside.

For an instant, Chiun remained.

Still young. Still arrogant. There had been times in the past when the most hazardous time for a newly invested Reigning Master were those first years as head of the village. The world was never more dangerous than when it seemed to no longer pose a threat.

All this and more did pass through the troubled mind of the Master of Sinanju in an instant. Praying to his gods that his words had had their desired impact, Chiun twirled through the gap in the door and was gone.

Behind, the police who had been tensed for an attack were jarred by the sudden disappearance of the two FBI men, as well as by the sudden sharp slamming of the metal door.

Somehow the keys came to a sliding stop at the

feet of Sergeant Jimmy Simon. His eyes strayed from the keys back to the closed door. He shook his head.

"When they get through with you, we're gonna need sponges for the remains," he announced.

Struggling over his wide belly, he stooped to snatch up the keys.

THE FETID AIR inside the lockup was thick with the smell of death. Remo and Chiun kept their breathing low. All the cell doors were ajar. The police had thought it safe to put normal prisoners in the lockup as long as they were separate from the more dangerous ones. With the keys taken from the late Officer O'Reilly, the creatures had made a feast not only out of the unlucky young police officer, but out of their fellow prisoners as well.

Greedy chewing issued from the dank corners of some cells. Sharp snaps came as strong jaws cracked brittle bones.

As Remo and Chiun made their way from the door, both men sensed hungry eyes tracking their every movement.

Noses keener than those of mere men fed the scent of fresh prey to watering mouths. Yellow feline eyes stared unblinking from out the shadows.

"You know the story of Daniel?" Remo whispered as they crept along. The cells opened right and left along the long corridor.

Chiun nodded. "Yes," he said. "And do not believe every Bible you pick up off the sidewalk."

A soft growl rose nearby.

"Sue me for finding comfort in a story where a guy who's tossed to the lions gets out alive."

"Find comfort in whatever nonsense you wish on your *own* time," Chiun commanded. "For the moment your unwillingness to accept the obvious has dragged me into this pit, so pay attention."

No sooner had the old man spoken than Remo felt a sudden displacement of air to his right.

There were six creatures growling within the nearest cell. As Remo and Chiun passed, one launched from the pack.

Until that morning, Remo's attacker had been an investment counselor who had spent an hour every night pumping away on a treadmill. The powerful legs his nightly workout had given him launched him from his jail cell bunk. He flew from the dark, fangs bared.

Outside the open cell door, Remo noted blandly that the man was coming in pretty fast. But for the Reigning Master of the House of Sinanju, pretty fast was not fast enough.

Remo watched the man come, gauged his speed and—at the last possible moment—slammed the cell door into the lunging creature's head.

Steel bars went clang, head went crack and the former investment counselor collapsed like a high-tech mutual fund after a lousy fourth-quarter-earnings report.

Instantly the five other creatures inside the cell surrounded the body. One kicked at the unconscious male with an experimental toe. When he didn't object, the five creatures began to nip and claw. As a pack, they began to tear off his clothes. They were growling and devouring chunks of flesh as Remo turned from the cell door.

"This might be easier than I thought," he said grimly to the Master of Sinanju.

His reply came not from Chiun but from farther up the cell block.

"Don't bet on it, kitten," purred a female voice.

Remo glanced over.

Elizabeth Tiflis stood in shadow two cells away. Her arms were crossed lightly. A knowing smile toyed at the corners of her very red lips.

There was still a gleam of deep intelligence in the eyes of the Vaunted Press employee, unnerving since it was clear she was something far more savage than man.

A few feet away from where she stood, six more creatures paced back and forth. Their yellow eyes stared with a predator's malevolence at Remo and Chiun.

"Who ordered chink food?" one of the females asked, her voice a throaty purr. Her hungry gaze was locked on Chiun.

"Quiet," Elizabeth commanded.

She had seen Remo's speed with the cell door. Elizabeth understood they were dealing with something different here. The creature Elizabeth scolded fell silent.

"Okay, here's the deal," Remo said. "We've had experience with your kind before, and there might be something that can be done to help you. But that doesn't mean we won't stop you if we have to. Now, you're not getting out of here, so why don't you be a nice kitty and get back in your cage?''

The harshness of Elizabeth's features melted into a malevolent, Cheshire-cat grin.

"Who says we want help?'' she said. "Besides…''

Slowly Elizabeth raised her hand. Around her slender index finger jangled the ring of cell-block keys.

"You're fast, sweetie,'' she said. "But I can let them out as quick as you can lock them up.''

This time it was Remo who smiled. "Don't bet on it, kitten.''

But even as he spoke he saw the slight nod from Elizabeth. The creatures behind her took the cue. A symphony of furious growls rolled up from six throats as the animals launched from the floor.

Unlike Elizabeth, they didn't view the two frail humans standing stock-still on the concrete floor as anything other than an easy meal. Humans were puny. Humans were weak.

Humans were also—apparently—missing.

The six pouncing creatures landed in the precise spot where dinner had stood only to find that the two men were no longer there. Curious growls rumbled up six throats.

When the nearby voice came, sounding like the voice of death itself, the creatures jumped in fear.

"The Master of Sinanju is not a meal, lowly beasts.''

The pack wheeled. Chiun was there, already moving.

The old Korean grabbed two creatures by the scruffs of their necks and hurled them deep into an open cell. They tumbled in a heap of limbs onto a bunk.

"Make that *Masters,*" said Remo, who was suddenly among the pack. A pair of elbows found two soft bellies. With a violent expulsion of vile breath, two more creatures flew into the cell, knocking back the first pair, which had scurried to their feet and were heading back for the door.

"Score two for the great white hunter," Remo said.

Panicked now, the final two attacked blindly. Jaws snapped viciously, teeth eager to tear flesh.

They chomped down on empty air.

And while their teeth clicked futilely and their bellies grumbled disappointment, the final two creatures felt a sudden jolting pressure to their chests.

They didn't see Remo's and Chiun's feet fly out. They only knew that one moment they had been charging; the next they were airborne.

Howling in rage, the last pair soared inside the cell, knocking over the first four, who were still in the process of scampering to their feet. Outside, Remo slammed the cage door shut. A paw tried to snatch at him through the bars.

"See?" Remo said, hopping clear of the swiping hand. "Only pantywaists use whips and chairs."

Chiun was already moving swiftly away from Remo.

"Hurry up, Great White Lunkhead," the old Asian snapped.

He bounded from cell to cell, yanking doors shut.

Remo raced along the other side of the block.

Until then most of the creatures had remained in

their cells, feeding hungrily on the unfortunate junkies, rapists and run-of-the mill murderers who'd had the misfortune of being arrested that day. None had been concerned with the two strangers, assuming they could be picked off easily at their leisure. But the clanging cage doors brought sudden realization. Roaring in anger, the beasts in human form abandoned gutted corpses, bounding across cells.

Too late. As the last of the creatures skidded to a frustrated stop, Remo and Chiun slammed the final two doors.

Snarls and howls of rage filled the cell block.

Remo scanned the last few cells for one face in particular. As he feared, Elizabeth Tiflis was nowhere to be seen.

''Where'd the one with the keys go?'' he asked.

As he spoke, panicked shouting suddenly erupted from the far end of the lockup. Gunfire rattled through the station house.

''This way,'' Chiun insisted.

The two men flew toward the disturbance.

A second door was around a sharp corner at the far end of a row of empty cages. When they turned the corner, Remo found that he and Chiun had not been entirely successful.

The door had been wrenched open. While the keys worked for the cells, the doors to the outside could only be opened from without. While Remo and Chiun had fought the rest, others had apparently been jimmying open the lockup door.

When Remo and Chiun exploded through the cell-block door, a dozen guns aimed their way.

Sergeant Simon stood with a SWAT team. He was panting and red-faced from his sprint through the precinct house.

"Are they after you?" Simon yelled.

"They're locked up," Remo snapped. "How many escaped?"

Simon didn't hear him. By the look on his face, Sergeant Simon was certain Remo and Chiun wouldn't be alone. Anxious eyes awaited the creatures that had to be chasing down the two FBI men. But no one appeared behind them.

"Where are they?" Simon asked.

"I told you, locked up. How many— Hey, Gunther Toody, will you knock it off and listen?"

Sergeant Simon was listening. Angry howls came from inside the cell block. But they sounded far back.

The SWAT team was already streaming past Remo, Chiun and Simon. They darted into the dank cell block.

"How many got out?" Remo pressed.

"Five," Simon panted. Numbly he holstered his gun.

The police had sustained casualties. Two men lay dead. A third was sprawled on the stairs, a row of vicious raking gashes across his chest. He groaned in pain as others tended his wounds, awaiting the arrival of paramedics.

"They could be anywhere by now," Remo said. "I guess we'll have to let the cops track them down again."

Beside him, the old Korean frowned somberly. "Perhaps," he said, stroking his thread of beard. "Do you not find it odd, Remo, that some chose to fill their bellies while others schemed to flee?''

"What am I now, the frigging Crocodile Hunter? Some eat, some run. It's what animals do. What?''

He could see his teacher was giving him that look. The "Remo, you're an idiot" look. But try as he might, Remo could not see what he'd said to deserve that look. And the fact that he couldn't see why he was an idiot, and the fact that Chiun could plainly see that Remo couldn't see why he was an idiot, only acted to further cement the expression of irritation on the wizened Asian's face.

"Animals flee as one and eat as one," the old Korean droned.

"And mares eat oats and does eat oats and little lambs eat ivy," Remo said. "So what? Hey, where are you going?"

The Master of Sinanju had turned away. Shaking his head in annoyance, he padded up the stairs.

"What did I not get?" Remo demanded of Sergeant Simon.

Jimmy Simon was staring down through the open cell-block door. Jungle roars echoed from out the darkness.

"Huh?" the police officer asked.

"Forget it," Remo sighed. "I need a phone."

Feet heavy, he climbed the stairs after the Master of Sinanju.

9

Mankind was destined for extinction.

No matter what bad human poets said, the end for mankind would not come with either fire or ice.

There would be no deep comet impacts or continent-sized holocausts. No massive gravitational or tectonic shifts to alter the geography of the planet over which he lorded his supremacy. Man's Earth would not be swallowed by a massive solar flare or turned inside out by cosmic collision with a spiraling black hole.

The ecologists who perpetuated the pollution myth would be proved wrong.

The climatologists would be mistaken about the bogeyman of global warming.

Even the entomologists and botanists who were predicting lower and lower crop yields with resultant mass starvation due to a dwindling population of pollinating insects would be proved wrong.

In the end, the thing that would doom mankind was something so small it couldn't be perceived by the naked eye. Mankind would be undone by his own vaunted technology.

The ultimate irony for a species that more and more valued science over nature.

The species that was Man would die out because the first female of the species that would supersede mankind as lord of the Earth wished it to be so.

While thinking thoughts of the end of human history, Dr. Judith White used her sharp white teeth to tug the stopper from the mouth of the test tube.

The open end exposed a textured black rubber ball.

With long fingernails, she delicately withdrew the eyedropper, careful not to lose a single drop of the brownish liquid that hung from its glass tip. With her middle finger, she tapped the hanging droplets back into the tube.

A charcoal filter rested in a shallow pan of water on the desk before her. With great care, she brought the dropper over the pan and gently squeezed the plunger.

Ten fat droplets of the brown solution plopped into the clear liquid in the pan. The pure Lubec Spring water darkened a deep brown.

Judith quickly replaced the dropper in the test tube, clamping the stopper back in place. Slipping the tube in her jacket pocket, she lifted the pan by the edges. With gentle movements, she swished the dark water around.

When she was satisfied that the compound had dissipated, she placed the pan back on the desk. She stood.

"Let it sit for an hour, then reinstall it," she ordered.

Standing before the desk, Owen Grude nodded understanding. "I think I can handle this now," he offered. "I've seen you do it dozens of times."

Owen was fidgeting. Agitated. As if at any moment he might try to spring in two directions at once.

Judith White had seen this sort of behavior in her young before. The cubs always had so much energy.

She shook her head firmly. "This is too critical. The filters have to be treated hourly. You're still a cub. At this stage stomach will always come before duty."

As if on cue, the quiet growl of Owen's rumbling stomach filled the room.

"Sorry," he apologized.

He was still trying to control his animal urges. But it was now against his nature.

Of course, Judith did not allow her base instincts to consume her. She had mastered both body and mind—harnessed them into a single, perfect being.

She could summon human intellect when it served her. She had the ability to squelch animal desire. And when it suited her, she could act on instinct better than any creature on the face of the planet.

She alone of all the beasts to ever walk and crawl and swim and run across the Earth had attained utter perfection.

Before her, Owen Grude shifted uncomfortably.

He was trying so hard to be strong. But the urges at this stage were nearly overwhelming. Owen had a long way to go before he attained the perfection of Dr. Judith White. But perfection was on the way. Not that Owen or any of the other new mongrels would be around long enough to witness it.

"You have a little time before this is ready. Go feed," Judith commanded.

Owen didn't need to be told a second time. Spinning on his heel, he prowled out of the office.

Once she was alone, Judith crossed over to a small, two-drawer filing cabinet. Beside it was a pair of pebbled black cases. She lifted one of the cases, setting it on a computer table below a long picture window.

The softly sighing conifers of the deep Maine woods were framed in the window. The beauty of the scenery had no meaning to Judith White.

Fingering the silver tabs on the case, she popped open the lid.

Inside was lined with the gray peaks and valleys of special packing foam. Large glass vials were lined up neatly on the egg-carton foam. There were now as many empty as full. Slipping the test tube carefully from her pocket, she set it delicately in its own recessed compartment.

There was a reason why she would not allow Owen or anyone else to handle the formula. There was simply no way she would *ever* entrust something so important with one of the others. The compound had to be measured just so.

Too little would take too long to affect the humans, if it worked at all. Too much would be a waste. The process would be accelerated to two seconds from fifteen.

And at the moment she didn't want to waste a drop. She could have more made, but it would disrupt her plan, which at the moment was proceeding precisely on schedule.

The intellectual part of her that remained knew that the odds were increasing in her favor with every passing hour.

"It's nothing personal, mankind," she growled to the whispering woods. "Just survival of the fittest."

Purring, Judith White slapped shut the case lid.

10

Dr. Harold W. Smith felt good.

For most people, feeling good was a normal sensation. Oh, sometimes it was fleeting, sometimes it lingered, but for the world at large it wasn't terribly unusual to simply feel good. But for the director of the secret agency CURE, feeling good was a strange, alien sensation.

A dour, lemony man, Smith's moods generally ran the gamut from mildly concerned to deeply anxious. Sometimes he was peevish; very rarely he was angry. At times—when his country or agency was threatened—there were moments of full-blown panic or, more likely, steadfast resolve.

Feeling good was definitely not part of his normal emotional repertoire. So on this day, as he steered his car onto the street on which he had lived for the past forty years, he resolved to savor the sensation.

Smith parked his rusted old station wagon in the driveway of his Rye, New York, home. He grabbed his battered leather briefcase from the seat beside him. After locking the briefcase in the back compartment alongside the spare tire, he headed up the front walk.

His wife had heard the sound of the car pulling in the driveway. She was at the front door to meet him.

"Hello, Harold," Maude Smith said. She was wiping her hands dry on a well-worn dishrag. Mrs. Smith had been in the process of scrubbing the old copper pots that had been a wedding gift from her long-deceased mother.

"Hello, dear," Smith said, giving the plump woman a peck on the cheek. He headed upstairs.

Smith generally stayed at work from before sunup until well after sundown. Seeing Harold home at any other time of day would ordinarily be cause of great concern to Mrs. Smith. But although it was only eleven o'clock in the morning, his wife had not been surprised to see her Harold today.

Smith had told her he would be home at this time. And since he said it, she was confident he would come. Maude's Harold was nothing if not reliable.

In the upstairs bedroom, Smith found his special clothes folded on a chair just where he'd left them.

His normal uniform was a three-piece gray suit, which he wore now. Smith changed out of the suit, hanging it carefully in the closet next to six other identical suits. He pulled on the powder-blue long-sleeved jersey and green plaid pants. There were some fabric pills on the shirt. Smith plucked them off, depositing them in the trash.

Sitting on the edge of the bed, he slipped his feet back in his dress shoes. He was lacing them back up when his wife stuck her head around the corner.

"Are you all right, Harold?" Maude asked, concerned.

"Yes, I'm fine." Smith asked, "Why?"

"That noise you were just making with your mouth. I thought something was wrong."

Smith frowned. "Noise?" he asked. "I don't believe I was making any noise, dear."

He picked up a pair of white shoes from the floor under the chair, just where he'd left them the previous night. Carrying the shoes under one arm, he kissed his wife on the cheek once more and headed back out into the hallway.

As he stepped down the stairs, he was unaware that he had started making the same horrible noise once more.

Behind him, Maude Smith watched from the top of the stairs. As he headed briskly out the door, she saw her husband's lips purse, saw his ashen cheeks puff out.

Maude recognized the noise this time. Her Harold was actually whistling. She shook her head in astonishment.

"Will wonders never cease?" she asked the walls with the old white paint that, although long yellowed from age, Harold refused to have repainted. The paint had been guaranteed to last thirty years, which would not be up for another two years. Even though the manufacturer had long gone out of business, Harold refused to pay to have the walls repainted until precisely thirty years had passed. Anything sooner than that would be an extravagance. Like whistling.

Maude heard the awful sound coming from outside. A dog two houses away was howling at the noise as her husband backed his station wagon out of the driveway.

Still shaking her head in amazement, but grateful to the Almighty just the same for her Harold's new outlook, Maude Smith climbed carefully back down the creaky old stairs.

SMITH COULD NOT THANK the Almighty for this morning away from work. Not that he didn't believe. A healthy fear of God had been inculcated in Harold Smith at an early age. But thanks to the requirements of his job as director of CURE, Smith had long before determined that he could not in good conscience involve the Deity in the matters of his adult life. Smith didn't bother God, and when the time of judgment came for him, Smith hoped the Almighty would understand the necessity of his many transgressions.

No, if any thanks were due at all, they went to Smith's assistant.

Mark Howard was a diligent young man who from the start had insisted that he relieve some of his employer's heavy burden. Thanks to Mark Howard, Harold Smith was able to take off two early afternoons every week to enjoy dinner with Maude. And thanks to his assistant, Smith was about to indulge in a guilty pleasure that he had given up long ago.

Smith's house bordered one of the most exclusive country clubs on the East Coast. As he drove along, he caught glimpses of well-tended greens between houses and trees.

Around the block and up through the gates, Smith

drove through the main entrance to the Westchester Golf Club.

There were plenty of spaces in the parking lot. Smith chose one recently vacated near the clubhouse. He changed into his golf shoes beside his car and took his wheeled bag of clubs from the back seat of the station wagon where he had carefully placed them earlier that morning.

He was whistling again as he headed for the clubhouse.

Although Smith had been paying his yearly membership dues without fail for the past forty years, he had been to the club only a handful of times in the past three decades.

When CURE had first been established by a President now long dead, Smith had been a CIA analyst living in Virginia. He had dutifully accepted his post, moving his family to Rye.

Smith had taken over directorship of Folcroft Sanitarium, a private mental institution and convalescent home in town. Folcroft was the cover for CURE, the agency that didn't officially exist. As part of his own cover, Smith had early on involved himself in his community. Not too much. But in the early 1960s, to be completely removed from one's community affairs was to invite suspicion, he reasoned.

One of the first things Smith did after settling in at Folcroft was join the Westchester Golf Club.

Almost straight away he was invited to be part of a regular foursome. It seemed three other members who happened to play on the same day as Smith—a doctor, a lawyer and a judge—had recently lost their fourth. The new director of Folcroft Sanitarium was more than welcome to join them.

It was perfect for Smith's plan of fitting in. He was the perfectly ordinary director of Folcroft Sanitarium, playing a perfectly ordinary game with perfectly ordinary companions. Nothing suspicious, everything aboveboard.

For almost two years in the early 1960s Smith had played regularly with the same three men. But then, slowly, he began missing dates.

The demands of his work. There was always some crisis that needed attention, always a catastrophe that needed to be averted. For a time the men would call his secretary asking where Smith was. Once or twice Smith did manage to get away to join them. Mostly he refused. Then one day he suddenly realized that it was the 1970s and his old golf companions had stopped calling almost a decade before.

It no longer mattered. Maude was active enough in the community for them both. And, luckily, over the years Americans had become more isolated. Gone were the days when neighbors knew every face on the block and the involvement of business leaders in the community was practically a requirement. As the century wound to a close, it was possible for people to live next door to one another for years without ever exchanging hellos. And the director of a private sanitarium could spend his every waking hour locked away in his office without ever venturing out to attend a city council meeting or to play even a single round of golf.

But things had changed once again—finally, blessedly—and Harold Smith, in the twilight of his life, was once more able to step out into the sunshine of the Westchester Golf Club. And to feel good in the process.

Drawing his clubs behind him, Smith entered the clubhouse. He found a smiling, fortyish woman with short blond hair and a tag on her jersey identifying her as staff.

"Good morning," Smith said. "Could you tell me if Dr. Glass is playing today?"

"Doctor who?" the woman asked.

"Dr. Robert Glass. He plays here every Wednesday."

"I'm sorry, but there's no Dr. Glass here."

Smith raised a thin brow. "You seem quite certain. You didn't even check."

"Actually, I don't really have to," the woman said. "I know everyone who's playing today. In fact, I know everyone who is a member at the club and we don't have a Dr. Glass."

Smith had met this kind of stubbornness before. He had seen it in all walks of life, from government bureaucrats to restaurant hostesses. People loved to see themselves as important and powerful. Obviously this woman's job as gatekeeper to the elite of Westchester County had gone to her head. But she had met her match today, for Harold Smith was in a rare good mood. The kind of mood where he would enjoy bringing an arrogant woman with clipboard delusions of grandeur down a peg or two.

He smiled. An uncomfortable twist of his thin lips. "Young lady, do you know who *I* am?" he asked.

"I'm sorry, no. Are you a friend of a member?"

"I *am* a member," Smith said. "Dr. Harold W. Smith. You will find that I have been a member of this club for over forty years. And since it is obvious you do not know me, we can safely dispense with your claim that you know everyone who belongs. Therefore you will concede that it is possible you've made a mistake and that Dr. Glass is a member, as well. Possibly he is even here today. Please check."

Smith's acid tone did not allow for refusal. The woman felt a red rash of embarrassment color her cheeks.

"I'm sorry, sir. I didn't mean—"

She quickly checked her reserved list. When she couldn't find a Dr. Glass there, she went behind the counter and checked the computerized membership rolls. Again she came up empty. Fortunately, the club director—a man Smith recognized from years before—happened to be passing by.

The club director had been a young assistant back then. He was older now, with white hair and a dark tan. Deep furrows of laugh lines crimped the corners of his eyes. When he was told there was a problem with a missing Westchester Golf Club member, the laugh lines blossomed, forming deep, sympathetic crevices. He frowned sadly.

"I'm sorry to be the one to tell you this, Dr. Smith," the man said, "but Dr. Glass passed away."

Smith blinked. "Oh," he said.

He was surprised he hadn't heard. His wife generally kept him up-to-date on such matters. Although Smith was the first to admit that as the years passed he found himself paying less and less attention to his wife's nightly reports on their community. Smith was usually distracted by CURE matters and generally tuned out Maude Smith, offering only a few "yes, dears" whenever they seemed warranted.

Obviously he had missed the death of his old golfing companion Robert Glass. He would have to send his widow a sympathy card.

"When did he die?" Smith asked.

The country club director checked his chart. "Ah, 1987," he replied.

"Oh," Smith said again. Perhaps it was too late for a sympathy card. "Is his wife still a member?"

"She moved to Florida. I believe she passed away last year. I could check if you'd like."

"Don't bother," Smith said, clearing his throat. "There were two other men Dr. Glass and I used to golf with. George Garner and Phillip Lassiter. Are they still, er, members?"

He could tell the answer from the fresh deeply sympathetic look that came over the man's face.

"I'm sorry, Dr. Smith. Judge Garner passed on about five years ago." He pitched his voice low. "Actually, it happened here. He'd just played eighteen holes and came back to the clubhouse. It happened in the locker room. He just sort of fell over. Eighty-six years old. In remarkable shape for a man his age. We were all shocked and saddened."

Smith's earlier good mood had long evaporated.

"Yes, thank you," he said tightly. "I'm sorry to have bothered you." He turned to go.

"Mr. Lassiter is still with us," the club director offered brightly. "An attorney here in Rye, correct?"

"That's right," Smith said, turning back.

"In fact, I saw him here this morning." The country club director's smile of optimism faded behind a somber cloud. "Oh, but you probably meant the father."

"Father?"

"Phillip Lassiter *Senior*. The name of the firm was changed to Lassiter and Lassiter years ago. The father and son are—were—both lawyers. Have you driven past their downtown offices in the last—oh, twenty years or so? That big sign out front?"

Now that he mentioned it, Smith had seen the name change driving through downtown Rye. He had noted it when it happened and then filed it away and forgot about it. The *Lassiter and Lassiter, Attorneys at Law* sign was now part of the background of his everyday life—just something he drove past and ignored.

"Yes," Smith said, already knowing where this was going.

"The second Lassiter is your Mr. Lassiter's son, also Phillip. Mr. Lassiter Junior is a member here, but I'm afraid Mr. Lassiter Senior is, well, no longer with us. Lung cancer, I'm afraid. He's been gone almost ten years. A shame, really. Such a gentleman. Never an unkind word for anyone. We all missed him dearly when he passed."

"Yes," Smith said. "Thank you. Excuse me, but I have a tee time."

Turning, Smith headed for the door, pulling his golf bag behind him. The wheels squeaked.

"Your clubs are wonderful, Dr. Smith," the club

director called behind him. "Very old. Almost antiques, really. You don't see very many like those around these days."

"Yes," agreed Dr. Harold W. Smith, who, as he headed out the gleaming glass door into the spring sunshine, no longer felt the urge to whistle.

11

The ivy-covered brick building that was Folcroft Sanitarium was nestled amid budding birch and late-blooming spring maples on the shore of Long Island Sound. In a small rear office on the second floor of the administrative wing, Mark Howard sat behind his scarred oak desk.

If he leaned over far enough, Mark could have just glimpsed the sparkling waters of the Sound out his office window. Mark didn't look out the window this day.

Intent brownish-green eyes were locked on the computer monitor on his desk. The monitor was attached by cable through the floor to four mainframes hidden behind a secret panel in the sanitarium's basement.

With a concerned expression on his wide face, Mark studied the data that scrolled across his computer screen.

At just under six feet tall, Howard was thin with broad shoulders. His face had the pleasant corn-fed wideness of America's heartland, ruddy at the cheeks. He lent the impression—even sitting—of a man who was always just a few seconds late for wherever he was going.

If some lost visitors were to accidentally step in from the hall, they would be singularly unimpressed by the average-looking young man in a small office. There were millions more just like him in banks and boardrooms around the nation. Bored at the seeming blandness of both man and office, they would have left, never realizing that the man they had so easily dismissed as average was arguably the second most powerful man in the world.

The assistant director of CURE was scanning the latest reports out of New York. He didn't like what he saw.

More cases of strange attacks were coming in hourly.

Dr. Smith had sent Remo and Chiun to investigate early that morning. Their plane had touched down in New York more than an hour ago. By then Dr. Smith had already left the office.

Mark was loath to call the CURE director back. After all, until Remo reported in, there was nothing Smith could do except sit and worry. For now, that was Mark Howard's job.

The assistant CURE director had gladly accepted that particular burden as just another one of his duties. For more than forty years Dr. Smith had worked tirelessly as director of CURE. When Mark had arrived at Folcroft more than two years ago, Smith had been showing all the signs of a man slowly surrendering to life's twilight. That was gone now.

Since Mark had come aboard, Smith had regained

his focus and energy. Only a small part of that had to do with having someone now to share the burden he had for so long carried alone. No, the thing that had most reinvigorated the CURE director was his protégé. He now had someone from a new generation with whom he could share thoughts, guidance and wisdom. In Mark Howard, Harold Smith was reborn.

Mark had seen the slow metamorphosis in his employer and understood the psychology behind the change. And in every way he could—large and small—he had determined to keep Harold Smith's burden light. America owed the older man that. And Mark Howard would do his part to repay the debt.

Howard pulled his eyes from his monitor. There had been another attack, this one at a delicatessen in Manhattan.

Mark's right eye was starting to ache. Staring at the computer was beginning to take its toll. He had always had better than twenty-twenty vision. Thanks to CURE, a few more years and he would have to think about glasses.

He was rubbing his eye with the heel of his hand when the black phone on his desk jangled to life.

Glancing sharply, he noted that it was the contact line. Dr. Smith had had all calls rerouted to his assistant's office while he was away, including the special line.

Mark grabbed up the phone, pressing the blinking blue light. "Hello," he said.

"We've got major problems here, kid," Remo said without preamble. "I need to talk to Smith."

"Dr. Smith isn't here right now," Mark said.

"What are you talking about? It's one in the afternoon. Smith's never not there at one in the afternoon. What is he, counting cotton swabs in the supply closet? Get off your duff and go get him. Now."

"He's not here, Remo," Mark insisted. "He's gone to play golf. He mentioned that he was going to try to hook up with some guys he used to play with."

"Oh, for Pete's sake. Perfect timing, Smitty," Remo grumbled to himself. "Can you page him?"

"Yes," Mark said. "Remo, what is going on there?"

There was an impatient hiss on the line. "You have access to Smith's computer records?"

"Yes."

Remo said only three words: "Dr. Judith White."

Mark spun to his computer. Short fingers moved swiftly over the clattering keyboard. In seconds he had pulled up the relevant CURE records.

"Judith White. Geneticist. Worked for a company called BostonBio on the Bos Camelus-Whitus." The stir of memory strained his voice. "Oh, no," Mark said worriedly. "I remember this. It was in the news right around Dolly the sheep. This Dr. White was into bizarre genetic engineering, wasn't she? She went on some kind of rampage three years ago in Boston. Oh. According to this encryption in Dr. Smith's notes, you and Chiun stopped her."

"Not good enough apparently. It looks like she's behind what's going on here."

Mark paused a beat. "Remo, it says here that Judith White is dead. I'm assuming you had a hand in that, too."

"And an arm."

"Excuse me?"

"An arm," Remo said. "As in I ripped her arm out of its socket just before she fell three stories and had a million tons of burning factory collapse on her. Sue me for assuming she'd gone to that great litter box in the sky."

Mark nodded. "Very well, I'll page Dr. Smith." He checked the time in the corner of his computer screen. "It will take him a good twenty minutes to get back here. Stay at this number. We'll call you back."

"Make it snappy," Remo said.

The assistant CURE director hung up the phone. He fished a scrap of paper with Smith's pager number from his jacket pocket. He glanced at his monitor. The blob of a cursor blinked over the *J* in Judith White's name.

"Sorry, Dr. Smith," Mark Howard lamented. "I hope you enjoyed your first five minutes off in forty years."

Exhaling, he reached once more for the phone.

ALL THINGS CONSIDERED, it had not gone as poorly as Smith had imagined.

He was rusty the first few holes, as would be expected. For working out the kinks, he had been generous keeping score—golf had always been the one aspect of his life where Smith's otherwise scrupulous honesty failed completely and utterly. But by the seventh and eighth he felt his game returning, almost as if he'd never given it up. By the ninth he barely had to cheat at all.

By the time he returned to the clubhouse, most of

his good humor had returned. He tipped his caddie a generous $1.25, adjusted for inflation from his old golfing days. As the young man muttered curses under his breath, Smith carted his own clubs up the stairs to the big shaded patio that stretched out at the rear of the main clubhouse.

Tables under umbrellas were arranged around the deck. Most were filled by patrons of the club's restaurant.

Through the patio doors was the more formal dining hall. To the left was the lounge.

Smith was passing the bar on his way out to the main lobby when he heard the disturbance.

A man at the bar was choking. At least he seemed to be. Hands clutched tight at his throat.

A club staff member—Smith noted that it was the same woman who had tried to help him earlier—was slapping the man on the back, a worried look on her pretty face.

A few others came to help.

Smith was going to ignore it. The last thing he ever wanted to do was attract attention to himself.

He was passing into the hall next to the lounge when he heard a terrible sound—a soft, animal growl. The noise was followed quickly by a woman's scream.

Turning, Smith found the choking golfer leaning back at the waist, hands raised and clutched like claws.

Smith watched amazed as, with a swat, the golfer threw back one of the men who had come to his aid.

It was an incredible display of strength. Far greater than should have been possible for a man that size.

The golfer spun on the female. Baring a mouthful of yellowed, middle-aged teeth, he sprang on her, knocking her to the floor. Sprawling on top of her wriggling body, he lunged at the screaming woman's throat.

There was panic in the lounge. And in that moment of panicked, paralyzed hysteria, no one seemed to know what to do. No one except one man.

The enraged golfer attacked purely on instinct. But so too did Harold W. Smith.

From his ancient golf bag, Smith grabbed a driver. Like a tired knight charging into the bloody fray, he ran back into the bar. Hauling back, he gave a mighty swing.

The club struck the woman's attacker hard in the back of the head. A swing that strong outside would have sent Smith's ball sailing nearly to the green. Here, it appeared to barely phase the growling man.

The golfer wheeled on Smith, wild-eyed. Blood dribbled down his chin, staining his white collar. He had ripped a gushing wound in the woman's neck. The look in his eyes was purely animal. He made as if to lunge.

Smith swung again.

The club cracked the side of the man's head. This time there was a reaction. A soft crack of bone.

The man growled, wobbling. Still he came.

Another swing. The golfer seemed finally to feel the combined effect of the three blows. His legs fell out from beneath him, and he toppled groggily to the floor.

When he finally dropped to his knees, the others in the lounge seemed to finally find their courage. The crush of heavy men fell on the semiconscious man, pinning arms and legs in place. Beneath the pile, the demented golfer whimpered like a wounded animal.

The club director Smith had earlier spoken to had raced into the bar for the end of the battle. A bartender had already called 911. Waiters from the restaurant held linen napkins to the injured woman's throat.

"What happened?" the white-haired club director panted. He stood next to Smith, surveying the terrible scene.

"I don't know," Smith replied. But there was a troubled edge to his acid voice. As he spoke, the pager on his belt buzzed to life. He checked it, noting the Folcroft number.

"Thank God, Dr. Smith," the club director was saying. "I mean— My heavens, thank God. If you hadn't stepped in, I don't know what would have—"

When he glanced over his shoulder he found he was alone.

The ancient bag of golf clubs was gone. So, too, it seemed, was the mysterious Dr. Harold Smith.

Breathless, the club director hurried to attend the injured woman and await the ambulance. On his way, he nearly tripped on an empty Lubec Springs water bottle.

Scowling, the club director angrily kicked the offending bottle beneath a nearby overturned bar stool.

12

Remo was sitting anxiously at one of the squad-room desks in the South Precinct Midtown station when the phone before him rang.

"Report," Smith said, his voice more tart than usual. It was as if his larynx had been soaked in lemon juice and had dried two sizes too small.

"We think it's Judith White, Smitty," Remo said.

Around him paramedics were still tending to police injuries. One officer was being carried out on a stretcher. The pandemonium of half an hour before had been replaced by mostly grim silence, interrupted by soft whispers.

"A strong possibility," Smith agreed tightly. "There was an incident at my golf club a few minutes ago."

"Anyone hurt?"

"Not seriously," Smith said. "The assailant was subdued. However, he displayed behavior consistent with the victims of genetic tampering that we've encountered before."

"We've got a bunch more here," Remo said. "Chiun's downstairs questioning them. I doubt he'll have any luck. They're like last time. Just worried about filling their stomachs. We're up to our armpits in half-chewed corpses.''

"I don't get this,'' Mark Howard's voice interjected. "Dr. Smith, your own files list this woman as dead.''

Remo could tell by the hollow tone of the signal that Smith had his assistant on speakerphone. He pictured the young man sitting at earnest attention on his usual creaky wooden chair before Smith's desk.

"There *was* a body found after Remo's encounter with her,'' the CURE director explained. "It was badly damaged, but the assumption at the time was that it was that of Judith White. And it still could be. Judith White was not the first to use her formula. Perhaps she had a protégé.''

"Maybe,'' Remo said. "We haven't met the big puss herself. But this has her paw prints all over it. Manhattan looks like freaking Lion Country Safari.''

"How is this possible?'' Mark Howard asked. "I read some of the information in the CURE database on this before you got back here, Dr. Smith, but I don't get how they're able to effect changes like this in people.''

"If we are correct in this, Mark, they are not people,'' Smith said gravely. "I cannot impress this on you enough. They might look human, but it is a deadly mistake to think otherwise.'' He took a deep breath before continuing. "As for the broad details, two decades ago a geneticist in Boston developed a gene-altering formula that allowed for rapid splicing of DNA from one species to another. She was able to lift specific characteristics from any animal and recode the existing DNA of another to incorporate the new genetic material. She was the first test subject, albeit accidentally. The resulting creature walked and talked and gave every outward appearance of a human female, but was something else entirely.''

''Mostly tiger,'' Remo supplied. ''That was what was in the goop she drank. And can we get the lead out, Smitty? You and the kid can do story time once I'm off the phone.''

Smith was not dissuaded. ''After several deaths in the Boston area, we managed to eliminate that woman. I had assumed that the case was closed. However, more than three years ago, a similar rash of killings took place in Boston.''

''Judith White,'' Howard supplied.

''So we came to learn. She had discovered the old formula and improved on it. Although she infused her DNA with primarily tiger genes, she had also included traits from several other species. Strength, speed, coordination were all enhanced. Her ultimate goal was to replace man as the planet's dominant lifeform.''

''And if she hadn't been such a whack-job, she might have succeeded back then,'' Remo pointed out.

''That is true,'' Smith replied darkly. ''The method by which she intended to spread the formula into the general population was diabolical. She hid the gene-altering material in the DNA of a laboratory-created transgenic creature, ostensibly designed to eliminate world hunger. Those who consumed the tainted meat would have, over time, become like her.''

"I remember reading about that at the time," Howard said. "But all those animals were destroyed."

"Yeah," Remo said vaguely. "All destroyed."

"That's true," Smith agreed. "Since the meat of the creatures was never consumed by anyone, the formula is being introduced in some other way."

Over the line, Remo heard the electronic beep of Smith's computer.

"One moment, Remo."

The rapid drumming of the CURE director's fingers on his keyboard ended in a rare, soft curse.

"I take it it's not good news?" Remo asked.

"The crisis is spreading," Smith said. "There are now reports of similar incidents occurring in other parts of New York, as well as two in Connecticut and one in New Jersey."

"Swell," Remo said. "Smitty, I called you hoping for some good news."

Smith gave a thoughtful hum. "Perhaps I can give you some small comfort," he said. "We cannot be certain it is her, but if Judith White did survive her encounter with you, she will not be what she once was. You did remove a limb, after all. That handicap alone will make her easier to find. I will begin a search. And with any luck the fall caused even greater damage. She may be an invalid. While able to direct things behind the scenes, hopefully she will not pose a personal threat to you or Master Chiun."

"It's not her I'm worried about, Smitty. By the looks of it, she's building an army for something."

"Yes," Smith agreed. "No matter her condition, our greatest concern is with the creatures she is creating. We need to find out the delivery method for the formula.''

"Maybe Remo could follow a trail, Dr. Smith,'' Mark suggested. "Maybe one of these...*things* can lead him back to the source.''

"That's a swell idea, kid,'' Remo said. "I'm gonna go out right now and stand in the middle of Times Square with a leash and a box of Meow Mix on my head.''

"That would not work anyway, Mark,'' Smith interjected. "It is not as if these creatures have a homing instinct.''

"So we're back to square one,'' Remo complained. He spied another stretcher being carted into the squad room from the rear stairwell. This one was draped in a white sheet.

The Master of Sinanju appeared in the wake of the two morgue attendants who were carrying the body of the dead officer. His wrinkled face was thoughtful.

"Look, now that you know what's going on, maybe you can find out something from there,'' Remo said. "I'll keep looking around. Maybe I'll get lucky.''

"We will try to find something from this end,'' Smith promised. "Call if you learn anything new.''

The line went dead. Remo was hanging up the phone as Chiun padded up.

"Anything?'' Remo asked.

Chiun shook his head. "I questioned a few of the beasts, but they are mindless mockeries of humanity. They do not know what made them thus.''

Remo leaned back against the desk, arms folded.

"Great," he complained. "Without a lead we're dead in the water."

The words had no sooner passed his lips than there came the sound of a sudden commotion behind them. A scuffle followed by a startled shout.

"Jimmy, knock if off. That ain't funny."

The two Masters of Sinanju turned to find Sergeant Jimmy Simon slowly circling Jeff Malloy at the precinct's main desk. The portly desk sergeant's nose was in the air, tracking a scent. Drool rolled down his chin, staining his collar.

"Oh, balls," Remo muttered just as the first inhuman growl rolled up out of the throat of Sergeant Simon.

THE HINT of high blood pressure on Simon's broad face had lightened to a mask of cold calculation. He bared his teeth at Sergeant Malloy.

"That's it, Jimmy," Malloy snapped, grabbing for his gun. He was too slow.

Simon sprang, cuffing Malloy on the side of the head. The stunned officer lost his gun. Bouncing off the side of his desk, he dropped to the floor. Jimmy Simon pounced on the stricken body. With a fearsome growl, he drew back his head, eager to bury fangs deep into the exposed throat.

He never got the chance.

Just as his head was snapping down, a strong hand grabbed a clump of sweaty hair at the back of his head. With a yank, he was off Sergeant Malloy's body and spinning in air. He came nose to nose with a very annoyed Remo Williams.

"Mr. Whiskers shouldn't play with his food," Remo said.

Growling, Sergeant Simon lashed out at Remo. Remo was holding the officer at arm's length. He dodged the swinging paw.

"Kitty go night-night," Remo said.

Frowning, he drove a pair of hardened fingertips deep into Sergeant Simon's jiggling neck.

Consciousness drained from Simon's body and he grew limp in Remo's hand.

By now, other uniformed officers had rushed over to help. Remo passed the unconscious desk sergeant off to them.

"Lock him up with the others," he ordered. "And if you don't want his liver pâtéed before he comes to, you'll give him his own room."

When he turned back around, Jeff Malloy was dragging himself shakily to his feet.

"What happened?" Remo demanded.

"I don't know," Sergeant Malloy said, panting. "He was just sitting there and he went nuts. He was still winded from downstairs. I told him to take deep breaths. I thought he was having a stroke. Then he just dropped his water and came after me."

Remo and Chiun looked down.

The disposable cup from which Jimmy Simon had been drinking was under his desk. Splattered water had turned the dirt on the floor muddy.

And, as one, they recalled the water dispenser standing in the corner of the Vaunted Press break room.

"It's in the water, Chiun," Remo announced, turning.

The Master of Sinanju was no longer beside him.

He saw a blur of black robes. The old Korean flew like a flash across the open squad-room floor.

A watercooler sat against the far wall. While Remo waited for Smith's return call he had seen a custodian install a new bottle. A plainclothes officer stood before the tank, raising a white disposable cup to his lips.

Before a single drop of water could touch his tongue, Chiun fell upon him. A vicious swat flung the cup from the man's hand.

"What the hell?" the cop snarled.

But Remo was already there, waving FBI ID. The angry detective wandered off, rubbing the crimson welt that was already blossoming on the back of his hand.

Shooing a few officers back, the old Korean placed a fresh cup beneath the cooler's spout. With a careful press of a solitary nail, he poured a short stream of water.

He brought the cup to his button nose, sniffing deeply. Face clouding, he looked to Remo.

"I detect nothing," Chiun said somberly.

Remo accepted the cup from Chiun's bony hand. He swirled around the crystal-clear liquid, looking for anything suspicious. There was nothing he could see. It was nothing more than a cup of spring water.

When he looked up, his brow was low.

"If we can't see it, either one of us could have drunk this," he pointed out.

"Do not remind me," the Master of Sinanju said. "As it is, you are barely housebroken, and I do not need you soiling the carpets or scratching up my good furniture."

"We'd better get some of this to Smith for testing," Remo said. He found a big aspirin bottle in a desk drawer. Dumping out the last few remaining pills, he poured some water into the bottle.

After Remo was through, Chiun turned to a patrolman.

"Remove these to a lavatory for disposal," he commanded, waving a hand at the boxes that were stacked next to the cooler. "And do the same with any others in this garrison, lest you end up like the beasts in your dungeon."

The officer was one of those who had seen Remo and Chiun pass through the cell block unharmed. He knew enough not to argue. Enlisting help of others, the group hauled the boxes of Lubec Springs water to the men's room for dumping.

"And say a prayer the alligators in the sewers aren't thirsty," Remo called after them.

13

The ozone layer was already taken. Hundreds of people had hogged the limelight on that one.

Greenpeace had claimed the seven seas for themselves.

Everything else good between heaven and earth had been laid claim to by someone.

HETA had dibs on animals. The Sierra Club had the trees. Earth First! had dirt. And the Brazilian rain forest was the private domain of one singer so selfish that others in the environmental movement didn't even like to mention his single-word name. Although he had been missing lately. Probably in for more hair plugs or—worse—in the studio recording a new album.

When it came time to decide which great planet-saving cause he would throw his support behind, poor Bobby Bugget was a man without an issue.

"You need *something,* Bobby," his agent had insisted.

His agent's name was Jude Weiss, but everyone called him St. Jude. Weiss found the nickname distasteful. First of all, he was Jewish. Second, he wasn't really Jewish. Not anymore. He had recently converted to Buddhism—this not long after converting to Poweressence, which had supplanted a deeply held, week-long conversion to Scientology. This was all part of the long-standing Hollywood tradition of religion as fad. If Madonna or Cher told Hollywood's movers and shakers that it was now hip to switch to high-colonic Amish, Jude Weiss would have dashed off to Home Depot for a horse and buggy and a length of garden hose. But one thing he had never been and never would be was Catholic. They actually had rules and, horror of horrors, expected you to live by them. So to Jude Weiss, recent Buddhist (or was it Hindu?) to be referred to as the Catholic patron saint of desperate causes was a grave insult. Unfortunately it was a nickname well-earned.

It had started with that one client. The Englishman with the shy stammer and bedroom eyes. Although he could have had any woman on Earth, he had settled for a cheap hooker in an L.A. alley. His arrest had been national news.

Jude Weiss and Associates had gone on red alert. There had been an all-out media blitz, culminating in a high-profile late-night talk-show interview on which the actor had stammered shyly, batted his bedroom eyes and—by the end of his first seven-minute segment—had made America forget all about his fondness for the French arts and his back-alley patronage of a twenty dollar Puerto Rican artist name Señorita Sugar.

If it had only stopped there, things would have been fine for Jude Weiss. But soon after that mess, another agency approached for help with one of its clients, a sports announcer who volunteered weekends at a home for troubled teens. Apparently the announcer did much of his charity work in a tutu and high heels. He also, it was learned, had a habit of taking it all the way to the end zones of both boys and girls.

This case presented a far tougher challenge than the first, given the nature of the criminal charges and the multiple lawsuits that were filed. But in the end, the announcer had not only kept his television job, he was awarded a seven-figure multiyear contract with a major cable sports station.

And thus was born St. Jude, patron saint of every desperate celebrity client that came along. Jude Weiss got them all. Every bed-wetting sicko and toe-sucking loser. There were only a few normal clients left. One of which was lounging nude on the patio beside his three-hundred-and-fifty-thousand-dollar Key West pool.

As Bobby Bugget smeared tanning lotion on his belly, he didn't even glance at Jude Weiss. He was staring out at the sea. The land on which Bugget's pool was built had been expanded out into the Gulf of Mexico in order to accommodate its great size.

"You need a cause," Jude Weiss repeated.

"I've already got something," Bobby said. Finished with his lotion, he settled cucumber slices firmly atop each eye. "I'm spokesman for the Save the Bottlenose Fund." Feeling blind for a glass, he took a sip of margarita.

"Even if that thing exists, the legends say it's ugly as the sales of your last three albums," Weiss said.

"My albums all go gold."

"Your fan base is aging rapidly. Yeah, you bring in college kids with your summer tours, but you lose them as soon as they grow up. Right now, you're a pirate pushing sixty. Your last hit was 'Daiquiri Dingy,' and you've been coasting on that since 1974."

The cucumbers came off. Bugget had to squint in the white-hot Florida sun. "What are you saying?"

"I'm saying, according to your accountants, your finances could be on the verge of a major reversal. Maybe even a meltdown."

Bugget's deeply suntanned face blanched. "I might have to give up all this?" he gasped, horrified.

"Not all of it. But you might have to start being more careful with how you spend your money. Sell off a few of your islands. Maybe unload a couple dozen sailboats. You crashed seven seaplanes last year alone, Bobby. Now, *that's* an expense you won't be able to afford if your finances keep trending like they have."

The prospect of even having to think about living within his means was too terrifying for Bobby Bugget. He downed the remainder of his drink, immediately summoning the nearest of three hovering topless waitresses to bring him another.

"Keep them coming," he snapped through his bristly gray mustache.

"You need something that will get you attention above the Panhandle," Jude Weiss insisted. "Something that will keep you in people's minds during the winter months when you're hibernating down here."

"Like what?" Bugget slurred, sucking down another drink.

Jude Weiss smiled. "Ever hear of Green Earth?"

"The big environmental group? Of course I have. Everybody has."

"Well, what everybody *hasn't* heard is that Green Earth has got a new cause it's supporting. There's a species that's being threatened with extinction. Right now it's only gotten some local support—a few protests, some write-ups in the regional weekly paper. But with Green Earth's involvement, it's going to go national. Maybe international. And they're offering the plum celebrity spokesman spots to clients of the Jude Weiss and Associates Agency."

"Wait, wasn't Green Earth in trouble a month or two back? Something about a stolen Russian submarine in South America?"

"Of course not," St. Jude promised. "That was a rogue organization member acting entirely on his own. He did not have the approval of the Green Earth hierarchy in San Francisco. Now, what do you say, Bobby? I'm offering you a chance to be out front on an issue of vital importance. The extinction of a species. Face time like that'll buy a whole fleet of seaplanes."

Bobby Bugget wanted to say no. He didn't like to change latitudes until the rest of the contiguous states shook off every last vestige of winter. But he had a mental image of an endless line of little dollar bills marching off a gangplank into a rising tide of red ink.

Swallowing the last of his margarita, the singer had reluctantly agreed. To jump-start his flagging career and preserve his fifty-million-dollar-a-year empire, he would have made a deal with the devil.

Unfortunately, he'd done worse than make a pact with Satan. He had signed on the dotted line with a double-crossing Jewish-Buddhist-possibly-Hindu-Catholic saint.

"This is *not* what I agreed to," Bugget groused to Jude Weiss.

It was two weeks since their poolside conversation. They were in a package store in rural Maine.

"What are you talking?" Jude said. "This is exactly what I told you it would be. You're saving a species."

Bugget almost dropped the second case of beer he was pushing up on the checkout counter.

"Worms," Bobby Bugget snarled.

"Leeches," Jude Weiss corrected. "Specifically, the Reticulated New England Speckled Leech. They've become very rare in these parts."

"Who gives a Havana hang? No one cares if an insect gets squooshed."

"Leeches aren't insects," Jude said knowingly. "At least I don't think they are. Anyway, who says an animal needs to be cuddly to merit saving? Ever hear of the kangaroo rat? Of the snail darter?"

"No," Bugget said glumly.

"Well, neither did I till I read this." Weiss slapped a shiny pamphlet on top of a case of beer.

On the cover were pictures of insects and animals only a Mother Earth could love. In the corner above the recycling stamp was the familiar Green Earth logo, a green-and-blue planet Earth. In a semicircle around the top—from equator to equator—was the legend It's *Your* Planet, People!

"Everything you need to know is in there, so read up," St. Jude said. He waved to the beer. "I'll pay for this. Lemme have your credit card."

Two minutes later they were back out in the street, each lugging a case of beer.

Some men were waiting curbside near a rusty old school bus. One of them opened the rear emergency door as Bugget and Weiss approached.

"And this is another thing I didn't sign on for," Bugget complained as they dumped the cases into the rear of the beat-up old bus. "You've got me touring with a freak show."

"Hey, they're clients, too," Jude Weiss said defensively.

Bugget glowered at Weiss as he tore open one of the cases and helped himself to a can. The two men went around to the front and climbed up inside the bus. As the door closed, dozens of faces looked up.

Only three were Weiss and Associates clients. The rest were rank-and-file members of Green Earth.

As the bus pulled away from the curb and Bobby Bugget popped the top on the first beer of what he hoped would become a short and forgettable bender, he scanned the three familiar faces.

The first was a famous movie actress who, though in her early thirties, looked all of thirteen. Erratic behavior off-screen had culminated in her most widely viewed performance—that of videotaped Rodeo Drive shoplifter.

Beside her was a hulking, potbellied brute with an

angry, dead-eyed stare. The former heavyweight champion's career had been troubled by teensy little problems such as rape charges, prison stays and his tendency to bite off the body parts of opponents whenever a fight was not going his way. With Weiss and Associates' crisis management, he hoped to have a second career in film and TV.

Finally there was the home-decorating and housekeeping guru, a soft-spoken woman who on her TV show and in her magazine told America to iron its underwear, build a Japanese garden out back near the trash cans and to always trim the toilet paper into decorative shapes just in case another country dropped by unexpectedly for brunch. What she didn't suggest was that America engage in insider trading with a resulting scandal that would rock its media empire and send it scrambling to the one agency that might be able to revive its tarnished wholesome image. That would be a bad thing.

The decorating expert sat in the corner behind the driver, trimming artificial roses from red felt. When she offered one to the boxer, he ate it. When she went back to her felt, she found her scissors had been stolen. The waifish actress had a guilty expression on her pale face and a scissor-shaped bulge in her Dockers khakis.

"Two cases ain't gonna be enough," Bobby Bugget said morosely, going back to get more beer.

The run-of-the-mill members of Green Earth were already delighted to be among such glitterati. They began to grow even more giddy as they approached their destination.

Bleary-eyed and slightly more than three sheets to the wind, Bugget was supremely indifferent.

"Aren't you excited?" enthused a young man.

"Sure thing, son," Bugget said. "Gotta save them worms. Some of my best friends—and agents—are worms."

"It's not just the leeches," a college-age girl insisted. "It's the water. The reason they're dying out is because they've tapped the water source."

"Honey, I'm all for preserving water, too," Bugget said. "People can do great things just stirrin' some hops and barley in a little cold Rockies springwater."

"We're not saving the water for *people*," the girl said. "Man treats the freshwater supply as his alone. He cages it up in reservoirs, harnesses its power to create dangerous electricity and drains streams, killing off beautiful, docile, harmless indigenous leeches."

"I agree wit you, little girl," the boxer interjected, his voice surprisingly high and feminine. "The man has done many bad and terrible things. Like prosecute and imprison innocent men who would never had done the lugubrious and ripricious malfeasance that they were unrightly accused of in court of doing by lying bitches who was only asking for it in the first place." He nodded deep understanding.

"Thank you, Mr. Armour."

"You're very welcome, young lady," the boxer said.

"Could you please stop squeezing my thigh now?" the girl asked, wincing.

A distracting shout from the front of the bus kept

the boxer from once more becoming a guest of the state prison system.

"Hey, get a load of this!" the driver called.

They had gone from small town to partially wooded farmland. To the right, the trees broke away into a wide field. A dead cow lay just inside a barbed-wire fence at the side of the road. A bloated tongue gave them a silent raspberry as they sped past.

"Was that a victim of ecosystem destruction?" the girl from Green Earth asked.

"Maybe," said the boy. "The poor animal could have died of thirst."

"It looked like it was eaten by wild animals," Bobby Bugget pointed out.

"Still," said the girl, "maybe it died of thirst, *then* was eaten. Maybe we should mention concern for cows, as well as the speckled leech."

"Don't get sidetracked," Jude Weiss warned. "Stay focused. Focus brings in TV crews and national coverage."

"I guess," the girl said. "But that poor cow. It looked like something tore it open and ate all its insides."

Everyone agreed that this was a terrible thing. All but the boxer. He was thinking of the half-chewed cow.

"Gawd, I miss the taste of boxing," he said, wiping back a sniffle. He found comfort by sticking his hand inside the girl's blouse.

Signs along the roadside every half mile took them from downtown Lubec deep into the woods.

The exit to the Lubec Springs bottling plant eventually appeared amid a small patch of landscaped trees. The bus drove onto the strip of tidy asphalt that cut through the thick pine forest.

A dozen yards in they came to a fork in the road. To the left was a gated, deeply rutted dirt path. The lane to the Lubec Springs plant was on the right. Glimpsed through the woods was a silvery stream that tied into the network of springs throughout the Lubec Springs property.

They parked the bus and climbed down to the road. Placards were passed out to the group.

Jude Weiss stepped down, accompanied by the waifish actress and former boxer.

"This is going to be perfect," St. Jude said. "The press should be here in about a half hour."

He tried to check his watch, but it had mysteriously disappeared from his wrist. That sort of thing seemed to happen a lot whenever his young, innocent movie-star client was around. Gold pens and brass bathroom fixtures vanished every time she showed up at his Beverly Hills offices. He made a mental note to check the poor maligned girl's backpack for his missing watch the first chance he got.

"Let's get a move on, people," Weiss warned the crowd. "Spontaneous protests don't just happen on their own."

On the road, Bobby Bugget couldn't find anyone to lug his beer. Hauling the cases himself, Bugget fell in behind the rest as they marched up the paved road to the bottling plant.

The aging singer's legs were nearly buckling by the time they reached the plant. When the low buildings finally appeared, he dropped his cases to the road and popped open a fresh beer.

"Okay, what's the drill?" Bugget panted.

"We wait for the reporters," Jude Weiss said. "No sense starting until they get here."

The TV homemaker was braiding pine needles into a decorative star-shaped ornament, perfect for Christmas or just everyday. "Maybe this is them now," she suggested.

Weiss glanced up.

They had come from around the building. So stealthy were they, none from the bus had heard them approach.

There were eight men in all, fanned out in a line across the parking lot. They moved quickly toward the band of protesters, heads down, chins parallel to the ground.

"Do you work here?" Jude Weiss demanded.

The men didn't answer. They continued to come. Faster now.

"Because if you *do* work here, I'd appreciate it if you hold off on any counterprotests until *Rough Print* and *Newsfotainment Now!* show up."

Jude Weiss heard something that sounded like a growl. For an instant he thought it was one of his clients. The boxer had a tendency to make animal sounds like that at mealtime or around the occasional unlucky female. Weiss was turning for the boxer, expecting the worst, when a strange thing happened.

The men running toward them from the bottling plant started flying.

It all happened so fast. One moment they were running across the parking lot; the next they had launched themselves in the air. Jude Weiss saw one flash toward him. The sun disappeared in the shadow of the lunging man.

Jude Weiss felt a sudden pressure on his chest. And then he didn't feel anything at all because one needed an intact spinal cord to carry nerve impulses to a functioning brain. The force of the attack against St. Jude Weiss had cracked the Hollywood superagent's spine and knocked his head clean off his shoulders.

As Weiss's head rolled, panic gripped the crowd. Men and women dropped protest signs and ran into the woods. More growls rose from others who had been lying in wait.

Screams filled the Maine woods.

Throats split, stomachs surrendered pulsing contents. Blood splattered like spring rain to the cold parking lot.

The boxer tried to take a swing. He was cuffed unconscious by a man half his size.

Bobby Bugget couldn't believe his eyes. When the attack began, the singer had been guarding his beer near some bushes. His booze was forgotten. The urge to flee registered in Bugget's beer-soaked brain.

He turned to run…

…and promptly flopped over his last full case of beer.

Sprawled on the ground, he heard a low growl behind him. Slowly, heart pounding, he rolled over onto his back.

Some of the Green Earth membership were being

devoured. Two of the attackers had separated from the rest. They were coming toward Bugget.

"The press is on its way," Bugget screamed.

If they heard, it didn't show. The men kept coming. Slowly stalking. Malevolent eyes focused hungrily on Bobby Bugget's throat.

"Grrr…"

Bugget heard the sound. Soft. Just above the range of human perception. It tickled his eardrums, made his heart rate quicken. The sound of ancient hunger. The sound of his own mortality.

He was up on his rear end. Scurrying back on palms and soles, he backed against the trunk of a tree.

"I ain't kiddin', son," Bugget said. "We're talkin' national exposure. They'll be here any minute. Now, I don't know who you work for, but if you're the people what wants to kill them worms, well, you can be my guest. Kill 'em all for all I care. Shoot, only good worm's the one at the bottom of a tequila bottle anyways."

His words seemed to have an effect. The two men stopped abruptly.

Bobby Bugget was beginning to think he'd survive this massacre. That he would get the exposure the late Jude Weiss had promised before his head came off, that he'd be able to hightail it back to Florida where he could spin this terrible day into TV appearances, songs and record sales.

All of this did Bobby Bugget think in the time it took to draw one terrified breath.

And then one of the two men before him disappeared.

He moved too fast. One moment he was standing three yards away; the next he was landing on Bobby's chest.

Bugget toppled over. He felt a rough tongue lick the side of his throat. He heard that terrible low growl and knew with sick certainty that the end for this old, washed-up pirate would not come at sea, but in a land-locked parking lot in the boondocks of Maine.

The slathering fangs of his attacker were a hair away from shredding Bobby Bugget's throat when the singer saw a sudden blur from the corner of his eye.

The woman had come out of nowhere. With an open palm, she cuffed the man on top of Bugget on the side of the head.

Although it didn't seem possible, the blow launched the man halfway across the lot.

"Down!" Judith White growled.

Their feast interrupted, the rest froze. Blood dribbled down chins. Shoulders rose in a parody of angry felines.

"Now!" she roared.

Hissing, the pack backed dutifully away.

On the ground, Bobby Bugget blinked. The near fatal assault proved to have an elucidating effect. For the first time in a long time, he almost felt sober. Under the circumstances, it wasn't a pleasant feeling.

Lying flat on his back, he gave Judith White a grateful nod. "This ain't the first time a woman's saved my life," he panted. "''Cept most of the others were whores or cocktail waitresses. Much obliged, ma'am."

When the woman who had been his salvation

turned her cold cat's eyes to him, the singer shrank from her gaze.

"What press?" she demanded.

"What?" Bugget asked. "Oh. National and regional. TV and papers. They'll be pouring in here any minute to cover the protest. Oh, the protest..." His voice trailed off as he glanced around the parking lot.

Many of the Green Earth members were dead and dismembered. Those who hadn't been devoured immediately had been knocked unconscious for later. Bugget saw that the boxer, homemaker, actress and several others appeared to still be breathing. They had fared better than those who had scattered into the woods. Pitiful cries were being drowned out by growls and the sounds of feasting.

"We were gonna have a protest," Bobby Bugget offered weakly. "Kind of hard to do with only six people."

"Quiet, human," Judith snarled. "I'm trying to think."

Bugget didn't see the hand that struck him. He only knew that he was suddenly tumbling end over end into a nearby tree, a sharp pain in the side of his head.

As Bugget was shaking pine needles out of what was left of his graying blond hair, Judith White was spinning to her pack. Owen Grude was huddled with the rest.

"I told you not to kill anyone unless I said so."

"We thought there was danger," Owen said.

"You thought with your stomachs," she accused. "Think with your *mind*. Humans are the greatest hunters in the animal kingdom. They can obliterate entire species and send us scurrying into the trees. The only way they'll be beaten is by superior intellect.'' She looked around the lot. ''Hide the dead around back. Cover the blood with sand. We need this mess cleaned up before the press arrives.''

The males began carting bodies toward the plant. Judith stopped Owen Grude. ''The ones left alive? Get them a drink of water.'' She pointed to Bugget. ''Start with him.''

Owen loped off across the lot and up the stairs. He returned a minute later carrying a Lubec Springs sport six-pack. A bottle was brought to Bobby Bugget, while others began pouring water into the mouths of the unconscious.

''Drink it,'' Judith White commanded.

Bugget licked his mustache nervously. ''You don't have anything stronger?'' he asked hopefully.

She moved in very close. Bugget could feel her warm breath on his damp mustache.

''Drink it,'' she demanded, ''or I'll split you open and chew your innards from stomach to spine.''

Bugget gulped. ''If you put it that way.''

Gingerly he squeezed his nose between his fingers. It had been a long time since he'd drunk plain old water. He never cared for the taste. Tipping his head sharply, he slugged the contents of the bottle down in a few big gulps.

When the foul-tasting liquid reached his stomach, a strange sensation seemed to come over him. The excruciating pain was more than he could bear. Dropping back to the ground, Bugget clutched his belly.

He was writhing in agony on the pavement as Judith White turned from him.

"I'll be inside," she said.

She prowled a few paces toward the building before stopping. She pointed at one of the bodies that was awaiting disposal.

"Bring that one inside," she commanded. "I think better on a full stomach."

Wheeling, she headed back for the bottling plant.

14

Dusk was creeping slowly in by the time Remo and Chiun arrived at Folcroft.

Long Island Sound was visible through the trees, slivered with shimmering streaks of twilight, as the cab steered between the great granite columns with their attendant stone lions. At Remo's instruction, the driver brought them to the sanitarium's main staircase.

"Why are we entering this way?" the Master of Sinanju asked suspiciously. Behind them the yellow taxi was making its crunching way back down the great gravel drive.

"Stairs are stairs," Remo said as they headed up.

"Yes," Chiun replied, padding up beside his pupil. "And the stairs that are the stairs we always use are on the other side of the building."

"I thought you liked front doors."

Remo held the door for his teacher. Chiun swept inside. As he walked, the old Korean stroked his thread of beard thoughtfully.

"I notice that this route avoids passing the Prince Regent's office," he commented.

"I know, Chiun," Remo sighed. "And before you

start on me, too, I admit it. I think the kid's okay. He was pretty stand-up for us in Sinanju when he didn't have to be. Smitty is doing a good job bringing him onto the team. He's working out. There, I said it. Happy?''

In the lobby Remo's raised voice caught the attention of a receptionist and two nurses. The receptionist recognized Chiun as a former patient who occasionally stopped back at Folcroft to visit. She thought Remo to be his nurse. Her frown of disapproval at Remo's raised voice was interrupted by a ringing telephone. She was answering the phone as the two men slipped by.

''I am pleased to hear that,'' the Master of Sinanju said. ''Since one day you will be the Regent's royal assassin.''

''Can't happen, Chiun,'' Remo said, shaking his head firmly. ''I'm not getting too chummy with the kid because Sinanju rules forbid me from working for Smith's successor.''

''Do not be so certain, white man,'' Chiun said knowingly.

''And here we go,'' Remo said. ''Back to that famous loophole you claim you discovered ages ago and refuse to tell me about.''

Chiun smiled slyly. ''Are you not the least bit curious?''

''Yeah, I guess. I mean, the way you manage to contort supposedly unbendable rules into pretzel shapes always fascinates me. But just 'cause I like to watch the magician saw the woman in half doesn't mean I'll be running to the nearest Tupperware party with a chain saw. Rules are rules.''

"They are not always as inviolate as you seem to think," Chiun replied. "Take your Smith, for instance. You agree that everyone finds him mad?"

"I don't agree with that."

"As I said," Chiun sniffed. "No one of consequence disputes his madness. And yet we have served him well lo these many years. Your House has not always had such tolerance for crazed emperors."

Remo's brow furrowed. "What does that mean?"

"It means that rules are only sometimes rules. Other times they are guidelines. It is for the wise to know the difference. Thankfully, you have me here to point the way."

He swept ahead of his pupil, through a set of fire doors and into Folcroft's administration wing.

Watching his teacher's purposeful stride, Remo smiled. "Amen to that, Little Father," he said, shaking his head.

Allowing the fire door to slip from his fingers, he trailed the wizened Korean up the hall.

SMITH ALWAYS KEPT a change of clothes at work just in case. He had been more than eager to slip out of his golf clothes and back into his more familiar uniform.

Back in his three-piece gray suit and starched white shirt—green-striped school tie knotted tightly at the collar —he was hard at work in his familiar Folcroft environs. Day had bled into night, and still Harold W. Smith remained at his desk.

The CURE director had scarcely noted the change of hour or scattering of daylight. He was far too busy monitoring the events taking place along the East Coast.

There had been many more incidents throughout the afternoon. And the tristate area was no longer alone. There had been like occurrences in Massachusetts and New Hampshire. To Smith, the pattern indicated a product being shipped by ground. He had already come to this conclusion even before Remo had phoned back to suggest Lubec Springs bottled water was the source of contamination.

Smith's desk was an onyx slab set before the big picture window at the back of the office. Beneath its surface was a canted monitor, visible only to whoever sat at the desk. A keyboard at desk's edge only became visible when it sensed Smith's touch. Keys lit obedient amber flashes in response to his relentless drumming fingers.

He had been working for hours nonstop. All at once, Smith paused at his workstation.

The lines of amber text on his special monitor were beginning to blur again.

Blinking hard, he removed his rimless glasses. He massaged his eyes with the tips of his arthritic fingers.

Looking to a point across the room, he tried to regain his focus.

The thing he stared at was a drab black-and-white photograph of Folcroft, taken some time in the 1950s. It had been hung in the office by the sanitarium's previous administrator.

Smith had never thought to take down the picture,

never considered bringing in something of a more personal nature from home. The CURE director felt that any infusion of one's personality into a work area had the effect of making that area too comfortable. And comfort bred lax work habits.

Besides, Smith's office *did* reflect his personality. It was cold, humorless and Spartan. The room was a direct, if inadvertent, gaze into the soul of the gray old man in the gray three-piece suit who sat in isolation at the loneliest posting in all of America's intelligence services.

Smith's eyes began to clear. The young saplings in the photograph, which had grown into mighty shade trees during Smith's tenure at Folcroft, were starting to come into focus.

He replaced his glasses and was turning back to his keyboard when the door to his office unexpectedly burst open. Smith looked up with a concerned start.

"Hope you're decent," Remo announced as he strode into the room. Chiun swept in after him.

"He is that and more," the Master of Sinanju proclaimed, personally insulted by Remo's choice of words. "He is decent, kind and generous. Hail, Smith, guardian of the sacred Constitution." The Korean gave an informal bow before sweeping across the room.

At his desk, Smith was still recovering from his initial shock. He offered a hurried bow of his head. "Please shut the door," he said to Remo. "And I wish you would knock."

"And miss that look on your face?" Remo said, swinging the door shut. "By the way, if you want to look a little more guilty, why not try wearing a black mask and an *I Violated The Constitution And All I Got Was This Lousy T-Shirt* shirt?''

As he crossed over to Smith's desk, he dug in the pocket of his chinos, pulling out an aspirin bottle.

''A little present from Catwoman,'' he said, tossing the bottle to Smith.

The CURE director caught it with both hands. Liquid sloshed inside. ''This is the police station sample you phoned about, I assume?'' he queried dryly.

''Yep. We dumped the rest down the drain.''

Smith placed the bottle to one side of his desk. ''We will test this if it becomes necessary. When you called, I sent Mark to my country club to collect samples there. They have been rushed off for analysis.''

''The kid's not here?''

''I instructed him to remain at the lab conducting the tests. I wanted him on-site the instant there is news.''

''The news is what Remo has already told you, Emperor,'' Chiun said. ''The creatures that have twice vexed your kingdom have returned. Fortunately, with Sinanju as sword and shield, you need not fear any common jungle beasts.''

Tucking his black robes around him, the Master of Sinanju sank to a lotus position in the center of the threadbare carpet.

''Yeah, go-go team,'' Remo said. ''In the meantime, you've put a stop to the Lubec Springs shipments. So once you have all the stuff that's been shipped recalled, I guess we won't have to worry about any more of those things.''

A troubled frown crossed the CURE director's face.

"You did have this stuff recalled, right, Smitty?"

"I have not," Smith replied tightly.

Remo's face darkened. "Why the hell not? In case you haven't heard, we've got *Daktari* breaking out on Main Street, U.S.A. and there's a run on safari jackets at Banana Republic. You've got to cut them off. While you do that, Chiun and I will go to that bottling place in Maine and pull White's plug."

"You can't," Smith insisted. "Not yet." He leaned back in his chair. "Remo, the nature of this crisis dictates caution. If Lubec Springs is alone in this, then we can focus on them alone. But if the contamination has reached other bottlers, then whoever is behind this could be anywhere. By focusing on Lubec Springs before we know all the facts, we could be alerting Judith White or whoever is responsible. We can't afford to tip our hand too early."

"You're just gonna let people keep drinking that junk?"

"Through CURE's facilities I have given an order ostensibly from the FDA. A new federal mandate now requires a forty-eight-hour waiting period before retailers can sell bottled water. This to allow for settlement of particulates. Given the relatively low number of cases so far, I would imagine that most outlets have not yet reached the contaminated shipments. They must yet have back stock to go through. With any luck, this should buy us the time we need to track down and eliminate whoever is behind this."

"We *know* who it is, Smitty," Remo said. "By

dicking around down here, you're giving White time to get away.''

"Quite the opposite," Smith insisted. "To err on the side of caution now should narrow her avenue of escape, assuming we learn that Lubec Springs is the only source of the genetic tampering. If we discover that this is the case, we will know precisely where to send you. You and Chiun may deal with Dr. White once and for all. If, indeed, it is her."

Remo leaned on the edge of Smith's wide desk. "I thought I dealt with her last time," he mumbled bitterly.

"An error that cannot be blamed on Sinanju," Chiun quickly pointed out from the floor. "For the cape in which it has cloaked itself is that of Man. We did not know then that the beast Remo battled had perverted nature by granting itself nine lives. We took but one before. This time, we will do away with the remaining eight."

"Just one of her was plenty tough, Little Father," Remo said. "I don't like the idea of a lion's den filled with eight Judith Whites. Even Daniel didn't have to put up with that."

Chiun shook his head angrily. His wisps of yellowing white hair danced above his ears. "Stop mentioning that troublesome wizard," he hissed.

Remo raised an eyebrow at the edge in the Master of Sinanju's voice. He shot a glance at Smith, but the CURE director had turned his attention back to his computer. Flint gray eyes studied the scrolling data stream.

"Okay—" settling on the floor next to his teacher,

Remo asked "—what gives with Sinanju and Daniel?"

The old man made certain Smith was not listening. Satisfied they weren't being eavesdropped on, he turned his attention to Remo.

"You remember the tale of Master Songjong?" Chiun asked.

Remo nodded. "Pupil of Vimu. Let his Master go to Egypt to slay a princeling when he should have gone himself. Vimu died away from Sinanju, leaving poor Songjong with the mother of all headaches once he reached the Void."

Chiun crinkled his nose. "That is essentially correct," he admitted slowly. Curious fingers clutched the tip of his beard. "But why would you think that Songjong was vexed when death carried him to the place of his ancestors?"

Remo shrugged. "Nothing pissier than a Master of Sinanju with a headful of self-righteous indignation."

"And on what, pray, do you base such an assumption?"

Remo cast a slow, careful glance up and down Chiun's robes of celebration. "Absolutely wild, unsupportable conjecture?" he asked hopefully.

The Master of Sinanju's eyes were slits of suspicion. "Kindly hypothesize on your own time," he said. He smoothed the knees of his black robes.

"Whatever happened to Songjong after death is his concern," the old Korean continued. "It is his life that is recorded in the annals of Sinanju." His voice assumed the cadence of instruction. "After the death of Vimu, Songjong traveled to Babylon, there to pursue employment in the court of Nebuchadnezzar. The death of his Master had brought great sadness to the heart of Songjong, for he rightly took the blame for the fate that had befallen Vimu. He determined to repay his debt in this life by amassing tribute so great as to wipe the stain of shame away from his name in the histories of our village.

"King Nebuchadnezzar joyously welcomed Master Songjong, for well he knew of the Pearl of the Orient and the assassins it produced. This because another Babylonian king of the same name had been blessed with the services of a previous Master half a century before. So Songjong found employment with Nebuchadnezzar, and great was his reign. For a time."

At his desk, the CURE director briefly looked up in mild annoyance. "You do not have to wait here," he said.

Remo waved Smith away. "We don't mind." To Chiun he said, "Did things sour in Babylon?"

"In a manner of speaking," Chiun replied vaguely. He continued before Remo could question further. "It was after the capture of Jerusalem. Thanks to the strategic use of the Master of Sinanju's skills and council, Nebuchadnezzar enjoyed a great victory over the Hebrew kingdom. The city was destroyed, and a large group of prisoners was taken away. Some were of royal descent. One of these was a troublesome young know-it-all named Daniel.

"Now Songjong saw mischief in the eyes of this young nuisance and, rather than allow him to work some wicked scheme of revenge against his captors, recommended to the king that the youth be put to death. But Nebuchadnezzar was flushed with his great victory and dismissed the advice.

"While in service to the king, Songjong did occasionally travel to distant corners of the kingdom. One night while Songjong was away, the king had a distressing dream. When none of his wise men could interpret it, he summoned the captive Daniel, who had a reputation as a sort of soothsayer. To the delight of Nebuchadnezzar, the slave was able to discern the meaning of the dream."

"No kidding," Remo said. "What did it mean?"

"What?" Chiun asked, annoyed that the flow of his narrative had been disrupted.

"The dream. What did it mean?"

"How should I know?" the Master of Sinanju said, scowling. "Dreams are baby stories created by the gods to keep the brains of dimwits busy at night—lest, restive, they scurry out ears and scamper away."

"I thought they were a wish your heart made."

The old man gave him a baleful look. "There are inmates under lock and key here at Fortress Folcroft who have greater attention spans than you. Perhaps I will go tell Songjong's tale to them."

"No fair," Remo said. "They're strapped to their beds. There's probably a law." An icy stare and he raised his hands in surrender.

Chiun resumed his storytelling tone. "Though a king, Nebuchadnezzar was not the wisest man in his kingdom. Rather than simply accept the fool words of his lying captive, he sought to reward the wizard who claimed to have insight into the dreams of men. By the time Songjong returned from his journey, Daniel had risen from the position of lowly captive to ruler of the whole district of Babylon.''

"That must have been one hell of a dream."

"Since it was the king's wish that Daniel hold this station, Songjong attempted to make the arrangement work. However, he soon discovered that all was not as it had been. Nebuchadnezzar soon began to rely more on the slave's counsel than on that of Songjong. Not long after Daniel's ascendancy in his court, Nebuchadnezzar was discovered attempting to milk a dog.''

Remo's brow dropped low. "Attempting to what a what?" he asked, voice flat.

"Songjong thought it strange, as well," Chiun agreed, nodding wisely.

"I should hope so," Remo replied.

"But the lapse in the king's sanity did not last. Soon Nebuchadnezzar was himself once more. He resumed his great work of cultivating the Chaldean Empire, which he had established with the aid of Songjong. In this time he also built the Hanging Gardens of Babylon for his wife. All was well. Until the day he was found cavorting naked with a leper in the pool of the god Marduk Bel.''

Remo sighed. "I'm beginning to see a pattern here."

Chiun nodded. "As did Songjong. He suspected that the Hebrew captive Daniel was responsible for the king's bouts of madness. He was a diviner and a wizard, as well as a man who had seen his homeland destroyed by Nebuchadnezzar. The deterioration of the king's mind coincided with Daniel's arrival. It was a logical assumption.''

''So was he slipping Nebuch a mickey, or what?''

''Songjong never found out,'' Chiun said, voice sad. ''Nebuchadnezzar was too steeped in madness to learn the truth. When he began to imagine himself an ox and journey into the fields to eat grass, Songjong shook the dust of Babylon from his sandals and left to seek out other clients.''

The Master of Sinanju stopped. Sighing with great sadness, he began to fuss with the knees of his robes.

Remo waited for him to continue, but the old man seemed finished.

''And?'' Remo asked.

''And what?'' the Master of Sinanju said.

''What happened to Songjong?''

Chiun seemed puzzled by the question. ''I told you. He went off to ply his art elsewhere.''

''So what about Daniel?''

''Daniel the Nuisance thrived in the court of mad King Nebuchadnezzar. Of course he fell out of favor in time and was thrown into a den of lions, as you are annoyingly aware, thanks to that Christian almshouse where you wasted your youth. He claimed after his safe deliverance that the God of Israel sent angels to shut the lions' mouths. It is more likely that the animals did not like the taste of ham.''

''So that's it?'' Remo asked. ''We hold a three-thousand-year-old grudge against Daniel just 'cause he outfoxed us?''

''While that is more than enough,'' Chiun said, ''there is another moral...'' He arched an eyebrow.

His age-speckled head tipped ever so slightly in Smith's direction.

The CURE director had remained hunched over his computer throughout the story. With the sudden silence, however, he raised his gray head.

"What is it?" Smith asked, brow creasing.

"Little Father, Smith isn't out grazing on Folcroft's back lawn," Remo said.

A look of dark anger settled on the old Korean's weathered face. "Of course he is not," Chiun said. "A shallow grave awaits the dastard who would suggest such slander. Emperor Smith is clear of eye, mind and spirit. Hail Smith. Sinanju serves on bended knee the ever wise guardian of the Eagle throne."

A hint of embarrassment colored Smith's ashen cheeks. "Thank you, Master Chiun," he said. Clearing his throat, he returned to his work.

When Smith's head was bowed once more, the Master of Sinanju turned angrily to Remo.

"Are you as mad as this one?" he hissed in Korean. "Never tell the lunatic that you think he is a lunatic."

"I don't think he is," Remo insisted, also in Korean.

"Do not make me question your sanity, as well, Remo Williams," the old Asian said.

"Give it a rest, Chiun. Smith isn't, wasn't and never has been crazy. If you think I'm going to ditch him like Songjong ditched Nebbitynuzzle, you can forget it. Smith's going to have to keel over for me to leave."

"Bah," Chiun said, waving a bony hand. "That time has passed."

Remo frowned. "What do you mean?"

"Listen," the Master of Sinanju instructed, nodding to Smith.

Confused, Remo pitched his hearing toward the CURE director. He heard the tapping of Smith's fingers on the keyboard. Beyond that he detected the strong heartbeat, a congenital heart defect having been corrected by a pacemaker implant some six years previous. There was nothing more.

"I don't hear anything," Remo said.

"Precisely," Chiun replied. "A year ago it was there. Two years ago it was stronger still. The dark cloud of life's end had settled. Once there were the creaks and sputters of a man ready to welcome death. Now that is all gone. Look at him toiling like a man ten years his junior."

Remo had noticed it before. Smith had seemed infused with new vigor. He had assumed it was wishful thinking.

"It's the kid, isn't it." It was a statement of fact, not a question.

Chiun nodded tightly. "At this rate Smith will last many more years. I might not be here when comes the time for you to choose your next emperor. Of course, we could remove the mad middleman by having this modern Nebuchadnezzar committed to his own asylum. Smith could live out his remaining years in dignity, safe under the watchful gaze of Sinanju here in Fortress Folcroft. In the meantime, the Regent could assume his throne with us at his side."

"A perfect plan." Remo nodded. "Except Smitty won't go silent into that good straightjacket, his wife would have to have him committed and wouldn't, and I won't go along with it and neither will Howard."

"Yes," Chiun agreed. "The Prince is aggravating in his lack of ambition. I blame the old one. They are like two white peas in a pod." He sighed unhappily. "Thanks to his presence, Smith's natural end is now many years away. I can only hope that if I am not here when the time comes that you do the right thing."

"Right thing will be to leave, Little Father. No Master shall work for an Emperor's successor. It's in the rule book, loophole or no loophole."

Chiun's papery lips thinned. "Do not be certain," he said cryptically. "Thank the gods I had foresight to anticipate your obstinacy."

"What's that supposed to mean?"

"It means the loophole, as you call it, is already set. It is up to you only to not mess everything up."

And with that, the old man picked himself up on two long fingers. Still cross-legged, he turned from Remo, resettling on the threadbare carpet. As he studied the dust dancing in the shadows of Smith's office, there was a look of hard resolve on his weathered face.

Remo could see there would be no further questioning of his teacher. Wary now of what both the immediate and distant future held in store for him, Remo turned his attention back to Smith. To await news of Judith White.

15

The leggy anchorwoman was gushing over some new movie. On a stool across the *Newsfotainment Now!* set, a reporter for the program flashed a set of teeth as white as angel wings while nodding his agreement.

"Absolutely," the reporter enthused. "This is simply the greatest movie I've ever seen, Mary. Last night's star-studded L.A. premiere was the hottest seat in town for the film that already has Hollywood talking Oscar."

In the cluttered GenPlus Enterprises office, Mark Howard grunted at the small television.

"The Academy Awards are a year away," he muttered.

Mark hadn't brought his laptop with him. Dr. Smith's work ethic was now Mark Howard's own. These days, without his computer to occupy him, he was completely lost.

For a while he had picked through some of the books in the office. But they were virtually all dedicated to genetics, a subject Mark barely understood. He had finally given up on the books and snapped on the TV.

On the screen, the reporter's teeth were polished ivory.

"Producer Barry Schweid denies it, Mary," he gushed, "but the rumor mill is already talking sequel."

Eyes barely registering the TV screen, Mark shifted in the chair. He was going stir crazy.

He had been alone in this room for hours. In addition to the water samples from the Westchester Golf Club, which he had personally collected, Mark had made arrangements for samples of other bottled-water brands to be brought to New York's GenPlus facility. It was necessary to see if Lubec Springs alone was the source of the genetic mutation. The last sample of commercial springwater had arrived at the White Plains genetic-research facility at the same time as Mark. All had been whisked off for immediate testing.

Now, hours later, Mark drummed his fingers on a desk that was not his own and stared blankly at the television.

The office belonged to Dr. Andrew Mills, the top research scientist at GenPlus. A plastic toy that looked like a spiral staircase sat at the corner of the desk. The steps of the toy were colored in reds, yellows and greens.

Leaning forward, Mark picked up the DNA model. It was incredible to think that he lived in an age when the basic building blocks of life could be disassembled and reshuffled.

Mark had read news stories in recent years detailing cases of strange genetic experiments. There were the various cloning stories. These had been most prominent. But just one year before there had been the one about the spider-goat.

In a story straight out of science fiction, goats had been genetically crossbred with spiders. The resulting creature was only one-seventy-thousandth spider, but in its milk it produced a thin web. Researchers claimed that the web was proportionate in strength to that of a spider. Clothing spun from the web would be lighter than cotton and three times stronger than Kevlar. The military applications were obvious.

It was strange. Research of this kind—meant to benefit mankind—was not fundamentally different from that conducted by Judith White. How many other Judith Whites were toiling out there right now in dusty corner labs, waiting to release who knew what horrors on a human race that had put perhaps too much of its faith in science?

Mark was thinking wary thoughts about the future when the office door finally sprang open.

A breathless, middle-aged man burst inside, jowly face flushed. A white name tag pinned to his lab coat identified him as Dr. Mills.

Mark rose quickly to his feet.

"Good news, Mr. Marx," Dr. Mills announced, using the cover alias Howard had given him. He thought Mark was a special FBI agent. "The other samples checked clean. The contamination is limited to the Lubec Springs batch."

"You're sure?" Mark demanded.

"We tested twice. There were the usual impurities in the rest—most springwater isn't much different from ordinary tap water. But the transgenic bodies are present exclusively in the Lubec Springs samples you brought in."

Mark didn't need to hear more. He grabbed the phone from the desk. Shielding it with his body, he stabbed the 1 button repeatedly. Smith picked up on the first ring.

"Report," the CURE director announced crisply.

"It's only the Lubec Springs water that's affected," Mark said quickly. "All the other samples are clean."

"They are certain?" Smith pressed.

Mark turned to Dr. Mills. "Any chance—any at all—you could be mistaken?" he demanded.

The geneticist shook his head. "No, sir," he replied. "We knew what to look for. The other samples were clear."

Mark turned back to the phone. "He said—"

"I heard," Smith interrupted. "This limits our focus. I will dispatch Remo and Chiun to Maine at once. Report back here immediately. Tell the staff there to remain. We will coordinate to get more samples to them just in case."

"Gotcha. I'll be back soon." He returned the phone to its cradle and grabbed up his suit jacket from a nearby chair. "We need you to stay at work, Doctor," Mark said as he shrugged on his coat. "We only brought you a random sampling for testing. We'll be shipping some more. With any luck, your findings will hold. Thanks for your help."

Dr. Mills offered a nervous grin. "Thank *you* for the chance," he said. "Our molecular biologists are fascinated. None of them were around the first time. You know, Boston, 1978. And the BostonBio research data from a few years ago was confiscated by the government I think. I've heard it's surfaced on the Internet, but I wouldn't trust anything I found on Usenet. Basically, what I've heard up until today has been largely speculation and scientific hearsay.''

The geneticist was still smiling with nervous excitement. Mark Howard did not return the smile.

"You'll forgive me, Doctor, if I don't share your enthusiasm," he said, surprised at the coldness in his own voice. "We'll get those fresh samples to you as quickly as we can. Excuse me."

As Howard brushed past him, Dr. Mills's smile faded.

"I—I didn't mean…" he stammered. "I'm sorry. Anyway, the FBI shouldn't be too worried. Much of the material in the Lubec batch was already inert."

At the door, Mark stopped. "Inert?"

"Dead." Mills nodded. "It's still detectable, but the stuff is dying. It's more potent than the original batch from the seventies—at least from what we can tell—but it's weaker than the BostonBio stuff from three years ago."

Mark's brow dropped low. "It's been altered?"

"As far as we can tell, yes. We haven't cracked all the codes yet, obviously. That could take months or years. But it's definitely not the same stuff according to everything I've ever read on the subject. The biggest change is from the BostonBio batch. The mutational effect of that stuff was permanent. This is only temporary."

Mark was trying to wrap his brain around this.

There had been cases of gene-altering material stolen from BostonBio three years ago. He and Dr. Smith had assumed this was what they were dealing with. But substantial changes to the formula meant one thing: access to a lab.

"How temporary are the effects?" Mark asked.

"Ooo, not sure," Dr. Mills said. "Without an undiluted sample of the actual formula and subjects to test it on, I can't say for certain. But based on past cases, probably two weeks. Maybe three. Of course, they can be reexposed to the formula, extending the duration of change."

Howard nodded. "Thank you again, Doctor," he said. Turning, he headed out into the hall.

He was only a few doors along when Dr. Mills called after him.

"Mr. Marx!"

Howard almost forgot his cover name. When he turned, Dr. Mills was leaning into the hall.

"I think you should see this," he called worriedly.

Mark hurried back up the hall. Inside the office, Dr. Mills was pointing to the small television. On the screen, the entertainment program had fed into the news.

A female reporter stood on a rural road. Behind her, a group of protesters marched back and forth carrying large signs. The slogans H-2-No!, Water We Fighting For! and S.O.L: Save Our Leech were printed in bold letters.

Mark didn't know why the geneticist had called

him back. He was about to ask when the reporter began speaking.

"This was the scene earlier today outside the Lubec Springs bottling plant here in Lubec, Maine," the woman droned. "Environmental activists have gathered to protest the destruction of the natural habitat of a local species threatened with extinction. Supporters have poured in from around the country in the hope of raising awareness and to stem the tide of what has, for many, become the latest victim in the rising flood of man's cruelty toward the species with whom he shares the Earth."

The scene cut to protest footage shot earlier in the day. Mark Howard immediately recognized the celebrities featured in the segment. Bobby Bugget took center stage, flanked by the kleptomaniac actress and the stock-fixing happy homemaker.

"Alls I know," Bugget drawled, "is that mankind'd better watch out who on the food chain he decides to stomp on. You never know when the worm you squish today might turn around and bite you on the ass."

There seemed a look of exhausted desperation on the singer's tan face. The camera cut back to the reporter.

"Sober words from Bobby Bugget, a man who cares. Live in Lubec, Maine, I'm—"

The TV snapped off. Mark Howard withdrew his hand.

"Is this a problem?" Dr. Mills asked worriedly.

When he turned, Mark Howard was already heading out the door. The assistant director of CURE was fumbling his cell phone from his jacket pocket.

The look on the young man's face was that of someone who had just been told the exact date and time of Armageddon.

16

Dr. Emil Kowalski plodded slowly up the east wing hall of San Diego's Genetic Futures, Incorporated building.

Though a small man, he moved with the swaying, lazy pace of the obese. At some point in the recent past, someone had dubbed him "The Cow." His walk, as well as his sad brown eyes and deep, slow manner of speech, cemented the nickname among the other scientists at Genetic Futures.

A wall of windows on Kowalski's left looked out on a small enclosed courtyard. Sunlight poured in, illuminating name plates and door numbers. All the men and women on this floor were scientists, and all were beneath Dr. Kowalski, Genetic Futures's premier geneticist. A voice here and there called hello as Kowalski passed open doors.

Each time, without turning, Dr. Kowalski gave a long hello. Drawn out on the last syllable, it sounded like a human parody of an animal lowing.

Dr. Kowalski didn't look in any of the open doors. His droopy eyes were staring out the window.

The courtyard was so green, so lush. Always well

tended. During the worst California droughts, it was always as fresh as a country meadow.

By the time he reached his own office, Emil's stomach was growling.

He let himself in and shut the door behind him. Plodding across the room, he sank in his chair. He pulled out a small plastic sandwich bag from a brown paper lunch bag tucked away in his bottom desk drawer.

The contents weren't as green as the succulent courtyard grass. They weren't even as rich as they had been when he'd clipped them in his backyard that morning. But they were good enough to settle his longing stomach.

Dr. Kowalski fished in the back and pulled out a fat clump of grass clippings. He stuffed it greedily in between cheek and gums. He was in heaven the instant he started chewing. Moaning in ecstasy, he sat back in his chair. Eyes closed, he savored the sweet sensation.

Over the past two years he had become a grass connoisseur.

He liked the simple heft of orchard or meadow grasses, the body of Bengal grass, the tang of Kentucky bluegrass and the insouciance of the haughtier millets. He reveled in the seductive danger of sword grass.

It hadn't always been this way. For most of his fifty-two years on the planet, he had seen grass as a forgettable part of the scenery. Nothing important. A nuisance, really. Something that he hated to mow since childhood and for which a few years earlier he'd finally hired a professional service to care for when the dandelions and crabgrass in his own yard eventually got too wild.

Not anymore. Two years ago he had fired his service. He was back to caring for his own lawn.

No one else was allowed near it. Emil obsessed over it. He was out there every night and all weekend long. He had put up a fence to keep out unwanted animals and neighborhood children. He mowed it personally, working for hours with an old-fashioned push mower, lest a single poisonous drop of gas or oil touch soil or grass. And once it was mowed, he saved every little clipping in dated bags in freezer and refrigerator. He had even had a brief, unfortunate flirtation with canning. Grass had become his life.

He had brought in a fresh bag today. Emil had earned fresh. After all, now was a very stressful time. Although he no longer felt stress quite the same way as normal people.

Chewing on a wad of grass always gave him a feeling of wonderful isolation. As if he were the only creature in all of creation. He never used to get that. Life was always a crush of people and daily stresses. But now he could stare into space for hours, his mind completely blank, with no thought of the intruding world.

And he owed it all to one amazing, wonderful woman.

At a genetics conference in Atlanta two years ago, he had met the woman who would change his life.

She had kept to herself mostly. Talked to a few geneticists here and there. It almost seemed that she was interviewing potential employees. When Emil Kowalski met the raven-haired, beauty he didn't know what to make of her.

She was undeniably brilliant. She could discuss genetic theory and practice better than any mind he'd ever met. The men she spoke to weren't able to keep up. No slouch in his field, Emil Kowalski was made to feel like a freshman high-school biology student by this unknown female scientist.

She called herself Dr. Judy Fishbaum. No one at the conference had ever heard of her.

Despite the Atlanta heat, the woman kept a coat draped over one shoulder. That struck Emil as very odd.

She stood differently. Not like other people. It was as if she were keeping her one visible arm free to lash out. It was a stance for a prison, where one expected attack at any moment from any direction.

And the way she held the hidden arm. Shoulder down. So protective. For a little while Emil thought that she might be a recent amputee, embarrassed by a missing limb. But he dismissed that theory when he saw something move beneath the jacket. Whatever might be wrong, there was *something* there.

When she got Emil alone in the lounge of the hotel where the conference was being held, the woman who called herself Judy Fishbaum finally took off her coat.

He knew at once where she'd gotten her fascination with genetics. Her right arm was not fully formed. Undoubtedly a congenital defect had guided her into her current field.

Dr. Kowalski hadn't been prepared. He couldn't

help but look. When she caught him staring, he was surprised by her reaction. He had assumed most people who had lived all their lives with a deformity would react to insensitive stares either with some level of embarrassment or anger. There wasn't a flicker of either on her pale face.

She didn't even look away. She continued to stare Emil straight in the eye.

"You're interested in this?" she asked, with not a flicker of emotion in her voice. The arm was raised. It was half the size of an adult arm. "It's not finished growing yet," she confided.

Emil Kowalski got a good look at the limb. There was a purr of pleasure from his companion when she saw the look of surprised understanding that crossed his face.

The arm didn't match. For one thing the skin was far too young for a woman somewhere in her late thirties. It was a child's skin. It was smooth and unmuscled with soft baby fat. The limb wasn't deformed in the least. Just small. As if the aging had been arrested years before.

"Oh," he said, his own embarrassment changing over to fascination. "It's not yours."

"Of course it is," she replied. "It's just not part of the original equipment." She flexed five pudgy fingers.

"Is it a graft?" Dr. Kowalski asked.

Doctors were doing that now. Grafting limbs. The success rate wasn't great, due to rejection by the body's immune system, but the work held promise. However, in the cases Emil had heard about, great care was taken to match the donor limb to the host. He had never heard of anyone grafting a child's arm on an adult's body.

"No," she replied. "Do you ever wonder—"' she read his name tag "—Emil, why one strand of hair will fall out, only to be replaced by another? Or why one set of teeth is replaced by another in childhood, but a lost tooth in adulthood doesn't grow back?"

"Simple," Emil said. "Encoding. The body does what it's programmed to do."

"Yes, simple," she said. "It seems so odd to me. Hair is nothing. A throwback to another evolutionary stage. Human beings no longer need hair to survive. Yet why does nature still give priority to replacing worthless hair and not to vital organs? Or limbs?"

It was the way she said it. The stress she put on the last word, accompanied by another flex of that child's hand.

The truth hit Dr. Emil Kowalski like a hard fist to the stomach.

"That isn't a graft," he whispered, awed.

Winking, she offered another contented purr. The coat came back on, covering the limb that Dr. Kowalski knew should not be, but was.

This was big. Research was heading in this direction, but results were still decades away. He needed to hear more.

Later, in a dark corner of the hotel bar, he heard her theories on transgenic organisms. Science was becoming involved more in the creation of new species. It was easier to mix genetic material and start from scratch. She explained that inherited genetic traits from one organism could be spliced into an existing organism without rejection by the host.

By this point it was very late. The bar had cleared out. She had ordered a martini at one point during the evening, but had taken not a single sip.

From the start she insisted that Emil drink only springwater. She told him she wouldn't waste time sharing thoughts with him if he wasn't stone sober. Dr. Kowalski agreed. He wasn't about to refuse an order from the most beautiful, brilliant companion he had ever gone out with.

They were whispering. Dr. Kowalski felt like a spy. It was all so exciting, so dangerous.

"There was research going on in this field before," he said. "You must have heard about it. In Boston? But it didn't work out. Both times there were deaths. After the last time, Congress passed a law against human testing."

"Human laws don't apply to us," she said.

Dr. Kowalski wasn't sure exactly what she meant by that. And at that moment he didn't really care.

He put down his glass of water.

He was dizzy. His tongue felt too big for his mouth.

By the time he realized she had slipped something in his drink, it no longer mattered.

He soon learned that his companion was the notorious Dr. Judith White, the infamous madwoman of BostonBio. She had used her own formulas to alter her features slightly—just enough so that none at the conference recognized her. And that wasn't all.

The change came over Emil Kowalski rapidly. In the first terrible moments, the last vestiges of his humanity conjured images of bloody, half-eaten corpses like he'd heard about on the news. But when it was done, he had no desire to eat human flesh.

"I feel different," he said, puzzled. "Am I like you?" His voice was slower now than before. A low, contented moan rose from deep in his throat.

She shook her head. "I need someone with your brains, Emil, but with no ambition and total loyalty," Judith White explained. "If I'd made you like me, you'd be like all my young. Thinking with your belly. I couldn't have bodies piling up around your lab. That would draw the authorities. I've made you a totally new hybrid. I drew on a few different species. You're now as indolent as a cow. No Nobel ambitions from you. I'll tell you what to do and you'll do it. The rest of the time you'll do pretty much nothing. And you're as loyal as a dog. You won't dream of turning on me. Feel proud, Emil. You're a totally new creature, unlike any other on the planet."

Emil liked the idea of that. Almost as much as he liked the woman who sat across from him in the bar. He would die before he betrayed her. Knew it on an instinctive level. He wondered what his new wonderful friend wanted from him.

"I need a lab," Judith White said. "A good, permanent one. I can't keep moving from place to place, plundering equipment here and there, afraid of being caught. I need a base of operations, sweetcakes, and Genetic Futures is it."

And so began Emil Kowalski's relationship with Dr. Judith White.

Emil was satisfied just to do what he was told to

do. For the past two years he did his work, and when he wasn't doing his work he spent his time either caring for his lawn or—better yet—staring blankly into space.

Dr. Emil Kowalski was staring at the wall of his San Diego office when there came a sudden knock at his door.

Emil wiped some lawn drool from his chin.

"Come in," he called.

A young Genetic Futures scientist stuck his head in the room. The man seemed hesitant when he saw the dull-eyed look on Dr. Kowalski's face. He tried not to stare at the drying green dribble stain on his boss's white lab coat.

"We're all set to go," the young man said. "Whenever you get the specimen in, we'll be ready."

Kowalski nodded. "It might be days. Keep shifts on around the clock. Time will be vital when it arrives."

"Yes, sir. I'll let everyone know."

"Is there something else?"

The young man hadn't realized he was loitering in the doorway. He just couldn't believe it. There was a piece of grass sticking out of the mouth of Genetic Futures's senior geneticist. He had never believed the stories, always assuming "The Cow" nickname was just a play on Dr. Kowalski's name.

"Um, no, sir. Sorry, sir."

The young face disappeared and the door closed.

Emil sat behind his desk for a short time longer, munching grass from his bag. When he finally looked at his wall clock, two hours had gone by.

That happened a lot these days. No track of time.

"Oh, well," he said. "Things will get busy soon enough. Better make sure we're ready."

Adam's apple bulging, he swallowed the big lump of grass that was still in his mouth. It would be even better once it had settled in one of his stomachs for a few hours. He'd bring it up as cud that afternoon.

Mooing contentedly, Emil Kowalski plodded lazily from his office.

17

By the eleven-o'clock news cycle, reports of new cases of feral behavior among humans had begun to die down. News reports were focusing mainly on New York, with mention of a handful of other cases in the Northeast.

In the family quarters of the White House, the President of the United States watched the late news with deep concern.

It was an hour past his normal bedtime. This President preferred to go to bed early and to rise early.

He trusted in the old "healthy, wealthy and wise" adage. It seemed to work for him. Although the wealth didn't matter so much—he was from a well-off family and had taken a substantial pay cut to become President—his health was fine.

As for wisdom…well, if the late-night shows were to be believed, he had none. According to the media, the folks from the other side were always the brilliant statesmen, the towering intellects. It was accepted as gospel that those on the President's side of the aisle were busy frantically rubbing their two brain cells together trying to make fire.

The thought always gave him a chuckle. This President was confident enough to not let such nonsense rattle him. It didn't matter to him what a handful of comedy writers in Los Angeles or anchormen in New York thought of him. Besides, he avoided network news and was normally in bed long before the late-night comics were on.

Not this night. This night there was a crisis and the President of the United States was staying up past his bedtime watching the late news.

The scenes shown were gruesome, the eyewitness accounts frightening, if true. The President had poured himself a drink, but it sat sweating in his hand. He watched the news recap with pursed lips and furrowed brow.

When it was over, the President got up from the sofa.

Walking briskly from the living room, he headed down the long hallway to his private bedroom.

His wife was away visiting family in Texas. There was no one to bother him as the President sat down on the edge of the bed and removed the cherry-red phone from his bottom bureau drawer.

He hated to make this call. He had been using this phone far too much in the past year. But the weight of the world had been dropped on his shoulders only eight months into his fledgling presidency.

With a deep appreciation for what it meant, he lifted the red receiver.

There was no need to dial. As usual, the phone was answered on the first ring.

"Yes, Mr. President?" said the familiar lemony voice.

"Hello, Smith," the President said. "The situation in New York and New England."

"Yes, sir," Smith said. "We are already working on it."

"Oh." The President was always impressed by the older man's efficiency. In a way, the lemon-voiced man reminded the President of his own secretary of defense.

"It is a complicated situation, but we believe we know who is behind the product tampering. My people left here an hour ago to put an end to the source. With any luck, the worst part of the crisis should be over by morning."

"They're now saying on the news that it resembles the case with that White woman in Boston a few years back."

"We believe she is the source," Smith said. "Either that or someone following in her footsteps. We have confirmed that it is a formula similar to hers."

"Great," the President muttered. "Another fine mess I've inherited. I'll add it to the pile." Sighing, the President took a sip from the glass he'd carried in from the living room. The ice was all but melted.

"Hopefully, we will end this by tomorrow," Smith said. "I have issued orders that all shipments of Lubec Springs water are to be intercepted. Once store back stock has been destroyed, there should be no more new cases."

The President stopped drinking. "Water?" he said. "That's what they're dumping this stuff in?"

"Yes, sir."

The President looked at the water in his glass.

"You might have given a guy a little warning, Smith."

"The problem has not spread farther down the East Coast than northern New Jersey. Washington is not a focus."

"My lucky day," the President said. Even so, he put his half-empty glass on the bureau. With his fingertips, he pushed it to a safe distance. "So why the Northeast? Lubec Springs is national. They could have shipped from coast to coast. There aren't any cases anywhere else, are there?"

"Not so far."

"Then what's so special about there?"

"We have not yet determined that," Smith replied. "If you'll excuse me now, Mr. President, my assistant has just returned."

"Smith?" the President called before the CURE director could break the connection.

"Yes, sir?"

"The FBI director mentioned something in my morning briefing about al-Khobar terrorists at an airport in Arkansas. Was that you?"

"My special person was involved, yes, sir," Smith said, obviously impatient to end the call.

"Good work, Smith. We've got them on the run. I'm sure you'll do the same with this new problem."

With a tight-lipped smile, he replaced the phone and slid the drawer shut.

There was no doubt that there were messes in America these days. This was just another tossed on the heap. But messes could be cleaned up. And despite the perilous times he lived in, the President remained an eternal optimist.

Standing, he carefully picked up his water glass and brought it into the presidential bathroom. A moment later came the sound of a flushing toilet.

UP THE EAST COAST in Smith's dimly lit office, Mark Howard had shut the door quietly and slid into his plain wooden chair. He waited for the CURE director to hang up the special phone in his bottom desk drawer before speaking.

"Is there some new catastrophe?" Mark asked warily.

"No," Smith replied, rolling the drawer shut. "And I wish I shared the President's confidence that we will prevail. I have had no luck since your second call."

He had been searching for potential research facilities with a Judith White connection ever since Mark had called from his cell phone in the GenPlus parking lot an hour ago.

Smith removed his glasses, touching them to his desktop with a soft click. "The President raised a question that has puzzled me," he said, massaging his tired eyes. "Why the Northeast alone? Aside from a single case in New Jersey late this morning, it hasn't extended beyond New York. There has not been one case in any other part of the country."

"Maybe it's just where the stuff happens to have been shipped so far," Mark suggested. "Maybe she's planning on expanding. Or maybe she ran out of formula."

"Perhaps. Although if it is as you suggested in your phone call and she has a facility for producing her formula, she would not have started without first having all she needed on hand."

"The guy I spoke to was certain there were alterations to the old formula, Dr. Smith."

"Then it is a certainty she has a lab." Smith replaced his glasses. "She had to know Lubec Springs would eventually be identified as the source. If simply increasing the numbers of her species was her goal, it would have made sense to blanket as wide an area as possible. She would have wanted to infect the greatest number of people before she was found out. Yet she seemed to concentrate in only one part of the country."

A thoughtful look on his face, Smith picked up the aspirin bottle of formula from the corner of his desk.

"I thought you usually used children's aspirin," Mark noted, nodding to the bottle.

"The sample Remo obtained in New York," Smith explained. He shook the bottle. Liquid sloshed inside.

"Do you want me to get rid of it?"

"No," Smith said. "For now I'll store it downstairs. In fact, it might be wise to save some frozen form of the genetic material she used in perpetuity. Perhaps from this one day an antidote or vaccine could be found."

"I notice we're both using 'she' a lot," Mark said.

Smith nodded as he tapped a gnarled thumb on the bottle lid. "Given what you have learned, I am leaning more toward Judith White herself as mastermind," he said, putting the bottle aside once more.

"After all, she did not turn any of the people in her lab three years ago. None were implicated at the time and they all underwent testing after the fact. Those that she recruited at that time were not scientists. Therefore we are not now dealing with a leftover creature from that time, since they would not have her knowledge of genetics."

"It still might not be her," Mark suggested. "One of the others might have laid low for a while and then found a geneticist to turn—someone who could help. You said those briefcases of her formula were never found. They wouldn't have needed her science background to turn new recruits."

"It does not fit their pattern of behavior," Smith insisted. "They would be like all animals. Driven purely by instinct. To feed, mate. They would live in the moment. They wouldn't worry about covering their tracks all this time. Only Judith White had a vision of a greater future for the abominations she had created. She alone would have the patience to wait this long. It must be her." His frown lines deepened. "But what her plan is I have no idea."

"Well, lucky for us Remo injured her last time."

"Yes," Smith agreed. "Still, she will not be unprotected. It is not cliché to say that an injured animal is most dangerous when it is cornered. I urged Remo and Master Chiun to caution before I sent them to Maine."

"What about the protesters?" Mark asked.

Even before Mark had called, Smith's computers had pulled up reports of the Reticulated New England

Speckled Leech protesters outside the Lubec Springs bottling plant.

"They should not be a problem. Our biggest concern would be exposure to the press. But there has not been great interest in their protest. The news cycle being what it is, I doubt they will get more coverage than they did today. Still, Remo and Chiun will be arriving just before dawn. Things should be quiet enough at that time for them to do what they need to and get out."

"Dr. Smith, just so you know, I'm a little worried that the protesters are from Green Earth," Mark said.

They had recently encountered the environmental activist group in South America. Back then it was in the form of a former Soviet president high up in the organization. That man's foolishness had resulted in environmental devastation throughout a large part of the Caribbean.

The CURE director caught the subtle strain in his assistant's voice at the mention of Green Earth.

"It is a large organization, with interests all around the world," Smith said cautiously. "Since this and our last encounter with them seemed unconnected, I was going to chalk it up to coincidence." He peered over the tops of his rimless glasses. "Unless you think we should look deeper into their group."

Mark met the older man's level gaze.

It was a subject that gave them both discomfort. Mark had a special, almost precognitive ability that had in the past given him early insight into potential CURE problems. For the assistant director of CURE, it was like peering into a puzzle box and seeing part of the picture where others only saw a jumble of pieces.

Mark shook his head. "There's nothing right now," he said. "But there might be something coming. I don't know for sure. But we should keep an open file on them."

"Very well," Smith said. "I'll have the mainframes collate any Green Earth data they find."

With a few sure strokes on his keyboard, he issued the proper commands to the basement computers.

While Smith typed, Mark got to his feet. His back was sore from sitting around the GenPlus offices all evening.

"If there's nothing else, I'd better get back to work," he said. "I'll try to find that lab. You should really go home, Dr. Smith. I'll stay here tonight."

Smith glanced up, shaking his head. "If I need to, I will take a few hours' sleep on the sofa." He ignored the look of concern that passed across his assistant's face, turning his attention back to his computer screen.

Mark could see there would be no arguing. Without another word, he headed for the door.

"Mark."

Smith called him as he was opening the door. When Howard turned, he saw that the CURE director wore a thoughtful expression. Light from Smith's buried monitor cast ghostly shadows on his gray face.

"Judith White is highly intelligent," the older man said. He leaned back in his chair, considering for a long moment. "Rather than look for the lab itself, I want you to do a search for mysterious deaths. There would be no mutilations like today or back in Boston. To do so would have tipped her hand long before this, and she is much too smart for that. Given her, er, appetite, they would have to be bodies missing organs or limbs. Perhaps cases that have been attributed to a serial killer and that remain unsolved. Begin with newspaper reports, police and FBI records and expand out from there.''

Orders crisply delivered, he returned to his keyboard.

It was a familiar pose. One that Mark Howard had grown used to over the past few years. The gaunt, gray man in the austere office typing assuredly at his computer. Mark didn't know why, but he found comfort in the image.

Smiling to himself, Mark gently closed the door, so as not to disturb America's last, great patriot.

18

A Navy jet carried Remo and Chiun as far as Bangor. A waiting Coast Guard helicopter brought them to a field just outside of Jonesboro.

Smith had arranged delivery of a rental car. The helicopter was lifting off into the predawn gray above Route 1 as the rental keys were being dropped into Remo's hand.

The pair of federal marshals who had been awakened in the dead of night with special orders to rent the car left the two Sinanju Masters beside the road. Yawning, they returned to their own vehicle as Remo and Chiun climbed into the rented car.

Both Coast Guard helicopter and U.S. Marshals took off down the coast. Remo headed in the opposite direction.

The minute they were on the highway, Remo had his foot jammed down on the accelerator. The car was soon tearing up the road at speeds in excess of one hundred miles per hour.

Chiun watched the road with some concern.

"Your driving being what it is, I cannot say that you are operating this vehicle in a more reckless fashion than usual," the old Korean said as Remo nearly sideswiped his third car. "Since you have not yet crashed, flipped or otherwise mangled either it or me, one could say you are doing better than usual. However, your speed might be considered excessive by the local constabulary."

"Cops schmops," Remo said, tension tightening his jaw. "Let them catch me if they can. Besides, most cops on duty at this time of the morning are either napping in their cruisers or their mistresses' apartments."

Luckily traffic was thin so early in the day. Remo beeped and jerked the wheel, scraping out between two cars and into the left lane. He accelerated past another speeding vehicle. With another honk and twist, he was back in the right lane.

From the passenger's seat, Chiun watched the display with disapproval. "How much did Smith pay you to assassinate me?" he asked abruptly.

"Huh?" Remo said. "What are you talking about?"

"He has put me in the death seat of this carriage with maniac you behind the wheel. Obviously he wishes the Master dead. Why else did we not take the aircraft farther?"

"He was afraid White would hear the chopper, realize it wasn't supposed to be there and bolt. The last thing we want is for her to get away again."

"No," Chiun pointed out. "While that would be bad, the last thing we want is for me to be killed."

"We've all gotta go sometime, Little Father."

"Speak for yourself, Round Eyes," the Master of Sinanju said. He sighed. "I suppose my leniency in training is to blame for your poor driving skills. I noticed a marked deterioration in your skills while we were living in Castle Sinanju, which I did nothing to address.''

"Yeah, Boston does have a tendency to bring out the worst in most drivers. Fortunately, I avoided the curse." He laid on the horn and drove onto the median strip to avoid a bread truck on its early-morning rounds.

Chiun shook his head sadly. ''The location of Castle Sinanju should have had no effect on your driving skills. A duck may live every day of its life in a stable, but it will never try to be a horse. And do you know why?''

"Dunno. Maybe it knows how stupid it'd look herding cattle in a cigarette ad. And did you ever try to saddle a duck? Plus the Kentucky Derby would be just plain silly. Although I'd probably tune in if the jockeys were riding mallards.''

Chiun gave his pupil a baleful look. ''Are you quite finished?'' he droned.

Remo sighed. "Why, Chiun, beyond the obvious, does a duck who lives in a stable not become a horse?''

"Because, ignoramus, the duck does not let his environment influence what he becomes. He is clever enough to remain a duck. Unfortunately, Remo, you are not as blessed as the duck. You allowed the bad drivers of that bean-eating province to influence your driving skills. If you were the duck, after one week you would leave the stable whinnying.''

"Boston driving was an education," Remo insisted. "If you can survive that demolition derby, you can race a Ferrari through St. Peter's without dinging a pew."

"Go ahead. Joke if you wish. Live recklessly. Play the part of the fool and forget that an entire village lives and dies with you."

Remo glanced at his teacher. The old man was staring stonily out the windshield at the empty road ahead.

"At what point did this stop being about my driving?" Remo asked.

Chiun shook his head angrily. "The risks you take," he complained quietly. "Being Master of Sinanju does not make you invulnerable."

Remo could hear the deep concern buried beneath his teacher's angry tone. "I know that, Little Father," he said reasonably. "But I'm more than good enough for pretty much anything we're likely to meet."

"Good enough?" Chiun said. "Good enough?" he repeated, voice rising in fury. "Is that what I trained? Good enough? Is that what the villagers of Sinanju must now rely on for their daily sustenance? Good enough? Thank you, Remo, for setting all my worries to rest. And I now have your epitaph, for with that attitude I will not only be alive to write it, but I will be able to do so soon. It will read, 'Here lies Remo the Pale. He was good enough until the one day he was not.'"

The old Asian threw up his hands, hissing frustration.

"This has to do with that legend, doesn't it?" Remo asked as Chiun muttered a string of harsh Korean at the Maine countryside. "The one that says I have to be careful going through the forest where the tigers live?"

Eyes dead ahead, Chiun nodded. "It was prophesied by no less than the Great Wang himself. The forest holds danger for Shiva's avatar."

Remo could see this was important to his teacher. Still, he couldn't see the risk. He was fully Master now, whole in Sinanju. And he had encountered these creatures twice before and vanquished them both times. Still, for the sake of his teacher and father, he offered a reassuring smile.

"Don't worry, Chiun," he vowed. "I won't let my guard down."

When he turned his full attention back to the road, he missed the look of dark doubt that passed like a cloud across his teacher's face.

He pressed hard on the gas once more, and the car raced up the road for the Lubec Springs bottling plant.

JUDITH WHITE SENSED them coming. Smelled them on the air. Felt the familiar, new presence through the dense wood.

For a long time as they came, she paced back and forth in the small Lubec Springs office.

The lights were off. Through the wide picture window, her keen eyes could see far into the depths of the dark, predawn woods. Here and there she saw them. Shadows moving ever closer.

The rest wouldn't have noticed yet. When the protest had ended and the cameras had left, the others who had stood in for the dead Green Earth protestors had skulked back to the warehouse.

Probably sleeping and eating. They were mostly males, and that was nearly all the males did.

Her human memory told her she'd had the same complaint about men even when she was living her old life.

The males were virtually useless. Dumb and lazy, only concerned about their immediate desires.

Judith was glad she had used a weaker version of the formula. So far, there wasn't one male in Maine she would want to keep around forever. All of those she'd altered would change back or die. She alone was perfection. She alone would usher in the age of animal dominance.

And there was another reason she was glad these particular males would not be with her very long. Who knew? If there were others who were turned permanently, a dominant male might very well emerge to challenge her.

Although she had many answers, this wasn't one of them. The truth was, Judith didn't know for certain what would happen to her under those circumstances. Would the instinct of the creatures whose DNA she now carried compel her to take a submissive role? She doubted she could ever follow the lead of a male. And for a very simple reason.

The humans would call it jealousy. But for Dr. Judith White, it was really pure animal resentment. This was *her* species. *She* had created it. And it was she and she alone who was molding it to take its rightful place as the preeminent animal life-form on the planet.

No, the males of her kind would never rule her world. She wouldn't allow it. And once she was successful with her work here, the best humanity had to offer would fail, as well.

Alone in Owen Grude's office, Judith's head suddenly tipped sharply. Ears far more acute than mere human hearing focused on a single sound.

A soft growl. Followed by cautious footsteps the others would not hear. The shadows in the woods were closer.

Abruptly she turned, gliding in silence from the office. She moved with feline confidence through the bottling plant.

When Judith White prowled into the warehouse, the others were lounging lazily.

The few Green Earth protesters who had survived the previous day's slaughter had joined the others Judith had turned since her arrival in Maine. Some lay sleeping on crates, arms and legs dangling over the sides. Others picked through the remains of victims.

The woman who had been a TV homemaking expert was weaving human veins into edible doilies for a special breakfast treat. She had already made a lovely centerpiece from pine cones and a human heart.

In one corner, the young movie actress slept in a nest of toilet paper and bones that she'd pilfered from around the complex.

The boxer was nowhere to be seen. Already wild in his human life, he had reacted more strongly than any of the others to the formula. He was keeping to himself, prowling the road and woods outside the bottling plant.

Judith picked her way through the gathered pride. One cautious foot stepped before the next. She sniffed the cool air, tracking a fresh scent.

At her appearance, the males rose dutifully to their feet. Owen Grude came to her side.

Far behind the others was Bobby Bugget. Ever since he was forced to drink the formula, Bugget had kept to the fringes of the pack. The singer was chewing nervously on a thumb he'd scavenged from the floor.

"What is it?" Owen asked Judith.

She kept her nose in the air. "We've got company."

As she spoke, the small side door next to the big loading bays nudged slowly, cautiously open.

A female face appeared. She was bent at the waist, her chin low to the floor. She sniffed questioningly as she came into the warehouse.

A second and third came in behind. They were quickly followed by two more.

The scents in the big warehouse seemed to relax the female. Here was familiarity, safety. She didn't know why. But there was a sense of home to these surroundings.

Her strides grew more confident. As she relaxed, so too did the four males. Their aggressive hunch eased as they trailed the female into the dimly lit building.

The creatures lounging in the warehouse were

roused from their torpor. Climbing out of nests and jumping down from crates, they moved to intercept the newest arrivals.

Judith White was pleased to see that, of these latest arrivals, the four males were obviously subservient to the female. This had seemed to be the case all during the night. Perhaps it wouldn't be necessary to tinker with the formula as much as she had feared.

The female broke away from her pack. The others dropped away behind her, skulking off into the shadows, yellow eyes studying the growling line that was protecting Judith White.

The new female stopped in the middle of the floor, rising proudly to her full height.

Judith's pride came forward slowly. Peering, sniffing, they nuzzled the new arrival curiously.

They quickly determined that she wasn't a threat. When the inspection was through, they broke away, fanning back out around the warehouse.

Some of the new arrivals took the acceptance of their leader as a cue. They came out of the shadows. When they tried to eat, they were chased away with growls and snapping jaws. Slinking off to the edge of the group, they gnawed the scraps that had been tossed to the concrete floor.

Judith White paid no attention to her cubs. She was sniffing the air almost as an afterthought.

"You're from New York," she announced with certainty.

"Yes," replied Elizabeth Tiflis. There was a hint of puzzlement in her deep, throaty voice.

Judith sensed her confusion. "You want to know

why you're here," she said. "Eschewing the boring human notions of the metaphysical, you are here because I *programmed* you to be here. Just the tiniest leech DNA. Green Earth is right to want to save them. Those things have one of the strongest homing beacons for the few square feet of swamp they were born and bred in than virtually any species I've ever come across. It's pretty useless in a leech. It's not like they can migrate. But then, they can't drive. I assume that's how you got here."

"Yes," Elizabeth said.

"Did you feed along the way?"

"No, we ate before we left."

"Good," Judith said, more to herself than to Elizabeth. "I want them here, not wasting time investigating every half-eaten corpse at every Mass Pike rest stop."

Elizabeth growled confusion. "Who?" she asked.

A flicker of self-satisfaction crossed Judith White's face. "In good time," she promised. "For now, you're only part of the equation. Get something to eat."

She waved at a few uneaten Green Earth bodies that had been stacked against the wall. The men who had come with Elizabeth didn't need a second invitation. They pounced on a body, dragging it out onto the floor.

As they began to feast, Elizabeth made a face.

"I prefer a fresh kill," Elizabeth complained.

"There will be plenty of time for that later, once more of the others have arrived."

"*If* they arrive," Elizabeth said. "If the same thing

happens to them as happened to us, they'll be lucky to get here at all.'' With the words came a soft shudder of fear.

Judith felt it in the woman. Fear was unusual for her species.

Elizabeth had chased back two of the males who had accompanied her from New York. She had settled in with the others at the protester's corpse. Her rounded bottom settled back on coiled legs.

"What do you mean?" Judith asked.

"We were taken captive. Two humans nearly stopped us from escaping."

Judith sensed it again. The fear.

"Describe them," Judith ordered.

"They were fast," Elizabeth said. "And strong. They weren't like the others. I sensed no fear in them."

"What did they look like?"

Judith was surprised at the urgency in her own voice. The others noted it, too. Worried eyes glanced up.

"One was Asian," Elizabeth said. "Too old for a meal. No meat on his bones at all. The young, white one had dark hair. About six feet tall. Deep eyes, high cheekbones. He had very thick wrists."

With the description came a cold shudder that passed like ice through her body. This time, Elizabeth was not the source. Her meal was abruptly forgotten.

Elizabeth was instantly alert. Back arched, she stood up on hands and feet. Brown eyes darted to empty shadows.

It was instinct. Elizabeth didn't know why she was

searching the corners of the warehouse. Only that her body had picked up a telegraphed dread.

And Judith White was the source.

The others sensed Judith's alarm. A thrill of panic rippled through the drafty warehouse. Males and females alike stopped whatever they were doing. They pawed the floor and sniffed nervously at the air for some unknown fear.

But while the rest didn't know why they feared, Judith White knew. It was those two. The men Elizabeth Tiflis had described could be no one else.

Judith was angry at the instinct that made her fear. If she were to succeed, she would have to master the panic.

Animal noises filled the warehouse. The creatures that had once been men and women paced and snorted at shadows.

"Calm yourselves," Judith growled loudly. "There's nothing to worry about."

Spinning, she left the fearful creatures growling at the walls of the big warehouse. Judith White hurried back to the safety of the front office. To quell the fear.

19

The bare bulb was snapped on from a switch above. A moment later, Harold Smith climbed down the basement stairs.

A set of keys from his desk drawer was clutched tight in his hand as he made his way around the bottom of the staircase. Nearby was the secret wall behind which CURE's mainframes hummed. Smith bypassed that part of the room.

He found a small steel door tucked away behind the ancient boiler. Grimy letters on a discolored brass plate read "Patient Records." A note written in Smith's hand instructed any Folcroft staff who wanted to enter the room to see Director Smith for the keys.

The paper was yellowed from age. Smith had posted the note thirty years before. No one ever asked for the keys.

He unlocked the heavy bolt and pushed open the door.

Inside was another bare bulb.

Smith rarely came into this room. The last time was a year ago when he had finally gotten around to showing it to Mark Howard. Before that it had been years.

The only person to come down here with any regularity was Smith's secretary. Whenever Eileen Mikulka needed to access old patient records, she used her own set of keys.

Six big filing cabinets held a century's worth of Folcroft medical records. In addition to these, three small stainless-steel drums sat against the far wall. There was a temperature gauge on the side of each tank.

When Smith peered at the dial on the nearest container he saw that it was holding steady at −196 degrees Celsius.

The other two tanks were no longer functioning.

Smith considered pulling the plug on the third tank. For a moment, his hand hovered near the off switch. After all, it had already served its purpose. For all the good that had done any of them. He had explained that to Mark the previous year, as well. But the pragmatist in him won out.

There might yet be a need. He left the tank running.

A small refrigerator—the kind used in college dormitories—sat unplugged in the corner. Smith plugged it in. Fishing in his pocket, he took out the aspirin bottle of Judith White's formula and put it in the fridge.

He'd find out proper storage later on. Perhaps he'd have to start up one of the other liquid-nitrogen tanks. And with any luck, Remo would get him an undiluted sample of the formula. That would be best for a vaccine.

When he was done, Smith shut the refrigerator door and took one last look around the room to make certain he hadn't forgotten anything. Satisfied, he closed the storage room door, locking it up tight once more.

In the dark closet, the old fridge chugged softly.

20

The deer carcass lay in the wet grass at the soft shoulder of the road.

There had been a feeding frenzy. Virtually all but head and legs were gone. As Remo and Chiun sped by in their rented car, Remo saw many footprints amid the scattered brown fur around the creature. Although the prints looked human, they were softer, with the weight more toward toe than heel.

"That's the third one we've passed in two miles," he commented grimly.

The Master of Sinanju had remained silent for the past few miles, concern for his pupil weighing heavy on his shoulders. But when his eyes strayed from the dead deer to the road ahead, a spark of life lit his dour face.

"Your persistent stubbornness is too stressful on my delicate senses," the old Asian announced from the passenger's seat. "Stop for a moment that I might collect my frazzled nerves." He tapped an urgent fingernail on the dashboard, pointing to a tiny strip mall that was speeding toward them on the right. "There is a good spot."

Remo followed his teacher's extended finger. "That's a real estate office, Little Father."

"Is it?" Chiun asked innocently. He pretended to see the sign for the first time. "So it is."

For a time two years ago the old Korean had been on Remo's case to buy a house in Maine. The rocky coast and bitter winter reminded him of his native Sinanju. Remo thought he'd won that battle when they'd moved into their new town house in Connecticut.

"We're not stopping," Remo said firmly.

"A good son who did not cause his father in spirit to worry for his well-being all the time would stop."

"We're not buying a house in Maine. Case closed."

Chiun watched the building zoom by. He sank back into his seat, folding his arms inside his sleeves. "You are an evil man, Remo Williams. We are already in the emperor's potato province. What harm would come of looking?"

"Walking out with a deed for one thing," Remo said. "Look, Chiun, I'm happy where we're living now. Living in Connecticut is close to Smith, but not too close. We've got a couple of airports nearby. It's convenient. Maine is too far off the beaten path."

"I am not surprised that *you* would be content with our current accommodations." Chiun sniffed. "I have never known a pig to complain about the quality of the mud he is wallowing in. I, on the other hand, am not happy. For one thing, it is only a matter of time before squatters take up residence in the home adjacent to our own. At my age I do not need to worry about Gypsy horse thieves keeping me awake until all hours of the night with their smelly cooking and rowdy tambourine banging.''

The other side of their duplex had remained vacant the entire time they'd lived in Connecticut. The Master of Sinanju had done yeoman's work chasing away any potential neighbors. But since their work for Smith sometimes kept them away for extended periods of time, the old Korean had been growing more concerned that the empty town house next door would be rented while they were away.

"I'm not worried that we'll get neighbors," Remo said absently. He had caught sight of something up ahead.

"Of course not. You would let any undesirables move in. It is up to me to maintain the quality of our neighborhood."

Remo was about to say something on the nature of racism, freedom in America to live wherever you wanted and Chiun's definition of undesirables, which included—on a good day—everyone in the world who wasn't Korean and—on a bad day—them, too. But he was too distracted to speak.

At their approach, the thing that had caught his eye had turned into several things. As they rounded a bend in the road, the several became several hundred.

In the passenger's seat, the Master of Sinanju's spine became more rigid as he sat up stiffly in his seat.

The winding road passed by a dairy farm. On both right and left wide grazing fields stretched to dark woods.

Intermingled with the smell of manure was the stench of death.

"Holy cow," Remo said softly.

Throughout the predawn fields were scattered the carcasses of hundreds of dead dairy cows. The animals lay in mottled grass, sightless eyes staring up at the brightening sky. Flanks were chewed; bellies were gaping black wounds.

Fences had been broken near the road. Some of the cows had been tossed out by a tumbledown stone wall.

A battered truck was parked at the side of the road. Three farmhands were struggling to load a dead cow into the rusted back. Two more of the animals were already sprawled on a blanket of damp hay. With a final heave, they shoved the dead animal into the rear of the truck.

The men watched in suspicion as Remo and Chiun drove by.

A lone dead animal was dumped a few dozen yards down the road, its milky white eyes staring blankly at oncoming traffic. A sign near the gutted cow pointed the way to the Lubec Springs bottling plant.

"That's not just White that did all that," Remo commented as they passed the last cow. The farmland fell away as woods closed in darkly around them.

"Animals seek their own kind," Chiun said. "In this they are like men. She has created more like her elsewhere. Did you not think that she would here, as well?"

"I guess," Remo said. "I just didn't think there'd

be so many. That was a hell of a lot of dead cows back there.''

As they drove, he found himself more and more studying the deep forest that lined the road.

He found the turnoff for Lubec Springs. They parked their car near a house that seemed abandoned and headed up the road to the bottling plant.

''Perhaps we should not have parked so close,'' the Master of Sinanju suggested as they walked the forest-lined road. ''The animal may attempt to flee if it feels threatened.''

Their steady, gliding feet made not a sound on pebble or sand as they slipped like shadows through the dim light.

''She won't run at the sound of every car,'' Remo said.

''Unlike you, she retains a hint of human intelligence. She surely knows the difference between a car engine stopping and one that has driven by.''

''Maybe,'' Remo said. ''But even if she's skittish, it looks like we don't have to worry about the rest of them taking off.''

His senses were trained on the woods around them.

Remo had been aware of them ever since he parked the car. A rustle of fallen leaves, the soft crack of a twig. Stealthy sounds that—except for the two men walking along that lonely Maine road—would have gone unnoticed by human ears. The sounds of animals circling prey, closing ever tighter. Their numbers continued to swell the closer Remo and Chiun came to the bottling plant.

Remo spent a few moments picking out individual

heartbeats. He lost count at three dozen, finally giving up.

"Okay, so there's even more than we thought," he said as they walked along. He pitched his voice so low only the Master of Sinanju would hear.

"Do not include me in your assumptions," Chiun replied, making a show of ignoring the woods around them. "And I will remind you once more to have a care."

"Relax," Remo said testily. "So there's more than we bargained for. Four, four dozen. Big schmiel. In case you forgot, I *have* met these things before, you know."

Chiun nodded gravely. "And it is apparent that my memory is better than yours. I recall the first time your belly was split open. In your second encounter, your chest was torn apart."

"Blah-biddy-blah-blah-blah," Remo said. "I lost some ground, but I rallied in the end."

"Only after your Sinanju training all but disappeared."

"That was only the first time."

All at once, Chiun stopped. Remo halted beside him.

The woods around them hummed with animal life. Remo could feel the heartbeats closing in.

Chiun ignored the forest and the creatures within it. In his unwavering gaze, his entire world seemed to compress until all that remained was the man standing before him. His hazel eyes were fixed on his pupil, burning deep.

"Do not gather false security from our past successes against these creatures," the old Korean hissed. "Whatever happens, remember well the prophecy."

Remo's attention was torn between his teacher and the woods. Through the trees he saw a shadow, then two. Moving stealthily, they came ever closer to the road.

"I remember," Remo promised. "'Even Shiva must walk with care when he passes the jungle where lurk other night tigers.' Don't worry, I got it."

A bony hand gripped his forearm. In the early days of training, it would have been a slap or some other inflicted pain to impress on his pupil the importance of what was being said. Another of the many things that had changed over the years. But Remo's fundamental nature had not changed.

"It is not enough to speak the words," Chiun insisted harshly. "You must understand their importance. You are in a difficult time now, Remo. In the book of Sinanju are the names of many good Masters who failed but once and paid with their lives, for such is the price of failure even for those from Sinanju. Yet you are more fortunate than Master Pak, who lost his life to the drinkers of blood. Or the second Lesser Wang, who was the first Master of Sinanju to encounter the dreaded succubi of the Nile. Or Master Tup-Tup, who was defeated on his first day as Reigning Master—yes, his first day—by the unholy magics of a Dravidian conjurer. You are blessed because you have their lessons, often learned in blood, to guide you. And, praise the Great Wang, you have prophecies like this one. Listen to them, learn from them.

But do not think yourself invulnerable because you benefit from the wisdom of the ages. You are not the end of history. It will take but one time, Remo—one fatal moment—for you to become an eternal lesson for all the Masters who follow you.''

With that, he released his grip on Remo's arm. Turning, his eyes slivered as he scanned the woods to his left.

Remo felt the heavy sense of dread that came like waves from the frail form of his teacher. When he spoke, his own words were filled with soft reassurance.

''I'll remember, Little Father,'' he vowed.

Chiun didn't take his eyes from the nearby trees at the side of the road.

''Good. Do not forget it when some new daydream flits through your wandering mind. Prepare.''

And the creatures appeared from the forest.

They came up all around. As if possessed of a single mind, they passed out of the thorny underbrush on either side. Low to the ground, they came onto the road.

''Stay alert,'' Chiun cautioned. Spinning, he pressed his back to Remo's and raised his hands. Ivory nails like shards of sharpened bone were directed at their stalkers.

Remo matched his teacher's pose. Senses stretched far out around them, he watched the creatures exit the woods.

Growling and hissing they came. They came and came until the road was clogged forward and back, blocking advance and retreat. Even though there were more males than females, the females seemed dominant. In each of the small groups the males stayed close to a single female.

As they circled, Remo searched the sea of faces for Judith White.

She might look different. He was prepared for that. The same formula that had made her the monster that she was could be used to alter appearance. Remo had seen it before. But Judith White was more than just a face. She wouldn't need to look the same for him to sort her from the pack.

In the sea of movement he detected not a single female that carried itself in quite the same way as Judith White.

Despite his disappointment, one woman caught his eye.

She was off to one side, watching intently. A hint of malicious glee brushed her beautiful face.

"Hey, Chiun, isn't that the chick from New York?" Remo asked, directing his chin toward Elizabeth Tiflis.

The questioning confusion in his voice was matched by the puzzlement on the face of the Master of Sinanju.

"It is," Chiun said, eyes narrowing suspiciously.

"How would she know to come here?" Remo asked.

ELIZABETH TIFLIS SENSED that she had drawn the attention of both men. She found her way to the head of the massive pack. Feline eyes settling on Remo, she extended a lazy finger his way. And the words she spoke surprised both Masters of Sinanju.

"You," Elizabeth announced. "It's about time you got here. You're wanted inside."

And the animal purr of satisfaction that rose from deep in her throat chilled the spring morning.

21

"Excuse me?" Remo asked. He shot a glance at the Master of Sinanju. Chiun's expression was stone.

"Don't waste my time, sugar," Elizabeth warned. "Get down on the ground now and you'll get out of this alive. Of course, I've seen you in action so I know enough not to take any chances. For our own protection, we'll have to make it so you can't harm us. A few broken bones, cut hamstrings. But I promise you'll live."

One of the males nuzzled Elizabeth's hand. His eyes were trained on the Master of Sinanju.

"What about the old one?"

She smiled. "Use him as a scratching post."

Remo frowned at Elizabeth. "What do you want with me?"

"Me?" Elizabeth replied. "Nothing. If it was up to me, you'd be nothing more than a meal. But this isn't my show. So do we have a deal? Or do we take you down the hard way?"

Remo's face steeled. "I don't deal with vegetables, minerals or animals."

"Suit yourself."

A subtle nod. The pack began to close in.

Elizabeth was the focus for those in front. The others circled in around her. Following her moves, mirroring them. The same was true for the larger groups. Eyes flicked from prey to their respective leaders and back again.

In the pack to the left, Remo spied three familiar faces.

The TV homemaker had found a pair of work gloves in the bottling plant. She thought they would be a pair of good things that would keep her hands clean for craft work, vegetable gardening or everyday disemboweling. Unfortunately she'd misplaced one. If she had looked a bit closer at her neighbor, she would have noticed a suspiciously glove-shaped bulge near the AA brassiere of the kleptomaniac actress.

Behind all of the others lurked Bobby Bugget. The singer seemed as out-of-place as he did frightened.

At the front of the closing pack, Elizabeth nodded to the Master of Sinanju.

"He looks even stringier in daylight. Looks like we'll be cleaning our teeth on your bones, Grandpa."

Chiun's neck craned from the collar of his simple black robes, offering a tempting target. "You are welcome to try, perversion of creation," the old Korean replied.

Smiling, Elizabeth stopped abruptly, still several yards shy of Remo and Chiun.

"Don't assume just because a species is new that it's necessarily stupid," she warned cryptically.

Her dark eyes flickered for an instant to the blind spot beside Remo and Chiun.

Remo nodded, a tight smile on his thin lips. "And

don't assume that just because a species has been around the block a few times, it can't hear what's going on right behind it.''

And as he spoke, the thing behind him lunged.

Remo caught the flicker of movement, felt the pressure waves as it flew for his throat.

Without looking, he reached out and plucked the creature from the air. Forward momentum brought it up and around. Its spine cracked loud against the toe of Remo's loafer.

The creature exhaled like a punctured air mattress.

"Chalk one up for Homo sapiens," Remo said, tossing the carcass aside.

A thrill of fear and confusion rippled through the frozen ranks. It culminated in the full-throated roar that rose from deep in the belly of Elizabeth Tiflis.

As one, the pack charged. Remo and Chiun became swirling blurs in their midst.

Long claws tried to rake Remo's throat. He redirected the talons into the soft belly of a charging male.

The television housekeeping expert tried to lash Chiun with her gloveless hand. Animal rage became incomprehension when her arm came back, minus the hand.

She howled in pain at her bloody wrist stump, which, as far as she was concerned, was the very worst of bad things. The cry of terror and animal fury lasted only as long as it took Chiun's long nails to pierce her forehead.

More creatures flooded in. Dozens upon dozens crushed toward the two men in the center of the maelstrom, all fangs and claws and hissing evil.

A male vaulted over the rest in a dizzying leap, paws extended, mouth eager to tear out Chiun's throat.

Chiun's flashing nails—more sturdy and lethal than any mere hunting blades—speared the creature in midflight. Ivory talons opened skin and muscle.

When the male flipped in midair, landing on feet and knuckles, the soft impact of its body caused his exposed organs to flop to the road. He joined them an instant later.

At the Master of Sinanju's side, Remo caught the nearest with a spinning toe to the chin. Vertebrae cracked like snapping twigs.

A thrum of uncertainty washed through the pack. The leaders had already begun to fall back. With them was Elizabeth Tiflis, fear wide on her ashen face.

This should not have been happening. She had been too busy making her escape back in New York. She hadn't seen enough. She had assumed that sheer numbers would overwhelm these two. Yet here they were, darting left and right. More bodies fell before their flashing hands.

Elizabeth was ready to concede defeat, ready to run for the safety of the woods. But to her great relief just as she was about to make a dash for the underbrush, there came from the forest a terrible, ungodly roar.

It was like thunder from the depths of Hell, echoing through the Maine woods. At the frightful sound, birds in treetops took terrified flight, scattering to the heavens.

On the road, Remo and Chiun felt a new fear wash

over the dozens of gathered creatures. It was terror mixed with reverence. Heads lowering to sniff the ground, the beasts ceased their attack. One by one they fell away, passing to the sides of the road.

The underbrush deep in the woods cracked and snapped as something made its way toward the road.

Whatever it was wasn't small. The ground shook with pounding footfalls. For a moment Remo wondered if Judith White had found a petri dish of Tyrannosaurus DNA. And as the thought flitted through his mind, the trees finally parted and the unseen behemoth stomped out onto the road.

An awed, frightened hush fell over the other creatures.

Remo glanced from the monster on the road to the Master of Sinanju and back again. He put his hands on his hips.

"You gotta be greasing my pan," he said at last, shaking his head in disbelief at the sight of the world-famous boxer.

The Weiss and Associates client had abandoned the rest of the creatures. He had been stalking the woods for the past day, only to be drawn out by the sounds of fighting.

"This is a terrible situation that you have unwantingly rendered upon my quietude," admonished the boxer loudly, in a voice far too delicate and high-pitched for his three-hundred-pound frame. "I will remedy the ignomoronious conflagration by bitin' your noise-making head off."

And with a roar that could be heard from Bangor to Portland, he charged. The earth trembled. Shivering trees rained fragile leaves. The other creatures watched in anticipation.

Remo yawned, checked his fingernails and—when the lumbering behemoth was within striking distance—reached out and snagged the charging boxer by the chin. As the dangling man thrashed, snarled, bit and kicked, Remo turned to the Master of Sinanju.

"See, this is what I'm talking about," he insisted. "I know I'm supposed to be careful and all that, but *look.*" He waggled the snapping boxer in Chiun's face.

The old Korean's expression grew irritated. "Do not point that thing at me. Hurry up and finish it off."

Remo remembered a rhyme from childhood that used to work with dandelions.

"Momma had a baby and its head popped off," he recited.

And with a thumb under the chin he proceeded to pop the boxer's head off his shoulders. He bowled it up the road where it got stuck under the front tire of a Dodge.

He held out the body of the boxer, shaking it like a headless Kewpie doll for all the others to see.

"Where's Judith White?" Remo demanded.

For an instant, three dozen sets of eyes darted toward the bottling plant. And in the next moment, three dozen sets of legs flew off in every direction.

There was a mass stampede for the woods. Elizabeth and the other pack leaders were first to vanish. Brush crunched under running feet as the creatures rushed to put distance between themselves and the two terrifying humans.

Back near the bottling plant, a lone creature turned tail and ran back for the building.

In a matter of seconds there was only one left on the road. He stood near the Master of Sinanju, shaking fearfully in his clam diggers and Hawaiian shirt.

"Holy guacamole," Bobby Bugget muttered.

When Bugget saw Chiun's leathery death mask turn his way, he let out a terrified yelp. Like an Olympic diver who had misplaced his pool, he dove head-first into the thorny bushes at the side of the road.

"What about that one?" Remo snapped, pointing to the nearby bushes where Bugget's bloodshot eyes stared out in panic.

"Leave it. Come! One has fled to her lair!"

Spinning on a black sandal, the old man bounded up the road toward the low concrete building that was the Lubec Springs bottling plant. Remo flew after him.

Behind, Bugget's frightened eyes watched them go. He scanned back from the two fleeing figures to the dead scattered across the road. Howls of fear filled the woods.

"Sweet shit-in-a-shoebox," he gasped.

With a whimper, he began desperately trying to extricate himself from the brambles. Before the two men who were scarier than any old run-of-the-mill half-human tiger returned.

22

Moments before Remo and Chiun began racing toward the bottling plant, the object of their wrath slipped through the shadows of the Lubec Springs warehouse.

Dr. Judith White had been drawn from her office by the scent of blood. One silent foot dropped assuredly before the other as she crept across the drafty room.

Her acute sense of smell was focused on the familiar metallic tang that clung, rich and heavy, to the clean Maine air, guiding her to the place of slaughter. Judith padded up to the pool of dark, coagulating blood.

The truck driver's face was wax. Glassy eyes stared at the iron rafters. His chest was an empty red husk. Huge toothy tears shredded the meat of biceps and thighs.

She knew the man. He had come to the plant twice to pick up loads of tainted water. With an angry glare, she noted the wedding ring on the man's left hand.

The ring meant family, meant this human would be missed.

A soft growl formed at the back of her throat.

''Idiots,'' she said to the silent walls.

As if in response to her growl of complaint, the side door of the warehouse suddenly burst open.

Owen Grude bounded inside, eyes wide and frightened.

Judith sneered at his approach. So clumsy. Yes, he was stealthy by the pitiful standards of humans, but he was still light-years from being completely like her.

But that was part of the plan. This wasn't about creating an army to combat man. Not yet. Emil Kowalski and Genetic Futures had helped her create a watered-down version of the formula. Without the genetic material that had made her whole, Owen and the rest were not like her.

Owen had yet to shed the extra weight he'd inherited from a lifetime of slothful humanity. Loping, panting, the spring bottler raced up to Judith White.

"They're here!" Owen announced.

Her cat's eyes narrowed. "Who?" she demanded.

"The two you told us about!" He glanced back, as if he expected the two men to appear on his tail at any second.

The fresh blood of the dead truck driver had distracted her. Smell conquered all other senses. She redirected her attention to the front of the building.

And she felt it. The thrum of fear from her creatures.

Judith was surprised by her own reaction. She thought she would be cool and ready when the time came. Instead, the oldest animal instinct overcame all else.

Panic washed over Judith White.

"You're certain it's them?" she demanded.

Owen nodded frantically. "They've killed many of us. I barely escaped. What should we do?"

Judith sensed the male's fear. The bottling plant was Owen's den, his shelter. Instinct told him that he would find safety here. But Judith knew that it was only a building. With wide-open doors and easily shattered windows.

"*We* aren't doing anything," Judith replied. "*I'm* escaping. And since I know you'll try to follow me…"

Her hand was up faster than he could see. Thick, hard claws attacked. With a violent tear, she ripped the life from Owen's bulging, throbbing neck.

Even as Owen was falling to the floor, Judith was wheeling. Alarm collapsed her pupils to yellow pinpricks of fear as she vaulted to the open loading dock.

Nose in the air, she sniffed deeply.

The smell of blood came to her. Soft wind blew from the front of the building to the forest. They were still out front. Out back was woods. The woods were safety.

Powerful legs tensed. Judith flew from the dock to the driveway. She was running the instant her bare feet touched the ground. She headed for the woods.

Branches snapped at her face.

Animal instinct she had thought she could control compelled her to put distance between herself and the very men she had schemed to bring to this place. But in her heart she was still an animal and her animal mind screamed *flee!*

Judith White ran like the wind. Away from those she knew could deal her death.

23

The Master of Sinanju avoided the stairs. Sandaled feet left the hard-packed front path and the tiny Asian vaulted to the porch in one bound. Plain black robes billowed around pipe-stem legs. He marched for the door.

By the time Remo flew up to join him, Chiun's hands were already blurs. With sharp strokes of savage fury, he reduced the front door to kindling. Both Masters of Sinanju swept inside the Lubec Springs offices.

Nothing seemed out of the ordinary in the foyer. Receptionist's desk and outer offices were empty as they moved deeper into the building.

Each man understood he was facing prey beyond the ordinary. Both strained their already heightened senses to the maximum as they headed along. But though they pressed to feel, they detected no telltale signs of life.

Owen Grude's office door was open. Ever alert, Remo peered inside.

The room was clear. A wide picture window looked out on forest at the rear of the building. There was no sign of Judith White or any of her cubs inside.

"She's not in here," Remo said thinly, ducking back into the hallway.

Chiun's face was dark. Wisps of hair were trembling thunderclouds as the Master of Sinanju turned from his pupil.

The next door they stopped before was closed.

An odor came from within. One with which both Masters of Sinanju were all too familiar.

It was the smell of death.

Remo raised a foot, striking hard with his heel dead center in the heavy door. With a shriek, the door whistled around on twisting hinges, burying itself with a vicious crack into the interior wall.

Even before the door struck, Remo and Chiun were sweeping inside.

The scene within was a vision torn from the darkest depths of Hell.

Judith White and her cubs had used the office to nest. Bales of hay stolen from a nearby Lubec farm had been broken open and spread around the floor. Animal smells mixed with the stink of rotting flesh.

The gristle-smeared bones of Burt Solare mingled with bits of dried grass. Tipped back in a carefully arranged hay bed, the grinning skull of the dead co-founder of Lubec Springs stared with hollow sockets at the two Masters of Sinanju.

Near Burt Solare's remains, a second skull peeked timidly from out of the grass. Wet hay clung to broken bone. All that remained of Helen Solare.

Arm and leg bones had been chewed to sharp fragments. They littered the room's damp floor. Against one wall, nestled between a small desk and a filing cabinet, a half-eaten cow carcass lay rotting.

"Puss has been busy," Remo commented with thin disgust as he surveyed the sick tableau.

Chiun's face was impassive.

There was no one in that small room but ghosts. Leaving the dead to their final rest, the two men moved back into the hallway. On the way out, Remo tugged the door out of the wall, swinging it back into place.

The few remaining offices were empty. At the rear of the attached wooden structure was the connecting corridor to the bottling plant and warehouse.

The plant was free of life, as well.

Even before they stepped through the door to the warehouse, Remo had detected the thready heartbeat. It came from behind a stack of cardboard boxes near the open bay door.

He didn't need to ask the Master of Sinanju if he had heard the sound. The old Korean's bright hazel eyes locked in on the source.

The heartbeat was almost but not quite human. It was the heartbeat of one of Judith White's monsters. But it was near death.

Side by side, the two men moved swiftly across the cold concrete floor.

They found Owen Grude tucked back from the main floor, chest rising and falling with shallow panting breaths. He had dragged himself up against a pallet loaded with boxes decorated with the familiar Lubec Springs waterfall logo.

Remo squatted beside him. Owen seemed barely to

notice his presence. Now in death's embrace, he had become fully animal. There was little pain. The look on his face was that of a creature confused by its own mortality.

"Where's White?" Remo demanded.

A glimmer of recognition. A flicker in his eyes.

Owen shook his head. A fresh gurgle of blood leaked from the claw marks raked across his throat. He tried to snap at Remo's neck, but there was no strength left. With a wet sigh, Owen's head dropped forward.

A final wheeze of fetid air and the creature grew still.

Remo stood. "There's no one else here, Little Father," he said.

The Master of Sinanju sensed nothing, as well.

Walking slowly, the two men crossed over to the open door to the loading dock. As they passed, they noted the freshly shredded body of the Lubec Springs truck driver.

Cool air carried the scent of pine as they stepped out onto the concrete platform. Outside, a truck half-filled with cases of Lubec Springs water sat silent.

Dense woods began only a few dozen yards from the back of the building.

Remo began to hop down from the platform, but a bony hand on his forearm held him fast.

"She is gone," Chiun said.

Remo hesitated. "Shouldn't we at least look?" As he spoke, he rotated his wrists in frustration.

"The forest is too vast, and there are too many others like her running through it now, creating false trails. That creature is fast and clever. She would gain distance from us with every step.''

The old man released Remo's arm. As the truth of his teacher's words set in, the fight drained from Remo.

''Dammit,'' he complained. ''She got away again.'' He tore his eyes from the woods, the light of hope dawning. ''Maybe we've still got one last shot.''

Turning on his heel, he headed back across the warehouse floor.

''OUCH, OWEE, ouch-ouch-ouch.''

Thorns dug deep into Bobby Bugget's bare legs. With thumb and forefinger, he gingerly picked them out one by one.

He was still carefully picking when Remo and Chiun appeared from the front door of the bottling plant.

''Crap on a crust!'' Bugget shouted.

Thorns forgotten, he ran from the bushes, away from the terrifying men who had slaughtered so many of Judith White's tigers. As he fled, his shoe hooked a root and he went flying face first to the driveway. He landed in a painful slide at the toes of a pair of hand-stitched leather loafers.

Bobby Bugget looked up into a pair of the deadest eyes he had ever seen.

''Oh, hiya,'' Bugget said. ''How ya'll doin'?'' He offered a big, disarming Southern smile to Remo and the Master of Sinanju, who stood in the driveway beside his pupil.

''Zip it, Goober,'' Remo snarled. He grabbed Bugget by the collar of his Hawaiian shirt and dragged him to his feet.

The Master of Sinanju was examining the singer, a look of deep mistrust on his leathery face. "He is not one of the beasts," the old Korean concluded.

Remo had noticed the same thing. Bugget didn't have the same sense of animal stillness or altered heartbeat as the other Judith White victims.

"You were with them," Remo said suspiciously. "Why aren't you one of them?"

Bugget's mustache twitched with his nervous smile. "They tried to turn me. They made me drink that stuff. What's it called?" He snapped his fingers, trying to jog his frightened memory. "You know. What ice comes from."

"Water, you nit," Remo said.

"Yeah, that," Bugget said. He shuddered at the memory. "As a rule I don't drink nothing fish pee in. Anyway, the stuff didn't work on me. Guess they musta thought it did, 'cause they accepted me as one of their own. Kind of like Jane Goodall living with them monkeys over in Africa."

Remo wouldn't need convincing that monkeys would have welcomed Bobby Bugget as one of their own. He had trouble, however, imagining Judith White being quite so accepting.

But as soon as he got a good whiff of Bugget's foul breath, he realized why the singer hadn't been mauled.

Chiun interjected before Remo could speak.

"This one has been consuming human flesh," the old Korean accused, face contorted in disgust.

"Hey, even Jane Goodall had to eat a banana every once in a while," Bugget said defensively.

Remo's face was death personified. "Where did she go?"

"She's gone?" Bugget asked, shoulders relaxing.

Remo smacked him on the side of the head. Bugget's shoulders tensed up again.

"I don't know where she is," the singer said. "She mostly kept away from the rest of us. Even when she came back to see us, I stayed as far away from her as I could."

"Okay, so what did she want with me?"

Bugget snapped his fingers. "Now, *that* I do know. I heard her talking to Owen—he's the guy who owns this place. She said something about seeing you in action a couple of years ago, and that you were like no other humans she'd ever seen. She said she tried to turn you into one of her little critters, and that you didn't cooperate."

That was true. In his encounter with Judith White near Boston three years before, she had tried to force Remo to drink some of the formula.

"That's it?" Remo asked. "She wanted to try again?"

"I don't know for sure," Bugget said. "I only know what I heard. It sounded like she was real keen on you."

Remo's lips thinned. "Ten words or less," he said. "Tell me why I shouldn't kill you and let something higher up the food chain than you eat for a month."

Bugget's tan face whitened. He thought very hard. When it came, relief dawned bright.

"Oh." As he spoke, he counted off each individual word. "I...know...where...she...keeps...her...genetic..." He paused at the eighth digit. "Hey, old-timer," he whispered to Chiun, "is *whatchamacallet* one word?"

"Oh, for the love of," Remo sighed, rolling his eyes heavenward.

He grabbed Bobby Bugget by one end of his bushy mustache. With a hard yank, Remo dragged the whimpering singer back across the parking lot to the bottling plant.

24

Mark Howard spent several long hours at his office computer in an attempt to find Judith White's lab. But a lengthy, frustrating search through the electronic reaches of cyberspace had yielded no success.

The first thing he had done was check for mysterious deaths which included missing organs or limbs, as Dr. Smith had suggested. Given Judith White's specific needs, he chose to start with the genetics field itself.

Mark had the CURE mainframes go through all unsolved murders for the previous three years in any way connected to genetics research facilities.

He hadn't given this much hope of success. He assumed that the ever vigilant CURE mainframes would have detected a pattern of murders in a particular scientific field.

He was right. The search came up empty.

Mark widened it to include unsolved murders merely in the vicinity of genetics facilities.

Since most labs were located in urban areas, this search generated hundreds of results.

Mark automatically sifted out all shootings, stabbings and anything else that wasn't out of the norm.

This reduced the number to a more manageable several dozen.

When he looked over the list, Mark noted that there was a disproportionate number of stories in the newspaper the *Super Nova*. Since that particular paper specialized in Bigfoot sightings, Bat-Gal attacks and other improbable news items, he disregarded those articles.

Of the rest there were only a few stories worth noting.

A body in a bad state of decomposition had been found on a hiking trail at Yellowstone National Park three summers before. Like the Judith White victims, the organs had been consumed. Park officials had attributed the death to a bear attack. The local medical examiner had agreed.

A similar story was reported in a local Arizona paper a few weeks after the Yellowstone article. A search for two lost college students had ended in a grisly discovery. The boys' remains were found at their campsite. According to the paper, both had been eaten by wild animals. It was concluded that they were victims of a pack of ravenous coyotes.

That was it. There were other deaths, but after those two cases—for the past two and a half years—there was nothing that fit Judith White's modus operandi.

Although they seemed pretty thin, they were all he had. Mark put both stories in the maybe file.

Sighing defeat, he began a more conventional search.

That the formula had been altered wasn't in question. Since Mark had returned to Folcroft, an independent lab had confirmed the GenPlus results. To alter the formula meant access to a laboratory. Mark reasoned that it was possible Judith White was staffing a secret lab somewhere.

He sifted through the personnel records of anyone who had worked for BostonBio or its earlier incarnation, the Boston Graduate School of Biological Sciences. Both had been involved in the research that had altered Judith White's DNA. It was possible that she had found an ally from one of the old research teams.

Much of the personnel had been scattered around the country. Some were in Europe. A few from BGSBS had died or retired. In the end, Mark had nothing more than a list of names. He dumped them into the mainframes for analysis. Maybe the CURE system could find something worthwhile.

Once he was done, Mark leaned back in his chair. His head touched the wall. For a minute, he closed his eyes.

It was like looking for a needle in a haystack. But Judith White's lab *had* to exist. And since his search had turned up no mysterious deaths or disappearances in the genetics field, it was safe to conclude the lab was still in operation. Judith White's pattern suggested that she would have severed the link once it was no longer useful to her. Which meant that she was keeping it open for some reason.

The thought gave Mark a chill.

A needle in a haystack. But this particular needle was there somewhere, waiting to be found. It was just a matter of weeding through each individual piece of hay to find it.

Opening his tired eyes, Mark looked at the clock in the corner of his computer screen. Just after three o'clock.

His blinds were closed tight on the night. Dawn was still a few hours away.

Climbing out of his chair, Mark stepped out of the office to stretch his legs.

Folcroft was asleep. The lights were off in the administrative wing. The glow of the stairwell exit signs was all there was to guide him. Through a hall window, he saw the nearly empty employee parking lot. His own car was parked in the last space far from the building. It was new, and Mark wanted to avoid parking-lot dings. Dr. Smith's beat-up old station wagon was parked in its usual place—the first spot near the building.

When he saw his employer's car, Mark shook his head.

The assistant CURE director didn't like the thought of Dr. Smith staying at his desk all night. The older man had been through more than his share of crises in his day. He had earned the right to a good night's sleep.

If nothing else, Harold W. Smith was a shining example of dedication.

"I hope I have as much stamina when I'm your age," Mark muttered quietly, leaning on the window frame.

From his vantage he could see down Folcroft's long driveway. Beyond the high walls, a pair of headlights sliced the night. A lone car was making its way up the road.

The driver was likely a Rye resident. How many times had he driven by the open gates of the ivy-covered sanitarium and never given it a second glance? Folcroft had been home to America's most damning secret for four decades, and yet no one in Rye had ever learned the truth.

Another example of the genius of Dr. Smith. When he was first setting up CURE, he had selected the perfect cover. He had not tried to hide out in the middle of nowhere, where remoteness itself might inspire curiosity. Folcroft was sitting right there for all the world to see.

"Hiding in the open," Mark said, yawning.

His tired mind drifted to one of the articles he had glanced at an hour before. Without even thinking, he breathed mist onto the window. One lazy finger squeaked through the fog. It moved automatically. Until he was finished, Mark hadn't been aware he was drawing a picture.

When he was done, Mark blinked.

The image was illuminated by the dull amber glow of the parking-lot lights. Mark's wandering finger had traced a small stick figure in a little dress. The arms were extended wide. Around them he had drawn a pair of bat's wings.

Judith White was highly intelligent. She'd know enough not to leave a visible trail. But if Dr. Smith's information was correct, she couldn't curtail her appetites. She would have to mask them. Hide them.

Make them look like something other than what they were.

Mark looked at the picture once more. It was fading now. As the fog evaporated, the wings disappeared. The bat creature he had drawn became a girl once more.

All at once, something clicked in Mark Howard's brain. Like the melting fog on the windowpane, his weariness fled.

"Hiding in the open," he repeated.

It was so obvious he was angry for not having seen it. And if he was right, he might have just narrowed the search for Judith White's secret lab.

Feeling the thrill of discovery, Mark turned on his heel and raced back up the dark hall.

THE WARM LIGHT of the rising sun brushed over the threadbare carpet, illuminating the figure asleep on the old leather sofa. The scattering night shadows were slinking slowly off into dusty corners as Harold W. Smith sat up.

Smith had stayed at his desk until the middle of the night, stealing just a few hours' sleep before dawn.

He checked his cheap Timex. Six o'clock on the dot.

He wasn't concerned that he had missed any fresh news.

As was his habit on those other rare instances when he had taken a few hours to sleep on his office couch, Smith had set his computer to beep loudly if the mainframes learned anything new. Mark Howard was also in the building. Since neither Mark nor his computers had awakened him, Smith assumed the crisis hadn't worsened.

Before checking the latest computerized digests, he allowed himself the luxury of a trip to the bathroom.

Ten minutes later, freshly shaved, teeth brushed and wearing a clean white shirt, he settled in behind his desk.

The screen-saver function switched off the moment his hands brushed his keyboard. As if on cue, a new message popped up on his screen. It was from Smith's assistant.

Smith opened the file. When he saw the contents, his brow sank low.

"What the devil?" he said to the empty room. He was still frowning a moment later when his office door opened.

Mark Howard hurried in, face flushed with excitement.

"Is this supposed to be a joke?" Smith asked, indicating his computer with a tip of his head. If it was a joke, his tone made it clear he wasn't amused.

Mark shook his head. "I think I found her," he blurted as he came across the room. "Or, rather, her pattern. She's been there all along, Dr. Smith. Right under our noses. Exactly like you thought. Did you have a chance to look at any of that stuff I sent?"

"Mark, most of these articles are from—" Smith paused, searching for the right word "—a *questionable* source."

"That's the most ingenious part," Mark insisted. "She's hiding right out in the open. We've all even heard stories about her victims, but no one's connected the dots.''

Smith glanced down at his monitor. When he saw the first article listed, he arched an eyebrow. The source was the *Super Nova,* a Florida-based supermarket tabloid.

''I do not understand.''

Mark stopped next to Smith so that he could see the angled monitor. The young man was wired from lack of sleep.

''See that?'' he said, pointing to the first article. ''Open that one.'' He continued talking as Smith clicked open and began scanning the first article. ''The story is probably familiar to you. There have been stories like it making the rounds the past few years. See, people get picked up in bars, or wherever. Doesn't matter where. The point is, they get taken back to a hotel thinking they're in for some fun. At some point someone slips something in their drink to knock them out. When they wake up, it's the next day and they're sitting in a bathtub filled with ice. And there's a note saying that they'd better call an ambulance because their organs have been harvested during the night.''

Smith took his eyes off the article. He was beginning to think that his assistant was in need of a vacation. ''That seems highly dubious,'' he said cautiously.

''It is,'' Mark insisted. ''It's just an urban legend. People trading in black-market organs. Nobody in their right mind believes it's true. That's what's so perfect about it. Did you read the first story?''

Smith had scanned it as Mark spoke. The article from the *Super Nova* was written by a reporter named Allison Braverman. She gave an account of an incident essentially the same as the one Mark had just told Smith. According to the tabloid, a body packed in ice had been found in a motel bathroom in Denver. However, this story had a more plausible ending than the one Mark had related. The victim had died.

Smith glanced up over the tops of his glasses. "Mark," he began, "you cannot expect a supermarket tabloid to—"

Mark shook his head. "Next one down," he interrupted. "It's an actual report from the Denver police."

Smith clicked on the highlighted line. As he read along, his expression grew more surprised. The report told the same basic story as the tabloid. A body had indeed been discovered. The murder was unsolved. When Smith was finished, he looked up at his assistant in amazement.

"It actually happened," he said.

"Not just once," Howard said. "*Dozens* of times. See?" He pointed at the list of articles from the *Super Nova*. "All these are similar cases. Same story. Guy dead in a bathtub filled with ice, organs missing. I verified each one of them with the local police. Every single one happened. The FBI is even tracking it. Except they think they've got a run-of-the-mill serial killer on their hands."

Smith couldn't believe what he was hearing. If this was true, it was operating so far below the radar that even CURE's computers had overlooked it.

"Why did this not make the legitimate papers?"

"It did," Mark said. "As far as that first story is concerned, the *Denver Post* ran it the next day. But the wire services didn't pick it up. I think they weed out this sort of thing. They're too savvy to run stories about dogs with burglar's fingers stuck in their throats or old people setting the RV on cruise control and then going in the back to make tea. Those are urban legends, too, just like this. Nobody suspected this one was real because they'd already heard it a hundred times. Editors killed it thinking it was a con job or tabloid junk."

Smith absorbed in his assistant's words. He had to admit it was clever, in a perverted way. However, on its own it was hardly conclusive.

"Mark, this alone does not implicate Judith White."

A tired grin surfaced on Mark's pale face. "There's more. May I?" He indicated Smith's computer keyboard.

The CURE director leaned back in his chair, allowing his assistant access to the keyboard. Mark typed quickly, closing out the first file. He pulled up another. A fresh list of articles appeared, these ones from the *Super Nova,* as well. He pointed to the top one.

"Get a load of that," he said triumphantly.

Adjusting his glasses on his patrician nose, Smith peered at the screen. The title of the new article, also by the Braverman woman, read *Mysterious Cattle Mutilations Continue! Are Aliens to Blame?* There was a long list of similar livestock stories. The headlines were each dated chronologically. Not one was more than three years old.

"I assume you've confirmed these, as well?" Smith asked.

Howard nodded. "For some reason—I have no idea why—the space-alien conspiracists think Kang and Kodos are flying all the way from Ork to chop up our cows. The articles about cattle mutilations are like crop-circle stories. They tend to get spiked by the legitimate press, too, since most editors put them in the same category of tabloid trash."

"And you believe Judith White is responsible for these, as well?" Smith said, nodding to the list of articles.

Mark attacked the keyboard once more. The folders of articles disappeared, replaced by a map of the United States.

On the map was a series of small circles shaded in dark red. Each of the small circles was surrounded by a larger pink circle. A date appeared within each of the concentric circles.

"These small circles are the cases where men were found dead in hotel bathtubs," Mark said excitedly, pointing to the smaller dots. "Farther out is where the cattle mutilations took place. Notice the dates."

Smith had already seen the pattern. In every set, the dates within the smaller and larger circles each took place within a month or two of each other. The dead men and cattle were killed at roughly the same time.

The circles moved slowly around the country. There were sets in virtually every state. They'd crop up for a few days, sometimes longer, before moving on to a new location. With a sinking feeling, the CURE director realized that he could have traced the path with his finger. It threaded through the nation in a single, unbroken line. Clearly it was the trail of a single individual on the move.

"My God," Smith said. "She's been here all along."

The excitement of discovery was fading for Mark Howard. The long night was finally beginning to catch up with him. Leaning back against the window frame, he rubbed his tired eyes.

"My guess is that she goes for cattle like fast food. It's not the fancy stuff she craves, but since she can't risk attacking people on the street she settles for good, full meals. They hold her for a month or two. But every now and then the craving gets to be too much for her. When that happens, she stages one of her bathtub specialties. After that she knows she has to move on. One death like that in a single city is dismissed as an urban legend, but two risks public outcries and curfews and added police patrols."

As he surveyed the map, Harold Smith could only shake his head in amazement. It was so obvious, so well researched. He had been impressed by his assistant in the past, but the young man had outdone himself this time.

"Excellent work, Mark," Smith said.

The thrill of discovery had passed, along with Mark's weary grin. There was a grim expression on his wide face as he looked at the map.

"There are two early killings I think are hers," he

said, pointing. "Here and here. A couple weeks after she was presumed dead in Boston, a hiker at Yellowstone and two campers were killed in Arizona. Then she got smart. The first bathtub story was some poor pizza delivery guy in North Dakota. After that you can follow her route. But, even though it's been happening pretty much all around the country for the past three years, notice where there *haven't* been any of these cases."

Smith had noticed. The Northeast was clear of circles.

"She has avoided New England," the CURE director said.

"According to the local paper in Lubec, there have been a bunch of cattle eaten by wild animals up there in the past few days," Mark explained. "I didn't bother to mark those. Assuming she's got some of those monsters running around loose up there, that was bound to happen. But for three solid years, she avoided the Northeast like the plague."

"Hmm," Smith mused. "I would say she was concerned about discovery, at least at the start. Since Massachusetts lived through this twice before, it would make sense for her to avoid that region of the country lest someone make even a tenuous connection as you have. Yet she has made it the focus now." He pursed his lips in thought. "If it was not animal fear that kept her away all this time, I would surmise that she kept clear of the region until she was ready to begin this latest scheme of hers." A fresh thought sprang to mind.

Smith quickly scanned the map. He found several

spots where the concentric red-and-pink circles didn't overlap. These in-between areas where Judith White had not left a trail were colored blue. Most were so small as to be insignificant. There were only two large areas shaded in blue. Besides New England, the largest blue spot was an area of California from south of San Francisco all the way to San Diego. The entire lower half of the state was untouched.

"There," Smith announced. "Why has she never gone to Southern California?"

Mark had noticed the blue area as he was making the map.

"I could only come up with two possibilities," the young man said. "It could just be that they lucked out and she left it off her route, or—"

Smith finished his assistant's thought. "Or that is where her lab is located," the older man said excitedly.

"I've compiled a list of facilities in California she might be using," Mark said. "It's still pretty long, but it's a start."

"Very good," Smith said. "We will begin straight away."

As he spoke, one of the two phones on his desk jangled to life. It was the blue contact phone.

As he leaned forward to grab the receiver, Smith's cracked leather chair retained an outline of his body.

"Smith," the CURE director said crisply.

"White got away, Smitty," Remo's voice announced.

Smith sat up more straightly. "Explain."

Remo exhaled angrily. "She was here, then she wasn't. Explanation over."

"Was she alone or were there others?"

"There were others, all right," Remo said. "And I know what you're thinking, but there's none left to ask where she might have gone to. The ones that aren't dead scattered like lab rats into the woods. They're probably halfway to Canada by now. But don't worry. As soon as they find out the whole damn country is on vacation thirteen months out of the year on America's hard-earned dime, they'll be back."

"So we still do not know what her ultimate plan was."

"Maybe we do," Remo said. "It's possible she did all this just to get me up here."

Smith frowned confusion. "Explain."

"Remember last time how she tried to get me to convert? I must be pretty hard for a gal to forget because I think she staged all this to draw me out. They seemed to be waiting for me. Only this time instead of just her, there was an army. She must have thought there would be strength in numbers."

Smith's mouth felt dry. He wet his lips with his tongue. "If that's true, it is a troubling development, Remo," he said slowly.

"Tell me about it. Beyond that, I don't think we have to stretch it too far for her ultimate goal. She's a consistent DNA-hole. Her turn-ons include world domination, subjugating mankind and Purina People Chow."

Smith shook his head. His face was troubled. "No," he said. "It does not add up. She remained safely hidden all this time. She could have continued to do so indefinitely. I don't think she would bait such an elaborate trap, risking exposure simply to turn you into one of her own. Beyond that the scheme falls apart. The formula is only temporary and does not affect a large enough area of the country.'' He tapped a hand on his desk. There was something more here. He could feel it in his rock-ribbed New England soul. ''It is unfortunate you didn't save one for questioning.''

''It was Remo's turn, Emperor Smith,'' the Master of Sinanju's voice called from the background.

''It's *always* my turn,'' Remo complained.

With a weary sigh Smith glanced at his assistant. Mark Howard had left the CURE director's side. The young man was sitting across the desk in his usual chair. He hadn't wanted to interrupt. He was watching Smith anxiously.

''One moment, Remo, while I include Mark in this.''

Smith switched over to speakerphone before replacing the receiver. When he sat back, the indentations of his chair accepted his angular frame.

''We do have one guy here, Smitty,'' Remo said. ''He's not one of them, but I still don't think he'll be much help.''

An unfamiliar, nasal voice came over the line.

''How y'all doin'?''

''Cork it, pinhead,'' Remo growled.

''Who is he?'' Smith asked.

''Florida's answer to the one-man frat party,''

Remo said. "He drank the formula but didn't turn into one of them."

"How is that possible?" Smith asked.

"I think it's because he was stewed out of his mind when White gave him that cocktail of hers. Two-hundred-proof blood must kill the stuff or something."

"Yes, that is possible," Smith agreed. "In the first case twenty years ago, the formula was susceptible to all manner of harmful agents. Since Judith White is apparently using a similar version of that formula, high quantities of alcohol in one's system could nullify the effects."

"Great," Remo said. "The only way to beat her is for all of America to get sloshed out of our minds."

"I'll lead the charge," Bobby Bugget volunteered. "Just gimme a musket, a sack of limes and aim me at the nearest liquor store."

"Chiun, do something about Good-Time Charlie, will you?" Remo asked, irritated.

"I am doing this because I want to, not because you ordered me to," the Master of Sinanju replied.

Smith heard a vicious slap followed by a loud yelp.

"Thanks, Little Father," Remo said.

"Think you could go a little softer next time, Little Father?" the voice of Bobby Bugget pleaded.

There followed a series of slaps and yelps that faded in the distance.

"That should keep them both busy for now," Remo said. "There's one silver lining in this cloud, Smitty. Bugget showed us where White stashed her case of tiger juice."

Very, very calmly, Smith placed a flat hand on his desk.

"Are you certain?" he asked.

"I didn't test it, if that's what you mean. But it looks like the real deal to me."

"Remo, that could prove to be invaluable. It is possible to trace her lab using the genetic fingerprints within the formula itself. There are labs working to do so right now, but an undiluted form of the formula could prove critical. You should return to Folcroft with the samples at once."

"That might be a problem, Smitty."

"Why?"

"I know you said these things don't home, but is it possible she put some kind of new homing signal in it? One of those things that escaped from jail in New York was up here. I don't think she could have found her way up here by accident, and I doubt White gave directions on the front page of the *New York Times*."

Smith tapped a finger on his desk, considering. "We know now that the formula has been altered. The introduction of a single biological imperative from a species indigenous to that region could theoretically affect the instincts of those under the influence of White's formula."

"I'm gonna assume that means yes," Remo said. "So there's our problem."

"I see," the CURE director said. "If there is a migratory instinct, there might be others, perhaps many more, en route to your location. You will have to wait there, at least until we can dispatch authorities in sufficient numbers to deal with whatever may yet arrive in Lubec.''

"That's what I figured. So should I UPS this gunk?''

"No. With Judith White still at large, I don't want it to leave our hands.'' Smith considered only a minute, nodding with certainty. "I'll come for it.''

"Dr. Smith.''

So engrossed was he in his conversation, Smith had nearly forgotten there was someone else in the room. He glanced up. Mark Howard was standing once more, a determined look on his face.

"What is it, Mark?''

"I'll go,'' the assistant CURE director said.

Smith hesitated. And in that moment of uncertainty, both men knew what passed through his mind.

The last time Smith had sent Mark Howard on a simple field assignment, the younger man wound up in a coma.

Smith pursed his lips. "Yes,'' he said slowly. "That's good of you to volunteer, Mark, but I'm not sure it's necessary.''

"Dr. Smith, this is what I'm here to do,'' Mark argued. "And anyway, it's just courier work. I'll stay in the car until I get there, collect the formula and get out. I won't stop for anyone or anything. Besides, if Judith White is smart, she wouldn't stick around after Remo and Chiun wiped out her protection. It'll be a piece of cake.''

Smith allowed a silent moment to pass.

"I, er—'' he began.

"Listen to the kid, Smitty,'' Remo interrupted.

At long last, Smith nodded his agreement. "Very well. Remo, Mark will collect the samples. Please wait there for him." He hung up the speakerphone.

Smith turned his full attention on his assistant.

"I issued a recall of all Lubec Springs water to coincide with Remo's arrival," he explained efficiently. "At the moment, every shipment is being impounded and destroyed. As far as White's creatures are concerned, our only problem will be existing cases. There will be no new ones. However, if Remo is correct, those that have already been changed might be converging on that area even now. I doubt the numbers are high, since we seem to have caught it in time, but the possibility exists that there are more."

Mark nodded anxiously. "I understand. What if I run into people who've already changed?"

Smith leaned far over, disappearing for a moment behind his desk. He pulled something from his bottom drawer. When he straightened, he held a cigar box in his hands. He placed the box between them.

"They are not people, Mark," Smith said firmly as he opened the box. "Do not forget that for a minute." As he spoke he removed a handgun and holster from the box. Gun in hand, he glanced up. "You don't have one on the premises, correct?" he asked, nodding to the .45 automatic.

Mark's eyes were locked on the weapon. He had a gun that he had used only once while with the CIA. It was stuffed in a sock on the bedroom shelf of his Rye apartment.

He shook his head. "Mine's at home."

"In future it might be wise to keep it at Folcroft,"

Smith said. He slid the weapon across the desk. "Please put it on in here. My secretary will be arriving soon and I don't want her to see it."

Mark did as he was told. He stripped off his jacket and shrugged on the shoulder holster. Smith's old Army pistol was heavy under his arm as he pulled his coat back on.

"Be careful, Mark," Smith said once he was through.

His assistant nodded. "I'll be back quick as I can," Mark promised.

He was heading for the door when Smith called to him.

"Mark?"

When Howard turned back to Smith, the CURE director's gaze was sharp.

"Misplaced compassion could get you killed," Smith said. "If you do encounter one of them, do not hesitate. Shoot to kill."

"Yes, sir." Nodding sharply, Mark left the room.

After the door was closed, the CURE director turned his attention back to his keyboard.

With luck he would find Judith White's lab before Mark returned from Maine. And end this madness once and for all.

25

Judith White ran.

Pure, unbridled panic propelled her. The men who had tracked her to Maine inspired a visceral terror in the cold dead center of what had been her soul.

Pine branches slapped her desperately pumping legs. With chopping hands she swatted away those near her face as they sprang up before her.

Feet raced swiftly, surely. Leaping over logs and rocks. A boulder appeared before her. With a bound she was on it. Another leap, and she was on the distant, mossy side. Still she ran.

It was the young one, Remo, who inspired the greater fear. She had used her intellect during their first encounter, had harnessed that part of her that was most human to outthink him. He was strong, but intellectually inferior.

But in the end he had shocked her. Despite his mental limitations, despite his inherent human frailties, he had beaten her.

Remo was some sort of special government agent. He had been sent to stop her before. She was certain before all this began that—once they knew who and what they were dealing with—they would send him again. After all, the survival of their species was too important a thing to entrust to the usual inept human hunters. They would send their best to track and kill her.

She had been right. Every step of the way.

Judith's mind—still analytical when called to be— made that conclusion even as she ran blindly through the Maine forest. She had fled the bottling plant only twenty minutes before and she was already miles away from it.

Distance bred safety.

Rationality was breaking through the veneer of panic. The fear was coming under control.

Her lungs and heart pumped in perfect concert, racing streams of altered blood to every modified cell in her body.

A thought sprang wild in the animal mind of Judith White. Her valises!

One moment she was running full-out; the next she had slid to a shuddering stop. Clumps of wet leaves and pine needles gathered around her bare soles.

In her haste to leave the bottling plant, she had left the formula behind.

She could always get more. Emil Kowalski and Genetic Futures could produce another batch in a few hours. But San Diego was on the other side of the country. She had chosen Kowalski partly because he worked far from the Northeast.

And if she had more formula made, then what? She'd had a specific plan here. One that didn't involve mass conversions of humans. Her plan was more insidious.

And most troubling of all, what if they used genetic signatures to link the altered formula at the bottling plant back to Genetic Futures? She'd lose them, Kowalski, everything she'd been working toward.

Alone in the forest, Judith hesitated.

Deep brown eyes tinged with flames of yellow scoured the tiny glade in which she stood, as if the answer to her problem were somehow hidden in birch or pine.

The two men from the government had killed and scattered her entire pride. They were efficient that way. While Judith knew she was better than the lesser creatures she had created, she knew that she couldn't stand up to the government men without assistance. She had hoped that numbers would work in her favor. Even though that plan had failed, she still couldn't let them find the cases.

The scientist that Judith White had once been accepted the conclusion as inevitable.

But the thing that Judith White had become could not quell the fear that pounded strong in her chest.

Still, she turned.

Swift feet made not a sound as she ducked back into the depths of the forest, running back in the direction of Lubec Springs.

26

"You know, if you fellas would help get me out of here, I can make it worth your while," Bobby Bugget offered slyly.

They were in the Lubec Springs warehouse. Remo had forced Bugget to drag all the bodies from inside and dump them around the loading dock. He hoped to bait a trap for any stragglers who might be arriving late for Judith White's party. But day had fed into night, and so far there had been no takers.

Remo and Chiun sat cross-legged on the floor. Judith White's gray case was at Remo's knees.

"Maybe we should switch over to live bait," Remo suggested to the Master of Sinanju. He raised an eyebrow toward Bobby Bugget.

Bugget had been pacing most of the day near the open loading-dock door. His mustache frowned at Remo's suggestion. "That ain't funny," the singer complained.

"Not trying to be," Remo said. "And you can leave any time you like."

"I ain't going out there on my own," Bugget insisted. "Now—no foolin'—name your price and it's yours. Within reason, of course. How 'bout clothes?

My fan shop in Key West sells the finest in official Bird Brain merchandise. I can fix both of you up nice in caps, sweatshirts, cotton Ts.'' He turned his attention to Chiun. ''What do you say, old-timer? You look like you could use some new duds, what with them pajamas you're wearing.''

The Master of Sinanju turned a gloomy eye to Remo. ''I must wear these drab robes for an entire year, thanks to my ingrate of a son. Unless he has reconsidered and has decided just this once to think of someone other than himself.''

''Nope,'' Remo said, shaking his head. His eyes were trained out the open bay door. ''Still just thinking of me. But thanks for asking.''

''Do you see?'' Chiun demanded of Bugget. ''Do you see how he is? Do you see how he treats me? I would not mind the selfishness if it were only directed at me. I have thick skin. But he has an entire village for which he is responsible. Yet does he care?''

''I care,'' interjected Remo.

''He does not care,'' Chiun insisted. ''If he did, he would not disregard hard-won lessons in favor of ignorance. Yet *you* try talking to him.''

Standing before the old Korean, Bugget tipped his head, as if seeing Chiun for the first time. ''You know, old fella, you seem like kind of an interesting character.''

''I am fascinating,'' Chiun replied.

''Don't forget humble,'' Remo said.

''Yes,'' Chiun agreed. ''You may live ten times your years and never meet another as humble as I.''

Bugget twisted his lip, chewing on his mustache.

"I think there might be the makings of a song in you."

Remo felt his stomach sink. When he looked over, he saw that the old Korean's face had brightened like a beam of misplaced sunlight in a moonless midnight sky.

"Oh, crap," said Remo.

"Do you really think so?" asked Chiun, suddenly warming to Bobby Bugget.

"Oh, crap," repeated Remo.

"Hush, Remo," Chiun said. "Forgive him, O minstrel. Rudeness is just another of his many failings. Tell me about the song you are going to write about me and are not going to write about Remo."

"I don't know yet," Bugget said. "But a lot of the songs I write are about folks I meet in my travels. I guess that's probably because of how I started out. Years ago I used to do country covers at a little bar in Nashville."

The Master of Sinanju gasped. He held a frail hand to his chest. "Dare I ask? Is it possible that you know the beauteous Wylander?"

This was a country music star for whom Chiun had developed a crush a few years before. She had the biggest hair and the fattest caboose in the Grand Ole Opry. Which, given the competition, was no mean feat. Somehow the Master of Sinanju was able to see past the surface to glimpse some deep, inner beauty. Remo, on the other hand, suspected if you dug that deep into Wylander, you'd strike nougat.

"Wylander Jugg?" Bugget asked. "Sure, I know

her. But don't beauteous mean good-looking?" Confused, he looked to Remo for help.

"Don't drag me into this. I thought he was over the Wylander kick." His ear was cocked toward the door. A dark notch settled in his furrowed brow.

"That is because all you think of is your selfish little self," Chiun said. He was listening, as well.

Without warning, the two men rose to their feet. Remo scooped up the case of gene-altering formula.

Bobby Bugget whirled around them worriedly as the two Masters of Sinanju swept past.

"What is it?" the singer asked.

"Do not concern yourself, my songsmith," Chiun said.

"A car," Remo said. "Probably just our delivery boy. But maybe you better stay back here out of the way just in case the fur starts flying."

Bugget hadn't heard a car. He strained his ears. All at once the soft sound of an approaching engine tickled the far edge of his hearing.

"If it gets as crazy as last time, I don't want this stuff getting spilled," Remo said to Chiun, patting the big case. He glanced around for a good spot to leave it, finally settling for the top of an eight-foot-high stack of bottled-water boxes. He slipped the case up on top just out of sight. "We'll be right back," he promised Bugget.

And with that they were gone. The door to the bottling plant swung shut behind them.

Alone in the drafty warehouse, Bobby Bugget's bare knees knocked anxiously together.

"Nothin' to worry about, Bobby," he promised

himself. "Them fellas scared off everything with sense enough to be scared."

For a moment, he looked out the open door, but he found the night too frightening. He looked at a fluorescent light instead. The fluorescent light was friendly. He wondered if there was anything cheerier than a fluorescent light. He decided that on his next gold-selling album he would write a song about the cheeriness of fluorescent lights.

As he stared at the light, he didn't see the glint of yellow that suddenly winked on in the trees outside.

Malevolent cat's eyes watched Bobby Bugget's back.

And as quickly as they appeared, they vanished. Absorbed by the night shadows.

27

Remo and Chiun slipped through the idle bottling
plant.

Soon the place would be crawling with federal
agents. Smith would need not hold them at bay much
longer. If this long day was any indication, there were
few if any more of Judith White's tigers migrating to
the Maine woods.

Remo, for one, felt little satisfaction. Most of those
who had been victims of the formula would change
back, but not soon enough. There would be other
murders in the next few weeks. And the cause of it
all—Judith White herself— was probably a thousand
miles away by now.

Bitterness deep, Remo pushed open the door that
led from the bottling plant to the Lubec Springs offices.

They had a clear view straight to the front of the
building. One chunk of the door Chiun had demol-
ished hung slack from the otherwise bare frame.
Through the opening they saw a car parked near the
steps out front.

From the foyer came a nervous heartbeat.

When Remo and Chiun rounded the corner from

the hall, they found a familiar figure standing near the empty receptionist's desk, his back to the two Masters of Sinanju.

"If you're going to interrogate the furniture, at least do it with the lights on," Remo said, flipping the wall switch.

Mark Howard wheeled toward them, Smith's heavy automatic clenched in a two-handed grip. He nearly squeezed the trigger as he blinked against the sudden stab of white light.

"Oh," Mark said, breathing a sigh of relief. "Remo, Chiun. I didn't know where you were. I was a little worried when you weren't waiting in front."

"Your concern for our welfare honors us," Chiun said, offering a slight bow.

"The real fun's happening out back," Remo explained. "We've got a trap set. No takers, though. It looks like you didn't have to waste your time coming up here after all."

Mark seemed to relax. With his free hand, he rubbed one tired eye. "I don't mind," he said.

"Yeah? Well, I do," Remo said, pointing at Howard's gun. "You mind putting that thing away? I've seen you in action with one of those before, and I don't feel like searching the woods for any toes you might accidentally shoot off."

Mark seemed to have forgotten the gun. "Oh, sorry," he said, slipping the pistol back in his shoulder holster.

Remo took special note of the weapon. "That Smith's?" he asked with a frown.

Mark nodded. "Mine was at home. He let me borrow it."

"Hunh," Remo said. "I didn't know he'd taken this adoption stuff that far."

"What's that supposed to mean?" Mark asked, puzzled.

The Master of Sinanju interjected. "It means, Prince Mark, that the Emperor smiles favorably on you. A ruler parts more easily with a limb than a favorite sword."

"It's just a gun," Mark said.

"Think what you want, junior," Remo said. "Just remember, Arthur didn't pass Excalibur around as an ass-scratcher for the other knights." He pointed down the hall. "The stuff's in the back."

The three men started up the hall, but as they passed a door, Mark paused. "I should check in with Dr. Smith."

Mark started to push open Burt Solare's battered office door. He stopped the instant he saw the roomful of human bones and bloodstained hay.

"Oh, my," he gasped.

Chiun reached quickly around, pulling the door closed. "There is a telephone in the next room, Regent."

"Was that a— Was that a *cow?*"

"Some of one," Remo nodded. "You make your call and try to hold down lunch. We'll go get the stuff."

Remo and Chiun headed down the hall. Behind them, the assistant director of CURE pressed a hand to his stomach.

"I think I just turned vegan," Mark Howard groaned to the silent corridor.

HER HEART SCARCELY BEAT as she pressed her chest against the slate roof.

Judith White could will her heartbeat slower. The mastery she had over the muscle kept it from registering to the ears of the two Masters of Sinanju. Even so, she knew luck was with her. Had their attention not been focused elsewhere, they still might have detected her.

An ear cocked to one side, Judith listened.

The two that posed the greatest threat to her began to move away. In a moment, they were gone.

A single, strong heartbeat remained behind.

Judith didn't know what agency they were with, but judging from the conversation she had just overheard, the human that remained below was connected somehow.

Judith had thought her plan was lost. But now— when all she was after was the formula that could link her to Genetic Futures—a new opportunity had presented itself.

Growling with soft delight, she began creeping, paw over paw, to the edge of the roof.

MARK HELD his breath. Fighting the urge to retch, he doubled back to the first office.

When he pushed the door open, light from the hallway spilled into a more inviting environment. The tidy office of Owen Grude was nothing like the ghastly scene he'd just left.

The stench was still in the air. His breathing shallow, Mark went over to the desk and switched on the light.

The wide picture window that overlooked the desk reflected the bright office interior. Beyond the gleaming pane, the cold Maine evening menaced the trees.

Sitting in Owen Grude's chair, Mark dialed the special Folcroft code on the old-fashioned rotary phone. It was answered on the first ring.

"Smith," the CURE director said tartly.

"Dr. Smith, Mark. I just got here a few minutes ago."

"What is the situation?"

Mark was looking out the window. The woods were disappearing, swallowed up by the night. He thought of every jungle movie he'd ever seen as a kid.

"It's awfully quiet out there," he said.

"That's good, I suppose," Smith said. "We'll have a clear field to send in other agencies to inspect the premises. Perhaps they'll turn something up in regard to White's lab."

"No luck yet?"

"No," Smith replied. "But it is there somewhere. It's only a matter of time until we find it. Until then, other authorities will have to deal with the creatures that scattered on Remo this morning. Since you left, there have been a few incidents, but nothing major. It seems the fear Remo and Chiun put in them is keeping them away from more populous areas for the time being. We can only hope it remains that way until they either change back or die out."

In the small office, Mark Howard's face darkened at the thought of all of Judith White's innocent victims. "I still want to know what she was doing," he said angrily.

"As do I," Smith said. "I still maintain that it is unlikely this was all done merely to bring Remo over to her side."

"It doesn't make sense," Mark insisted.

"Yes, it does, Mark," Smith replied firmly. "It is important in our work to realize that what makes little or no sense to us has almost always been meticulously planned by those we are up against. I guarantee you, her reasons for executing this plot in this manner make perfect sense to Judith White. We simply have not yet found out the details. Perhaps the answer is still there somewhere. I will have federal authorities go through that facility with a fine-tooth comb as soon as we are finished."

The logic and certainty of the CURE director helped to relieve some of Mark's anxiety.

"Well, I'm finished now," he said. "Remo's getting the stuff. I'm ready to come home. Do you want Remo and Chiun to head back with me?"

"No," Smith said. "It would probably be best to wait until morning. However, I will begin making arrangements for the authorities to move in."

As he sat behind Owen Grude's desk, Mark was beginning to feel cramped. The knee well was smaller than his own. He twisted in his chair. His knee bumped something hidden in the desk's well.

"I'll let them know," he said as he leaned back to see what was tucked beneath the desk.

"Return with the formula as soon as possible. We'll send it out for analysis as soon as you're back."

When the phone clicked in his ear, Mark hung up and pushed away from the desk. He tipped his head to get a better view underneath.

Tucked far toward the front was a gray plastic valise, roughly the size of a small suitcase. Getting down on all fours, Mark dragged the case out from its hiding spot. Standing, he placed it in the center of the desk.

Etched in the right corner, two printed *B*s were entwined with what looked like a five-rung spiral staircase. A single drawing of a DNA strand.

It was the logo of BostonBio, the company at which Judith White had developed her gene-altering formula. Mark recognized it from his research. Remo and Chiun's source must not have known of the second case.

Feeling the thrill of discovery, Mark popped the silver latches with his thumbs. Inside was lined with waves of soft egg-carton foam rubber. Recessed in smooth compartments in the packing material were six glass vials of brownish liquid.

Mark pulled one loose. Holding it up to the office light, he tipped the vial to one side. Like thick molasses, the gene-recoding substance rolled over the rounded interior of the tube.

"Hmm," Mark said softly. "You look so *ordinary*."

He watched light glint off the liquid. So engrossed was he, Mark failed to notice that one of the shadows beyond the office window had begun to move.

Mark only realized something was wrong when he heard scratching at his back.

It was gentle. Like a tree branch blown by wind scraping across the office windowpane.

Still holding the vial of formula, he froze. The wind. That was all it was. Still, the sudden appearance of the scratching sound caused his heart to beat faster.

He reached slowly under his suit jacket. Even as he put the vial of formula carefully on the desk with one hand, he drew Dr. Smith's .45 automatic. Gun in hand, he switched off the lamp.

He didn't breathe. Two careful steps brought him to the window. With the lights off inside, he was able to see out more clearly. As he squinted into the dark woods, he saw nothing but the black triangle tops of waving pines.

There was nothing nearby that might have made the noise. The trees were too far away to be the cause.

His palm was sweating cold on the pistol's walnut grip. Mark decided it might be wise to find Remo and Chiun.

He was taking a cautious step backward when there came a sudden blur of movement beyond the window. A cold shadow lurched up from the night. A face appeared, twisted in a grinning caricature of humanity.

Judith White's piercing yellow eyes locked on his.

Mark's heart tightened. He whipped the gun up to fire.

And then the world exploded all around him as the big picture window came crashing down like a curtain of doom onto the floor of the small office.

"IT WAS right here," Remo said.

From the top of the stacked cases of water, he glanced around the warehouse. The bay door was still open on the night. The case of formula was nowhere to be seen.

"Forget your nonsense," the Master of Sinanju demanded. "Where is my songsmith?"

"Bugget's the least of our worries right now."

"Spoken like a jealous someone who was not about to have a hymn written extolling his greatness and sung by the comely Wylander. Did you frighten him off? Tell me, Remo, why do you find it so difficult to get along with people?"

"I had the world's greatest teacher," Remo said, hopping from the bottle stack down to the floor.

"Jealous, selfish *and* hateful. I will remember that for your headstone, as well."

The Master of Sinanju's muttered complaints were stopped only by the muted sound that carried to their hypersensitive ears from the other end of the complex.

"What the hell was that?" Remo asked.

"It sounded like a window breaking," Chiun replied.

The next noise that came to them needed no explanation.

A gunshot.

Exchanging troubled glances, the two men took off at a full sprint across the warehouse floor.

JUDITH WHITE POUNCED into the room behind shards of scattering glass. Mark's bullet missed her by a whisker. His first chance proved to be his last.

Judith grabbed his forearm, slamming his gun hand against the wall. He struggled to hold on to the weapon.

If he could turn the barrel just a little. Get one clear shot.

Judith squeezed his wrist. Mark's hand popped open and the gun fell with a heavy thud to the glass-strewn floor.

A hand too fast to follow snatched Mark by the throat.

Mark grabbed at her arm with both hands, trying to tear it away. It was too tight. It wouldn't budge.

His oxygen was going. He was becoming light-headed. He saw Judith White reach out with her free hand. She grabbed up the vial Mark had left on the desk.

Popping the top with her thumb, she dipped the tip of her tongue into the thick liquid. Swishing saliva, Judith brought her mouth close to his. Her breath was vile.

"How about a kiss, darling?" Judith purred.

Her free hand pried open his mouth. It was easy now. The fight was gone. Even as his lips formed an O she was already spitting the sickly warm goo onto Mark's tongue.

She slammed his mouth shut and massaged his throat.

He knew he should resist. But the urge to swallow came anyway. She eased up the pressure just a little, and Mark felt the thick liquid slide down his constricting throat.

The world began to spin. She whispered a few quick words in his ear before letting him go.

As he fell against the desk, he caught a final glimpse of Judith White. She was crouching on the windowsill, the heavy BostonBio lab case dangling lightly from her hand.

She flashed a toothy smile.

"Be seeing you, precious," she growled.

And then she was gone.

Mark reeled. Somewhere deep within him, he felt a terrible, primal stirring. His stomach clenched. He pressed both hands to his gut, trying to hold back the pain, desperately trying to hold on to *himself.*

His head whirled. The room danced a kaleidoscope across his double vision. Through it all, one thought passed over and over through his mind.

One arm. Remo said she had one arm.

This Judith White had two.

They don't know. I have to tell them. Have to warn them.

But it was too much. Mark Howard felt all that made him human slip gently away. He fell. On the way to the floor, his temple cracked hard against the corner of the desk.

And a darkness greater than the cold, collapsed center of a dead universe washed over him.

28

Remo and Chiun felt the draft of forest air the instant they burst into the Lubec Springs offices.

They raced up the hall to the open office door.

The picture window was gone—shattered in a million pieces across the floor. A few shards stuck from the window frame like crooked teeth.

Afraid Mark Howard had been kidnapped, Remo bounded across the floor to the window. He nearly tripped over the young man. Howard was sprawled on the floor behind the desk.

Because Remo had not detected him the instant he entered the room, he was certain Howard was dead. But all at once, the younger man came back to life.

Howard sucked in a pained gasp of breath. Like a newborn testing its first gulp of air. His heartbeat seemed to reset. Like tumblers in a safe, the muscle fell click-click into a new pattern.

Remo had heard the pattern before.

"Christ," he hissed.

On the floor, the assistant CURE director stirred.

Remo glanced worriedly at Chiun. Standing somberly beside the desk, the Master of Sinanju looked down on Howard, his face gathered in a mask of wrinkled worry.

Remo had hoped he was wrong. But with the look on his teacher's face, his worst fear was confirmed.

"Watch him," Remo snapped.

In a shot, he was up on the windowsill. Loafer soles disturbed not a single fragment of glass as he launched himself outside.

He hit the backyard at a sprint.

It was mostly rotting leaves on scraggly weeds. Howard's attacker would have been easier to track through fresh grass, but there was no back lawn to speak of.

Here some leaves had been recently overturned. Over there something had kicked a stone.

Judith White was good. Judith White would not leave big, blundering tracks.

By the time Remo reached the tree line, he knew it was hopeless.

There were tracks in and out of the woods. Some a few days old, some as new as that day. White's creatures probably used the woods as cover for their nightly forays to the local dairy farms. He found a path that looked as if it could have been broken recently.

No, not her. Too old. Too clumsily formed.

Maybe with Chiun they could each go in a different direction. Expand their range by fifty percent.

But Chiun had his hands full.

Remo was forced to admit defeat.

Running back to the building, he bounded back through the broken window.

Chiun was kneeling on the floor beside Mark Howard. The cushion had been removed from Owen Grude's office chair. The Master of Sinanju had tucked it gently under Howard's head. A nasty red welt was rising on the young man's temple.

"She got away," Remo said, slipping up beside Chiun. He crouched beside his teacher.

"We must hie to Fortress Folcroft at once," the old Korean intoned solemnly.

"You put him under?"

Chiun shook his head. "There was no need. The Regent sleeps for now. But he is gravely afflicted."

As if to offer proof, a withered finger brushed Mark Howard's right eyelid. Folding back the thin flesh, the old man exposed an orb of twitching brown. All the green in the young man's iris was gone. When Chiun looked up once more, his mouth was a razor slit of worry.

On the floor, a soft sound came from the back of Mark Howard's throat. It was a contented purr.

29

Dr. Lance Drew had seen much that was strange during his tenure at Folcroft Sanitarium.

There had been the time many years before when the old Asian—who was either an acquaintance of Director Smith or a former patient; Dr. Drew could never figure out which—had succumbed to a hitherto unknown viral infection. Somehow he had been miraculously cured by a simple electric shock.

That was one for the medical books.

Then there were those dark days ten years back during a highly stressful IRS raid when mass hallucination had caused people within Folcroft's ivy-covered walls to see purple pterodactyls and pink bunnies. Dr. Aldace Gerling, head of psychiatric medicine at Folcroft, had wanted more than anything to present that episode at a national conference. His request had been denied. Folcroft's privacy policy.

Then there was the comatose girl whose brain showed no signs of synaptic activity whatsoever. Even so, the night she was brought in, Dr. Drew swore he heard her muttering in a voice that sounded like that of a thousand-year-old man. Not only that, her body reeked of a sulfur stench that would not wash away. And to compound the strangeness of that case, for a time the girl's body had released clouds of noxious yellow smoke. That had long since stopped, but the girl was still on the premises. Clearly she was a candidate for the supermarket tabloids. Any one of them would have made her their cover story.

In that as in each case, Dr. Smith would hear none of it. The families of Folcroft's patients, Smith maintained, had not entrusted the care of their loved ones to Folcroft so that their tragedies could be exploited or sensationalized.

There were times in the past when this stubbornness of Dr. Smith had almost driven Dr. Drew to resign. Nowhere else in medicine were healers forced to sign a draconian gag order like was required of the medical staff at Folcroft. At any other institution, he would be able to talk and write freely. But, unfortunately for a man as intellectually curious as Dr. Lance Drew, there was no other place he knew of on the planet that offered such fascinating cases as Folcroft Sanitarium.

And the best benefit of all, for the most part when he left work at the end of the day, he could put it all behind him. The sanitarium ran with such efficiency, thanks to its priggish director, that rarely was Dr. Drew bothered by work at home.

Folcroft Sanitarium was far from his mind as picked up the jangling kitchen phone in his Milford, Connecticut, home.

"Hello," he said absently. With the tip of his tongue he stabbed at the tiny bits of steak and corn that were stuck between his front teeth.

Dr. Drew had just picked up a new Barbecue King 3000 at the local hardware store. He had been enjoying a late supper with his wife, burned with his own two doctor hands.

He had assumed it was one of his grown children. Drew was surprised by the voice on the other end of the line.

"Dr. Drew, there is an emergency at Folcroft," the tart voice of Harold Smith said. "I need you here immediately."

Lance Drew could not remember Director Smith ever calling him at home before. Drew had been helping his wife do the dishes. When he glanced at her, she saw the look of concern on his fleshy face.

"What's wrong?" Drew asked into the phone.

"I'll tell you when you arrive. Please hurry."

The phone clicked in Drew's ear.

Lance Drew felt a tingle in his ample gut.

Another odd case. Had to be. It was the only explanation for Smith's troubled tone and the fact that the Folcroft director was personally calling him back to work.

"Sorry, hon," Drew said, tossing the wet dishrag in his hand to the counter. "Duty calls."

Grabbing up his jacket from the hallway coat rack, he hurried out the front door.

FORTY MINUTES LATER, Dr. Drew was on the sprawling side lawn of Folcroft, Director Smith at his side. Smith's rimless glasses were trained on the southern midnight sky.

It had gotten much cooler since Drew had left work

at five. Long Island Sound churned cold and foamy white at the shore. Drew could just see the old boat dock behind the building. It rose and fell with the waves.

Wind whipped across the water and up the back lawn of the sanitarium to where the two men stood. Dr. Drew's hands were shoved deep in his pockets. He was wiggling his cold fingertips when the rumble finally sounded in the distance.

The wind almost covered it. When the Navy helicopter appeared over the dancing trees, it did so in a shock of sound. Claws of yellow searchlights raked the grass.

As soon as the lights found Director Smith and Lance Drew on the side lawn—a pair of orderlies waiting with a stretcher behind them—it lowered quickly to the ground.

Even as the aircraft settled to its wheels, Dr. Smith was running toward it. The howling downdraft from the rotors blew his thinning hair wildly.

Dr. Drew and the others hurried in behind him.

Before any of them could reach the helicopter, the side door slid open. Two men Drew recognized from his years at Folcroft jumped to the ground. One was a young Caucasian; the other was the ancient Asian who had suffered the mysterious viral infection years before.

"It looks bad, Smitty," the younger one said. Although he didn't seem to shout, his voice was crystal clear over the helicopter noise.

The sanitarium director barely acknowledged the presence of the two men.

"Stand back," Smith demanded, straining to be heard over the roar of the blades. He waved for the orderlies to hurry.

The patient was lying inside the helicopter. Scampering inside, the two Folcroft attendants strapped him to the collapsible stretcher. Only when the man was brought out onto the lawn did Dr. Drew get a good look at him.

His jaw dropped. "It's Mr. Howard," he gasped.

Folcroft's assistant director was unconscious. A large purple welt colored one temple. His wide face twitched with spastic tics.

Smith's steel-gray eyes fixed on Drew's. "Treat him," he commanded.

Drew quickly recovered from his initial surprise. He spun to the orderlies. "Get him inside!"

Dr. Drew ran alongside the two men as they crossed back to the sanitarium.

"Smitty, I—" Remo began.

"Later," the CURE director snapped. Without a backward glance at his enforcement arm, he ran after the others.

As the Navy helicopter was lifting off, Dr. Lance Drew was flinging open the side door of the facility. Running up behind, Smith grabbed the door from him, ushering the doctor and the others hastily inside. He ducked in behind them.

There was nothing more Remo and Chiun could do.

Faces as cold as the wind from the Sound, the two men glided across the lawn and slipped inside the big building.

30

The examination took more than half an hour.

Harold W. Smith watched every second of it, face drawn in lines of paternal concern.

Even before Dr. Lance Drew finished the exam, he knew his original assumption had been correct. This *was* an unusual case. But while unusual, it wasn't unique. Dr. Drew was certain this was connected to the still unexplained incidences in New York and elsewhere.

When he was through, the doctor instructed an attending Folcroft nurse to draw additional blood for testing. As the woman did as she was instructed, Drew was pulling off his latex gloves. He stepped across the small examination room to his anxious employer.

"This man should be in a hospital," Dr. Drew insisted in a hushed tone.

Smith shook his head firmly. "Folcroft is adequately equipped for his needs, Doctor."

"I don't even know what his needs *are*." Drew shot a troubled glance at Mark Howard. "There's been a rash of cases like this in the past few days."

A thought occurred to him. "I assume you've read about them?"

Dr. Drew didn't mean to insult, but Director Smith gave the impression of a man not fully in touch with the events of the everyday world. Drew wanted to be certain that Dr. Smith knew what they were dealing with here.

"I am aware of what is going on," Smith said icily.

"Oh. Well, then you must know that this is more than we can handle here."

"I know nothing of the sort," Smith replied tartly. "Folcroft certainly has enough room for one more patient. And as I understand it, none of those other cases have been cured. Those afflicted like Assistant Director Howard have been sedated and warehoused in other hospitals pending a cure."

"That's true," Drew agreed slowly, "but if there is a breakthrough—"

"Then and only then will we send Mr. Howard for treatment if need be," Smith interrupted. "Until that time, Folcroft takes care of its own."

Dr. Drew could see there would be no arguing.

"Very well, Dr. Smith," he sighed. "But given what we know of those other cases, I insist we keep him under heavy sedation."

Dr. Drew nodded to the sleeping form of Mark Howard. He raised a bushy white eyebrow when he saw that the crazed twitches that had afflicted the young man since his arrival had stopped. A nurse continued to fuss over the unconscious young man.

"I not only agree, I insist," Smith said. "Do it. And report back to me hourly on his condition."

With that the Folcroft director left the room.

As the big examination room door sighed softly shut, Dr. Drew watched through the window as the gaunt, gray man hurried up the sterile hallway of Folcroft's security wing.

The creases of Dr. Drew's pronounced frown lines deepened. His employer had an unerring ability to make the greatest physician feel like a lowly janitor. Drew dismissed the thought the moment it passed through his mind.

"That's not true," Lance Drew muttered. "He treats the janitors around here like he cares whether or not they quit."

Grunting unhappily, he turned to the nurse.

"I need a walk. I'll be back with the patient's sedatives in a minute."

"Yes, Doctor."

Drew pushed open the door and stepped out in the hall.

Across the room, unseen by either Dr. Lance Drew or the Folcroft nurse, a pair of yellow predator's eyes peered at them both through razor slits.

31

Eileen Mikulka's thumbnail was bitten nearly down to the quick. Nerves, she thought as she chewed the ragged end. All nerves. All because of the terrible news.

Smith's secretary had been a nervous wreck ever since she'd found out that poor Assistant Director Howard had been brought back to Folcroft by some sort of emergency life-flight helicopter.

Mrs. Mikulka normally went home at five. But two long-term Folcroft patients had recently passed on and, as was her custom, Smith's secretary had dutifully retired their files to the storage room in the basement.

While downstairs earlier that week she had unhappily noted the condition of the rest of the patient records. It had been years since she'd given them a good going-over. She had gotten permission from Dr. Smith to stay on after normal business hours a few days that week to clean up the basement files.

She had been coming up from downstairs when she heard the frightful ruckus out on the lawn. There was a helicopter and flashing lights and a stretcher being hurried inside.

A night-duty nurse had told Mrs. Mikulka that the patient was that nice young Mr. Howard.

Fraught with concern, Mrs. Mikulka had returned to her own office. But she had been in such a distracted state she couldn't seem to keep her mind on work.

Now, forty-five minutes later, the plump, middle-aged woman puttered from desk to corner filing cabinet, not sure what she was even doing.

This was the state she was in—beside herself with worry, seemingly lost in her own office—when Dr. Smith came hurrying in from the hallway, his face drawn.

Smith seemed surprised to see his secretary still at work so late after five.

"Oh, Dr. Smith, how is Mr. Howard?" Mrs. Mikulka asked.

"Mark is fine," Smith said brusquely. "At the moment he is resting comfortably."

He tried to sidestep her, but the distraught woman wouldn't let him to his office.

"The poor dear. He hasn't had much luck since he started working here, has he? Someone said he has that awful thing on the news. The thing that made those people do those terrible things earlier today. It isn't that, is it?"

Smith's lips thinned in irritation.

It was apparent Dr. Lance Drew or the attending nurse had mentioned Mark's condition to others on staff. Smith made a mental note to reprimand the Folcroft staff members for their lack of discretion.

"You do not have to stay, Mrs. Mikulka," Smith said.

"Oh," she said, noting his sharp tone. "Yes, sir. I just have to make copies of these and put them downstairs with the rest." She held up a file of papers in her hand.

Smith nodded crisply. He stepped around her, heading for his closed office door.

"It's just awful about Mr. Howard," Mrs. Mikulka said. She was chewing on her thumbnail once more.

"Yes," Smith agreed. "But as I say, I'm sure he'll be fine."

"I hope so," she said absently. "He's such a nice young man. Not that I'm complaining, mind you, Dr. Smith. You know I've always enjoyed working at Folcroft. But things have been so much…lighter since he came to work here, don't you think? Oh, well. We hope for the best, don't we?"

File in hand and a worried look on her face, she headed for the hall.

"Oh," Mrs. Mikulka called as Smith was reaching for his doorknob. "Your two friends are waiting inside."

She shook her head, muttering to herself. Still clucking concern, she left the outer room.

The care lines of Smith's face faded as he pushed open his office door. It was as if all at once exhaustion and worry had finally taken their toll. His shoulders sank.

Remo and the Master of Sinanju sat on the carpet before Smith's desk. When the CURE director entered his office, both men looked up with troubled eyes.

"How is he?" Remo asked.

Smith's face was blank as he shut the door. He seemed robbed of the ability to display emotion.

"Not well," he replied.

Walking numbly past Remo and Chiun, he made a beeline for his desk. He sat down woodenly.

He didn't seem to know what to do with his hands. He nudged his black office phone as if to straighten it. After, he put his hands to the arms of his chair. He didn't turn on his computer. He just stared.

Remo glanced at the Master of Sinanju. There was a hint of sympathy on the old Korean's face. The look of a father who had himself once lost a son.

They all knew what Mark Howard had come to mean to Harold W. Smith. But this was the first time Remo *felt* it. His own heart went out to Smith, a man unaccustomed to emotion, whose numbness at this point now revealed an unexpected depth of attachment for his young assistant.

"I'm sure he'll be fine, Smitty," Remo said softly.

"Remo is correct, Emperor," Chiun echoed. Slender fingers rested in bony clusters atop carefully scissored knees. "Others have survived this trial in the past. Prince Mark has strength of body, mind and character. He is sure to pass this test."

Smith removed his glasses, placing them on his desk. "While it is true some earlier victims changed back, others could not take the strain, even with the earliest version of the formula," he said wearily. "We know that she has made some alterations. Without an undiluted sample of what she is using now, we can't begin to judge its ultimate effects. At least not until these latest victims begin to change back.''

He closed his tired eyes.

"The ones from Manhattan have been transferred to high-security facilities where they will be monitored around the clock," Smith continued. "We will learn from them whether or not humans exposed to this version of the formula are able to slough off the effects.''

On the floor, Remo heard the strain in the older man's voice. "I still can't believe she slipped through our fingers like that," he complained. "Now she's at large with that formula again. There's no telling what she'll do next.''

Smith opened his eyes. They were rimmed in red.

"For America, the greatest risk of White's tampering is not out there. It is downstairs.''

The true meaning behind his words was obvious. Remo felt the air of the room still.

"Smitty, you can't be serious," he said quietly.

There was not a twitch of emotion on the CURE director's face. He replaced his glasses.

"Given Mark's knowledge of our operations, I obviously cannot allow him to be remanded to the custody of another facility," he said. "Even here at Folcroft he is a potential threat. I have placed him in the secure ward, away from the general population. Still, in his current condition he is the worst kind of threat for us.''

There was a time when Remo would have welcomed Smith's words. But that now seemed a long time gone.

"The kid's been locked up downstairs before and you didn't consider pulling the plug on him, Smitty," Remo said.

Smith didn't look at Remo. He spun his chair to the window. His own reflection stared back at him from the dark pane. He was surprised at how old he seemed.

"That's not entirely true, Remo," he replied quietly.

Smith's voice seemed faraway. Given the current circumstances, he seemed almost to be looking back wistfully on the events that had twice before put Mark Howard in CURE's special basement isolation ward.

Despite his fondness for his assistant, CURE security overruled all other considerations. That was true for all of them—Remo, Chiun, even Smith himself. The CURE director was no hypocrite. In the pocket of his vest was a coffin-shaped pill that Smith intended to take on his last day as administrator of America's most secret agency. The pill had been procured for Smith by another CURE agent many years ago. That man had been Smith's only real friend and yet, when CURE security was threatened, Smith had ordered his death. Just as he would order the death of Mark Howard if circumstances deemed it necessary.

Remo and Chiun felt the heavy burden that weighed on the bony shoulders of Harold W. Smith. Again Remo felt a pang of sympathy for this taciturn man whom he did not always like, but whom he always respected.

"Let me know when you need me," Remo said softly.

Smith said nothing. Swiveling back around in his chair, he offered a crisp nod.

"Worry not about the health of your heir, Emperor Smith," Chiun said. "A fire burns in his soul. This have I seen. He will not slip easily into the Void. Concern yourself more with finding the fiend who has done this to him."

"I have been working on that, Master Chiun," Smith said. He seemed relieved to discuss something other than his assistant. "Mark narrowed our search for her lab considerably. I have been attempting to weed through the larger list, reducing it to the likeliest locations. Still, even if we find it, there is no guarantee that she will return there now."

Remo had already spent enough time sitting around Folcroft. He suddenly rose to his feet.

"All right, that's it," he said firmly. "She got away. So what? Everybody's got to be somewhere. I'll just go back to Maine and beat the bushes until I flush her out."

The CURE director shook his head. "We cannot know that she is still there," he said. "She has what she wants. She collected the formula she left behind. It would make sense for her to get out of the area now that she knows we are on to her."

"She doesn't have what she wants, Smitty," Remo said. "I'm fine, remember? She didn't turn me into some sort of Vicious Bearded Gagon in her freak menagerie."

"I still do not think that was her intention," the

CURE director said. "But what else it might have been, I have no clue. Her scheme was not merely to infect those who drank her tampered product. If so, she would have used the newer, permanent version of the formula. The kind she used suggests she only wanted a temporary army at her disposal. Still, one has to assume that she ultimately wants to transform all mankind into creatures like herself."

"Patience is not a quality exclusive to humans," Chiun suggested.

"Agreed," Smith said. "So we know her ultimate goal, and we know that she considers whatever it is she is up to to be a step toward achieving that goal. She does not mind the attention this will draw to her as long as she succeeds. I almost wish she simply wanted to make Remo one of her own. It would simplify things for us. Until we do know what she's truly after, we are all at a great disadvantage."

He was interrupted by the buzzing of his phone. It was the interoffice line.

"Excuse me," Smith said, reaching for the receiver.

Remo was still standing. As Smith answered the phone, he turned to the Master of Sinanju.

"I don't like just standing here doing nothing," he complained, clenching and unclenching his hands.

"The creature has fled. Smith's oracles have yet to locate the place where she created her wicked brews. What do you propose we do?"

"I don't know," Remo said, frustrated.

"Then by all means," Chiun said, "go waste effort and time running around doing nothing just to make yourself feel like you are doing something. In the meantime, I will remain here and pray to my ancestors that you are not so exhausted when you finally do meet her that she does not kill you and feast on your impatient innards.'' He patted the rug beside him. ''Or you could sit, my son, and meditate with me.''

Reluctantly, Remo realized his teacher was right. He was about to sink back to the floor when he was stopped by a sharp intake of breath across Smith's desk. When he looked over, he saw that the grayness had drained from the CURE director's face, leaving behind a sickly shocked white. The older man's arthritic knuckles bulged in pearl knots around the receiver.

''I will be right there,'' Smith choked.

He was on his feet even before he had hung up the phone. Seeing his urgency, Chiun rose like gentle steam from the floor.

''What's wrong?'' Remo asked. He and Chiun fell in behind Smith as the CURE director raced for the door.

Smith flung the office door open. ''There has been an incident downstairs,'' he blurted. When he cast a glance at Remo, his eyes were sick with fear. ''Mark has escaped.''

32

The room was a shambles. The examining table on which they had put Mark Howard was overturned. The straps that had bound him were snapped.

There was a blood streak on one wall. Mottled brown hair clung to the shiny strip.

From the hall, Smith's troubled eyes were drawn from the blood to the pair of white shoes sticking out from behind the toppled table.

Two nurses in starched white uniforms tended to the injured woman. With them were the two orderlies who had helped bring Mark inside from the helicopter. As Smith hurried into the room, accompanied by Remo and Chiun, a doctor ran past them. He flew over to the group near the table.

Dr. Lance Drew was leaning back against the wall near the door. He pressed a bundle of red-soaked gauze against his neck. Blood stained his fingers.

Smith quickly surveyed the scene.

"Master Chiun," he announced tightly, nodding to the injured woman, "could you please see if there is anything you can do?"

As the Master of Sinanju hurried over to the

stricken woman, Remo and Smith stepped over to Drew.

"What happened?" Smith demanded.

Dr. Drew seemed dazed. "I don't know," he said, shaking his head. "He just came out of nowhere. The nurse was about to administer the tranquilizer. But before she could, I heard that terrible snapping."

Smith glanced at the broken restraints. One frayed end lay across the ankle of the unconscious nurse. Gray eyes darted to Remo. The younger man's face was dark.

Another nurse came racing into the room. For an instant she hesitated, trying to take everything in.

"See to Dr. Drew," Smith snapped.

Nodding, the nurse led the zombielike Dr. Lance Drew out into the antiseptic hallway.

The Master of Sinanju was hurrying back to Remo and Smith, his face stone.

"How is she?" the CURE director asked.

"She will live," the Master of Sinanju said. "It is merely a concussion. Your quacksalvers believe it to be worse."

The group on the floor was lifting the nurse onto a portable stretcher. They carried the woman hurriedly from the examining room. Their frantic voices quickly faded down the long corridor.

"We must find Mark," Smith insisted once they were alone. His face was pleading.

"He doesn't have much of a head start," Remo said. "And we know for sure which direction he'll be heading in. Maybe we can catch up with him before he does anything stupid."

He began to turn, but Smith grabbed his arm.

"No," the CURE director said urgently. His mind was reeling. He tried to force his thoughts into focus. "Mark is highly intelligent. Do not assume he is heading north. At least not straight away."

"She's given them all the same call of the wild, Smitty. She had a million of those things somehow find their way up there. His brain is wired on automatic pilot."

"Perhaps," Smith said, worriedly. "But Mark knows we are aware of that aspect of the genetic programming. If it is not an overwhelming urge, perhaps he can fight it. If so, he could go in an altogether other direction at first, just to avoid the inevitable net he knows I will cast."

"There is some intelligence to the brutes," the Master of Sinanju agreed somberly. "If the Regent retains some small aspect of himself, the Emperor could be correct."

"Fine. We won't assume north."

Smith nodded sharply. The three men hurried out into the hallway. "In the meantime, CURE's computer systems are at risk," Smith said. "Mark knows the codes and could access them remotely. I will have to lock them down."

"One of us should remain with you, Emperor, in case the Prince is still in the building," Chiun said.

"No," Smith insisted. "I will be safe. There are two tranquilizer guns stored in the basement. I will get them once I am finished securing the CURE systems."

Smith headed for the stairwell doors while Remo and Chiun continued for the exit.

"And, Remo?" Smith called. When Remo turned, the CURE director's face was fraught with fatherly concern. "Please try your best to bring him back alive."

Spinning on his heel, he ducked through the fire door. His gaunt frame disappeared inside the murky stairwell.

If Remo didn't know better, he would have sworn Harold Smith's flint-gray eyes were moist.

33

Smith hurried alone through the darkened corridor of Folcroft's administrative wing. Cautious eyes studied every shadow as he made his way to his office suite.

His secretary was not at her desk.

Assuming she'd finally gone home for the evening, he hurried into his own inner sanctum. Settling into his chair, he did a quick security check of CURE's computer system.

It had only been a few minutes since he'd been summoned downstairs. Smith had assumed there wasn't enough time for Mark to access the system so soon after his escape. Still, he was relieved to find everything in order. CURE's files remained untouched.

Setting to work, Smith quickly altered the security protocols, changing passwords and initiating lockouts. It took only a few moments. With the changes he instituted, he was confident the mainframes would be safe.

Sliding open his top drawer, he grabbed up his special set of keys.

Before getting out of his chair, Smith cast a glance at his closed bottom drawer. Under the circumstances he would ordinarily have taken his automatic with him. But the cigar box in the back of the drawer was empty.

He had given the gun to Mark for protection. The old .45 had sentimental value to the ordinarily emotionless Smith. In more than fifty years he had never loaned his service weapon to another soul. Mark Howard was the first. And now Smith needed it to defend himself against the assistant he had hoped to protect.

Feeling a chill up his rigid spine, Smith dropped the keys in his pocket and hustled out into the hall.

In all probability, animal instinct had compelled Mark to flee the sanitarium grounds immediately. He was likely miles from Folcroft already. Still, just in case, on his way to the basement Smith crept past Mark's office.

He wasn't sure what he would do if he encountered his assistant. In his current condition Mark would be more than a match for unarmed Harold Smith.

Fortunately the door was locked and there was no sign of tampering.

Breathing a small sigh of relief, the CURE director hustled to the basement door at the far end of the hall.

Smith fought to keep his anxiety under control as he climbed down the stairs. His normally ordered mind swirled with competing thoughts. None of them good.

He had faced many disasters in his day, but this ranked up with the worst.

One of CURE's own had been turned.

Of course Smith understood that it wasn't Mark's

fault. Judith White's twisted tampering had not only drawn out the young man's animal instincts, it had suppressed his sense of duty, honor and loyalty. But although Mark wasn't to blame for what he had become, that didn't lessen Smith's concern.

Smith had invested much in his assistant. From the start the young man had showed great promise. More than anything else, Mark Howard had given Harold Smith hope. For CURE, for America. For the future.

Presiding over CURE had been Smith's mission and his alone from the very start. Oh, for the first few years he'd had some help. But Conrad MacCleary, Smith's right hand in those formative years, was more a field agent. MacCleary tended to blank out when it came to the mundane day-to-day aspects of running the secret organization. In a very real sense, Harold Smith had always been alone.

But over the past few years, Mark Howard had given Smith hope that the agency would continue after his own death. That knowledge had given the older man great relief. After all, when Smith was gone, America's problems wouldn't end. The nation would still need CURE. Mark was their best bet for the organization to continue.

But now he was gone. Lost to the enemy. Worse, the secrets in his possession could damn them all.

Jaws clenched tight, Smith hurried across the basement.

The cabinet with the tranquilizer guns was in the corner opposite the stairs. Walking briskly, Smith was reaching in his pocket for the keys when he heard a sudden noise.

He stopped dead.

For a moment he just stood there, uncertain of the sound, unsure if he had heard anything at all.

He strained to hear, but the basement was silent.

Thinking he had imagined the noise, he was about to take another step when he heard it again. A soft rustling.

Only then did he notice the scrap of yellowed paper on the floor.

It was the note he had taped to the storage-room door years before. The Scotch tape was brittle from age. There were pieces overlapping from where he'd had to replace them over the years. But the note had never fallen before.

When Smith craned to look around the boiler, he saw that the steel door was ajar.

A shadow in human shape spilled from inside the room. A scuffling footfall sounded from within.

Smith became aware of the pacemaker in his chest. He noticed it only in moments of extreme anxiety.

Holding his breath, he tried to will his heart to slow.

Pulling in a lungful of air, Smith pressed his back to the wall. He stayed there a moment, unsure what to do.

He could not possibly reach the tranquilizer guns. The cabinet was too far away, beyond the open door. He would have to pass in full view of the storage room. Even if by some miracle he made it past, he was certain he couldn't get his keys out and open the cabinet without being heard.

He contemplated turning back. He might be able to catch up with Remo and Chiun. Get help.

But whoever was in the room wouldn't stay inside forever. If Mark had come down to hide until he felt it was safe to bolt, he might be gone by the time Smith returned.

Smith was given little choice.

On the wall nearby hung a rack of old lawn tools that had for years been used by Folcroft's elderly groundskeeper. When that man retired back in the 1980s, Smith had hired a professional landscaping service. He was happy now to have saved the gardening equipment.

Hands veined from age took a pair of shears down from a hook. They were rusted shut. No matter.

Fingers tight on the twin grips, Smith crept for the open door. He held the blades out before him, ready for anything that might lunge at him through the door.

As he approached, the shadow that came from the open door made little movements.

And then, abruptly, it stopped.

Smith worried that whatever was inside had sensed someone creeping up from outside.

He was almost to the door. He raised his makeshift weapon. Ready for attack, ready to plunge the blades home.

A soft scuffle. Something stepping out from the storage room. The shadow congealed into a familiar shape.

It wasn't the figure he had expected.

Startled, Smith felt the tension slip away.

"Mrs. Mikulka," he gasped, lowering the blades.

"Dr. Smith?" Eileen Mikulka asked, glancing at the shears. There was no alarm in her voice or on her face. Smith's secretary seemed to take in stride the fact that she had just nearly been assaulted by her employer in a lonely basement in the dead of night. "Is something wrong?"

"I was—" Smith said. He cleared his throat. "That is, I heard a noise. I forgot you were still here."

"I'm nearly finished," she promised.

"Finish whatever you have to in the morning," Smith said. "It is not safe for you to stay here by yourself."

"Oh, dear. Is something wrong?"

Smith considered telling her about Mark Howard but decided against it. Mrs. Mikulka was fond of Smith's assistant. Having her standing around all night fretting would merely complicate an already difficult situation.

"A dangerous patient has escaped," Smith replied. "I'll see you safely to your car. Please lock the records room. I'll be with you in a moment."

Turning, Smith fumbled the shears up under his arm as he reached in his pocket once more for the keys. He was heading for the corner cabinet when he caught a flash of movement from the corner of his eye.

He twisted in time to see his secretary lunging.

Shocked, Smith dropped the shears as Eileen Mikulka roared. A loud, inhuman sound that chilled his marrow. Mrs. Mikulka's crooked talons flew for his throat.

IN THE INSTANT before the blow landed, Harold Smith's heart thrilled as he spied the flash of yellow in his secretary's brown eyes.

She was too fast. Too slow to react, the flashing, logical part of his brain fully expected the killing blow to register. He felt the breeze on his neck.

In the instant before her claws struck, Smith was startled when another hand darted into view. With a loud slap, it batted his secretary's hand harmlessly away.

"Hold, thing of evil," a booming voice commanded.

Smith's brain was still only vaguely registering how close he had just come to mortality when his lagging vision finally spied the flash of black to his left.

The Master of Sinanju shot in beside the CURE director. In a heartbeat, he was standing between Smith and his snarling secretary. Knotted hands rose before the old Korean like tensing cobras, ready to lash out.

Remo slid in on Smith's right.

"You okay, Smitty?" Remo asked levelly, a wary eye on Mrs. Mikulka.

"Fine," Smith insisted. He was still gathering his wits. The shock had begun to fade.

Eileen Mikulka had stepped back a pace. She hunched her head protectively down into her shoulders as she studied the wizened figure that had blocked her killing blow. She seemed to suddenly decide that he was no real threat.

Baring fangs, Mrs. Mikulka growled.

"Prepare to meet your doom!" Chiun declared, deadly hands raised.

"Don't hurt her!" Smith shouted.

Remo had to hold the CURE director back to keep him from throwing himself between Chiun and Mrs. Mikulka.

"I realize this was a favorite concubine, Emperor," Chiun said through clenched teeth. "But this one is lost. Allow me to dispatch her, and you may restock your harem with a dozen maidens more comely than she."

"No, Master Chiun," Smith insisted. "There will already be too many questions with Mark. I might be able to keep that confined to Folcroft, but if Mrs. Mikulka is killed, the police would definitely become involved. It is too risky."

The Master of Sinanju shot Smith an irritated look. The moment his head was turned, Mrs. Mikulka charged.

For a frightened moment, Smith thought his dowdy secretary's attack would succeed. But in the instant her claws should have ripped through Chiun's spindly neck, the old Asian was no longer where he had been.

Only Remo saw the perfect pirouette the Master of Sinanju executed around the charging woman. In a flash, he was beside her. As she lumbered past, a single whitened knuckle struck a point on her right temple.

Eileen Mikulka went down in a growling, wheezing heap.

Skidding on the dirty concrete floor, she came to a sliding stop at the feet of Harold W. Smith.

Smith looked up at the Master of Sinanju, his face wan. "Is she—" he pleaded.

"It lives," Chiun replied, gliding up beside Smith. His hands vanished inside his sleeves.

A low groan rose from beneath the rumpled pile that was Eileen Mikulka. Smith let out his own low sigh of relief.

"Thank God," Smith said. "We will strap her down more tightly than Mark and sedate her heavily. With luck she will pull through."

"I'll give you luck," Remo said. "You're lucky we found the loading-dock door open. Two seconds more and you would have been a midnight snack. What the hell happened here, Smitty?"

"It would appear Mark came down here after his escape," Smith said, checking the knot on his Dartmouth tie.

"We don't know where he went after. He didn't leave a trail outside to follow." Remo nodded to Eileen Mikulka. "So how did he change her? These things aren't werewolves. You said all the contaminated water was being collected."

For a moment, Smith seemed puzzled. "It is," he insisted, frowning. The light dawned. "Except—"

His face blanched. The CURE director stepped hastily over his secretary's body, hurrying inside the storage room.

The refrigerator door was open. On the floor the aspirin bottle Remo had brought from Manhattan lay on its side. The cap was off. Smith's bad knee creaked like crunching cornstarch as he quickly knelt. When he shook the bottle, a single drop fell out.

"Oh, my," Smith said.

"That explains that," Remo said. "Why the hell didn't you dump that stuff?"

"I was keeping it here for testing in the future if it became necessary or until a purer form of the formula could be found. Mark knew this was where it was stored."

"Why would the Prince risk his life poisoning the Emperor's concubine when he knew that Sinanju was but a stone's throw away?" Chiun asked.

"Probably wanted her to buy some time for his escape. Mission accomplished, by the way. He's long gone by now."

"I fear that was not his purpose here," Smith said. His eyes were trained on a silver object in the corner.

There were three similar, barrel-shaped devices lined up in a neat row. Only one seemed operational. Even across the room near the door, Remo and Chiun could feel the intense cold emanating from the device. A top lid had been popped open. Weird steam—like melting dry ice—rose from the open top.

While the three of them had been in the room, Remo had watched the temperature gauge on the side change. It had started at −132 and was now at −98.

"What's that contraption?" Remo asked.

When Smith looked up, his angular face had grown visibly haggard. Remo didn't like the older man's tone.

"Perhaps we should discuss this in my office," the CURE director said. He didn't look Remo in the eye.

34

"You son of a bitch," Remo growled.

They had returned to Smith's office. The CURE director had taken up his post behind his desk, hands folded neatly before him. Remo and Chiun stood in front of the desk near Mark Howard's vacant chair.

Smith had just finished telling them, in the most blunt, clinical terms possible, exactly what had been stored in the stainless-steel drum downstairs.

"You no-good, lying, coldhearted son of a bitch," Remo repeated. Knots of rage stood out on his neck. He clenched his hands so tight his digging nails nearly drew blood.

"I did not lie," Smith pointed out. "And you were aware that we took a semen sample from you the day you arrived here at Folcroft."

"Hold the phone," Remo said, a warning finger raised. "It's not like I was awake for that particular party. You didn't even let me in on the joke until twenty years later. And that was only *after* I found out you'd gone off and created a test-tube son for me without even telling me about him."

Smith's lips thinned. "That child was not created as a son for you," he said tightly, clearly uncomfortable with this aspect of the discussion. "He might have been your biological offspring, but he was brought into existence as a contingency plan for CURE. In case you were killed in the line of duty, Winston was to be our fallback."

"'Brought into existence,'" Remo scoffed. "Do you even hear yourself? You jerked me around so you could jerk some other poor slob around." A thought suddenly occurred to him. "How many more are there?"

"I do not understand."

"You used artificial insemination to make one. How many more little contingency mes are running around out there?"

"Winston was the only one," Smith said.

"How do I know that?" Remo demanded. "You've had that stuff stored downstairs in deep freeze for thirty years. You could have whipped up a hundred more in all that time."

"It is my understanding that you are able to tell when someone is not telling the truth. Remo, Master Chiun, I give you my word that there was only one baby born with the aid of Remo's, er, contribution."

"He does not lie," Chiun said. The old Korean stood at Remo's elbow, leathery countenance unreadable.

"Small comfort, you bastard," Remo grumbled.

A delicate touch to the wrist. Remo glanced at the Master of Sinanju. Chiun was shaking his head. His yellowing white puffs of hair stirred almost imperceptibly.

"Now is not the time, my son," he said in Korean. "We have a far greater problem on our hands."

In English he said to Smith, "Remo's seed was frozen for many years. Would it retain its potency after all this time?"

Smith exhaled. "I'm not certain. There is another sample that Mark left in the container. I can send it out for testing in the morning. For now I can only guess, but I do believe in the fertility field ten years is considered a long time for liquid-nitrogen storage. And we've tripled that time. However, I have maintained the environment meticulously over the years. I suppose it is possible."

"Swell," Remo said. "I guess we finally know now what she was really after this time. And now thanks to you, Judith White has a turkey baster with my name on it. You're unbelievable, you know that, Smith?"

There was no emotion on the CURE director's face. "I do that which is necessary," he replied levelly. "And might I suggest we put off the recriminations until we have retrieved the specimen?" He stretched his hands for his keyboard. "I will arrange a military flight back to Maine. Mark does not have access to CURE's facilities any longer, so if that is where he is headed, he will have to get there by conventional means. You should arrive there first."

Remo crossed his arms. "I can't believe this is what she was after all along," he muttered bitterly.

"Yes," Smith said as he worked. "It would seem that the chaos of the past few days was engineered just to satisfy some mating urge in Judith White. Of course she could not have known about the sample. She must have given Mark some sort of instructions after she fed him the formula.''

''The first time this happened years ago that other monster wanted to do the same damn thing,'' Remo said. ''What do they want with me?''

''You are Sinanju,'' Chiun said with a simple shrug. ''Other females sense it—why would these be any different?''

''Yeah?'' Remo grunted. ''Well, at least the first one had the decency to kidnap me and actually get in my pants. This one's satisfied to let science do her dirty work for her.''

''Judith White has—or at least *had*—a methodical, well-ordered mind,'' Smith said, eyes on his monitor. ''Given her scientific background, from her perspective this would be the most efficient way to handle her procreative needs.''

Remo didn't even look at his employer. ''Don't, Smitty,'' he warned. ''Don't even think about being matter-of-fact about all this.''

The CURE director could hear the strain in Remo's voice.

He glanced up.

There was something more beneath the anger. He could hear it in Remo's voice, see it on his face. Hurt and worry.

Smith understood the reason. Remo had been robbed of a life of wife and children many years ago. And the thief had been Smith. Now, thanks to Smith, Judith White might acquire the means to create something that would stand as a mockery to everything Remo wanted but could never have.

Clearing his throat, Smith refocused his attention on his computer.

He had made arrangements for a Navy jet to fly them from Connecticut to Maine. He quickly gave Remo the details. Once he was finished, both Sinanju Masters turned wordlessly.

Chiun padded from the office. Remo trailed behind. He was on his way out the door when Smith called to him.

"Remo, I understand that this is difficult for you. I apologize for that. But Mark is innocent. Please do not blame him for any of this."

Remo turned. His voice was flat.

"I don't. The kid's not responsible for what he's doing. This is all *your* fault, Smitty. Whatever happens from here on out is your doing."

With that he was gone. Leaving Harold W. Smith alone with his computers. And his guilt.

35

The car scrunched to a stop on the lonely access road. The thing that had been Mark Howard switched off the engine.

When he got out, he smelled the tantalizing blood aroma rising from the outside door handle.

He had stolen the car in Rye.

This new Mark Howard was no more fool than his human counterpart had been. He had wisely chosen from memory a man from the CURE computers. Mark's first real meal had been a minor player in organized crime. He might not be missed for days. And even then his associates would probably dispose of the remains themselves rather than involve the authorities.

Harold Smith wouldn't be able to track him.

Mark moved with catlike silence up the wooded access road.

He was pleased at his own thoroughness. When he was human and cared about such trivial human things, he had made a point of familiarizing himself with all possible routes in to Lubec Springs. Since it wasn't relevant, he hadn't bothered to mention it to the others. And so it was that Mark Howard had his own private route to the bottling plant.

A few dozen yards up the road, he glimpsed the low buildings through the trees. For the next half hour, he patiently watched for any sign of activity. Nothing.

Mark continued on.

The bodies that Remo had forced Bobby Bugget to haul from the warehouse were still arranged outside the loading dock. They were going on two days dead now. The smells were no longer inviting.

Mark circled the warehouse and bottling facility. Behind the offices, he stopped in the shattered glass beneath Owen Grude's window. Sprawled along the length of the empty frame, a lone figure waited, bored.

Judith White arched her back, shaking off slumber.

"It's about time you came back." She yawned. "I was starting to think I wasted my time on you." She rolled to a sitting position, legs dangling to the ground.

Wordlessly Mark dug in his pocket. He produced a small plastic tube, handing it to Judith White.

She accepted the insulated container. It was cold to the touch. Whatever was inside remained frozen.

Judith looked up, suspicious. "What's this?"

Mark Howard smiled. When he told her, he could see the look of delight blossom on her beautiful face.

"You're joking, right? I figured you'd tell me where he lived. That I'd maybe sneak in and get a follicle from his hairbrush next time he goes shopping. At best I thought maybe since you worked with

him you could get me some blood from his last physical.'' A cold edge crept into her voice. ''Is this a
joke? Because if it is, I swear I'll rip your liver out
and make you watch me eat it.''

''It's no joke,'' Mark insisted.

Judith White's grin broadened. Clutching the vial
tight in one paw, she hopped lightly to the ground.

''Just one thing,'' Mark asked. ''Why is Remo so
special?''

''Genes, sonny boy, genes,'' Judith said. ''Why do
pretty human females sniff out big, strong, pretty
lunkheads to make darling little pretty pink human
babies? Because pretty breeds pretty, and strong
breeds strong. I've got the brains but, sad to say, I
didn't come by the brawn naturally. But in all my
years I never met another human like your friend
Remo. Whatever he's got, it's in the genes.'' She held
up the vial like a trophy. ''And now I've got it, too.''

Judith smiled, victorious. In her mind were tantalizing images of a new world. Men and women sold
as livestock. Human children raised in pens like veal.
A single pack of creatures like herself—successors to
humanity—spreading out across the globe. And herself, Dr. Judith White, architect of the new age, ruling
over it all.

It was her dream, her vision. But the instant they
came, the images were swept away.

A voice from behind spoiled her moment of triumph.

''Is that all I am to you? A piece of meat?''

Judith and Mark wheeled.

Remo and Chiun were sliding silently around the

side of the building from the direction of the parking lot.

"Prepare to meet your end, perversion of nature," the Master of Sinanju intoned.

Judith had been shocked by their appearance, but quickly brought herself under control. "Sorry, no can do, Gramps," she said. "I've still got a lot of work ahead of me." With a malevolent grin, she waggled the specimen container.

"How did you two get here?" Mark demanded. "I didn't hear you drive up."

"We've been here right along," Remo said. "We've just been waiting for you to finally show up, junior."

"That's impossible," Mark insisted. "I couldn't hear you or smell you anywhere."

"How like all the lesser beasts," the Master of Sinanju said, his head shaking with pity. "You smell for the scent of man on the footpath to tell whether or not you should fear, yet you do not sense the arrow that from a distance takes your life. We," he said, nodding to himself and Remo, "are the arrow."

Judith nodded, impressed. Clearly she hadn't sensed them either. "What can I say. That's exactly why I wanted your input, brown eyes."

Despite her seeming calm, she was being cautious. With small sidesteps she was circling back.

Remo expected her to dart for the woods, but instead she inched closer to the building. The broken picture window was above her shoulder.

"Sorry to disappoint you, Mittens, but that stuff

you're holding isn't exactly the freshest fish in the tank.''

Judith's face clouded.

"How new is this?" she hissed to Howard.

"I'm not sure the exact date," Mark replied. "But it was taken some time in late 1971."

"This is more than thirty years old?" she demanded, a hint of worry melting the certainty in her voice.

"I feel your pain," Remo said. "I'm good, but even I'm not that good."

He and the Master of Sinanju continued to advance. They came slowly, as if trying not to spook an animal.

Judith White seemed to be doing rapid calculations in her head. Mark Howard stepped in front of her.

"There's no reason this new species and the human race can't live on the same planet peacefully," he said to Remo and Chiun.

"No deal, kid," Remo replied. "The human race wasn't born yesterday, you know. Mankind turns its back for two seconds and it'd wind up on a platter with an apple in its mouth."

"Be reasonable," Mark warned.

"Reason is for man, not beasts," Chiun said.

Remo was surprised Judith White hadn't fled by this point. Her behavior seemed to go against every animal instinct for self-preservation. He could sense her growing fear, as well as see her struggle to overcome it.

He and the Master of Sinanju were nearly upon her when they suddenly sensed another presence nearby. The third heartbeat had just registered to their ears when a new figure sprang into view in the open window.

The tan face relaxed the instant it spied the two Masters of Sinanju.

"Hell and damnation, fellas, am I glad to see you," Bobby Bugget said, breathing relief. "I got scarder 'n all hell the way you left me last night. I been hiding out all day in the—" His face dropped when he saw Judith White. "Uh-oh."

"Get out of here, Bugget," Remo warned.

But even as he spoke the words, he knew something wasn't right. The singer's heart rate was off.

They hadn't detected him as they approached. An average human had no such ability to hide his life signs.

Bugget had been alone in the warehouse. Bugget had disappeared along with Judith White's case of genetic material. Most important, unlike the first time he'd been dosed with the formula, this time Bugget had been *sober.*

Chiun had realized it, too.

"My songsmith!" the Master of Sinanju cried as Bobby Bugget hopped up onto the windowsill.

With a growl, the singer launched himself at Remo.

Bugget alone wouldn't have been too much to worry about. Remo had dealt with these creatures before. But simultaneous with Bugget's attack, Mark Howard lashed out.

He couldn't kill Howard. Not when there was a chance of bringing him home alive. And thanks to Bobby Bugget's fat songwriting yap, he couldn't kill the singer, either. Not without cheesing off the Master of Sinanju.

It was only an instant. A split second of thought, a mere fraction of equivocation.

But that minuscule moment of hesitation was enough.

And in that tiny moment of fractured time, Judith White's darting hand flew forward.

It wasn't intended as a killing blow. Had that been the case—Howard and Bugget be damned—Remo's system would have gone on automatic, dismissing the conflict of mind, killing her instantly. It was a tiny nick. Just on the forearm.

Flecks of glistening red speckled the clapboards of the Lubec Springs office wing.

Blood. Remo's blood.

And then she was gone. With a single leap she was up to the low roof of the one story building. A hand caught the rain gutter and she was swinging up and over.

Bugget was still in the air, flying for Remo. A howl of triumph rose from deep in his throat.

It was a triumph short-lived.

He had scarcely come within two feet of Remo when a flattened palm caught him dead center in the forehead.

It was as if Bugget had been hit by a bus. Bones shattered back into his brain. Eyes widened with the shock of death and the singer belly flopped to the ground.

Remo dropped his hand, whirling for Howard.

But the Master of Sinanju had already swept be-

tween them. The assistant CURE director didn't see
the fluttering hand that darted forward, nor feel the
slender fingers that pressed against his bruised temple.

Mark Howard's eyes rolled back in his head and
he collapsed into the arms of the Master of Sinanju.

"Chiun?" Remo pressed urgently.

"I will see to the Prince," Chiun hissed, nodding
sharply. *"Go."*

Remo didn't need to be told a second time. Flexing
calf muscles, he launched himself to the roof in a
single bound.

Judith White was gone.

"Not this time, sweetheart."

She wouldn't have gone to the road. Wouldn't risk
being seen. The forest meant safety. That eliminated
south and west. Picking east, Remo flew to that edge
of the roof. He spied a set of fresh imprints in the
grass below.

There were no others running through the woods
this day to confuse her tracks. These marks had been
made by White.

In a blur, Remo was back down off the roof and
racing full out for the forest. Broken twigs marked
the route she had taken. Remo dove in after her.

Fear had made Judith White clumsy.

As he raced through the woods, Remo easily spot-
ted the deep heel print that marked the spot where she
had changed direction.

He tore off the same way.

Two miles into the woods, Remo began to smell
the closeness of the Atlantic Ocean. The underbrush
grew thicker, and the ocean sounds louder as he drew

to the edge of the forest. When he broke through a patch of wind-whipped brush a mile later, he found himself standing at the edge of the world.

He was on a bluff high above the Atlantic. A blanket of drab clouds pressed down to the whitecapped waves.

Craggy black rock stabbed off in either direction along the rough shore. Perched at the farthermost point of the jagged finger of rock stood a lone figure.

Judith White's face registered no surprise when Remo emerged from the woods. Brown eyes trailed him as he stepped across the thin strip of tousled-hair grass that separated forest from rock.

"We've got to stop meeting like this," she called over the roar of the ocean.

Despite her seeming calm, he could hear the nervous thump-thump-thump of her beating heart.

"That's about to be arranged."

Remo was at the base of the outcropping. Although he was still far below her on the angled basalt, Judith took a cautious half step back.

A hundred feet below, the crashing waves of the Atlantic attacked the shore.

"It's kind of fitting that it would end this way," she called down. "For your species, I mean. Did you know that life here on Earth began in the sea? A couple of spontaneous aggregations of dissolved organic molecules that were born from inorganic chemical reactions. Three and a half billion years later, here we both are."

"Not for much longer," Remo commented, eyes dead. "I like the new arm, by the way." He noted the plastic container clutched in her regrown arm. As if protecting something even more valuable, her other hand was clenched tight, fingernails biting deep into the palm.

"Starfish DNA," she explained. "I'm from a species that likes to plan ahead. I just wanted to thank you for your contribution, Poppa. None of the other men I've ever met were worthy to become father of the new Earth. But between your genes and mine, look out, world."

Remo's voice was cold. "Not gonna happen," he vowed.

There was a faint smile at the corners of Judith White's perfect red lips as she held up the specimen container.

"Aw, darlin'" she purred. "Thanks to your buddy back there, it's already a done deal. Your boys and I will see you in a few years. Until then, I wouldn't get too comfortable around this planet. Toodles, brown eyes."

With that, she turned and jumped.

The air swallowed her whole.

"Dammit," Remo snapped. He bounded to the edge of the cliff.

Judith White had already slipped beneath the black waves that pounded in between the craggy rock. Though he strained to see a body, she didn't resurface.

It was too great a drop. She shouldn't have survived. But he remembered all too well her spectacular fall from a burning building last time they had met.

One arm missing, bleeding from the shoulder, building collapsing.

She had survived that time. Not again.

Remo kicked off his loafers. Bare toes curled around the edge of the rock promontory. Without a thought of the dizzying height, Remo launched himself out into open air.

In Sinanju it was called the Flying Wall. His forward momentum carried him out over the churning ocean. He soared parallel to the water's surface for fifty feet before allowing gravity to take hold. He descended in a broad arc, his body capturing rogue air pockets to lighten his landing. When he finally brushed the choppy waves, he was facing back toward shore.

His body skimmed the surface for about twenty feet before he allowed the sea to wash in over him. He disappeared near the spot where Judith White had vanished, not a single foamy bubble in his wake.

Below the ocean surface, the cold water of late spring clenched Remo's body like a fist of ice. He willed heat to his extremities as he knifed through the murky waves.

Eyes oblivious to the sting of salt and cold, he scanned the area near the shore. Judith White's body wasn't visible amid the slimy slabs of underwater rock.

The surging sea should have thrown her back to shore, crushing her against stone. It would have done so to Remo, but his arms and legs mimicked the waving skirt of a jellyfish, holding him in place. As his limbs danced in deceptively gentle movements, impossible for even the ocean to overcome, Remo willed the very core of his body still.

He stretched out his senses. The churning water around him became a conductor, carrying sounds and sensations of movement to his finely tuned body.

Even though summer had not yet warmed the waves, the dark world in which he was an alien visitor teemed with life. He felt many living organisms in the sea around him. All were small.

Except one.

About one hundred yards out, the creature that was big enough to be Judith White swam away from shore.

Remo's gentle resistance to the water ceased. He knifed back into the waves, pulling himself away from shore with sharp, powerful strokes.

The cold grew worse the farther he went from land. The creature he was following was leading him deeper and deeper out to sea.

He couldn't allow her to escape. Not this time.

Powerful kicks propelled him farther on. He shot through the water like a fired torpedo.

One hundred and fifty yards out, Remo got his first cloudy glimpse of her. She was knifing through the water, faster than humanly possible.

A few sharp kicks and he was on her.

There was no fighting, no finesse. A crushing blow collapsed the back of her skull.

The plastic container wasn't in her hand. She had to have dropped it when she jumped from the cliff.

Her fingers were open. Remo noted that they seemed a bit too long. More genetic tampering, no doubt. Although the skin didn't look quite right. This arm was younger than the rest of the body. He had noticed back on the bluff that the skin texture didn't quite match up with the other arm. But here, underwater, both arms seemed to match perfectly.

He felt a sudden sinking in his stomach.

Kicking in the waves, he flipped the body over. Long hair flowed in front of the face. When he pulled it back he found that he was staring into the dead eyes of Elizabeth Tiflis.

He released the body as if it were electrically charged. The current dragged it slowly away.

Remo stopped dead. This time when he extended his senses, he felt nothing except schools of small fish. Judith White was gone.

A single bubble of frustration escaped his thin lips into the cold gray ocean.

Turning his back on the empty sea, Remo began the long swim back to shore.

36

When Remo emerged from the woods beside the Lubec Springs bottling plant, the Master of Sinanju was waiting in the front seat of Mark Howard's stolen car. The assistant CURE director lay unconscious on the back seat.

On his way back through the forest from the ocean, Remo had raised his body temperature to dry his clothes. The last of the steam was whirling wisps as he slid in beside Chiun.

The old Korean had salvaged Smith's automatic from the Lubec Springs offices. The gun was on the floor at his sandaled feet. Remo glanced at the weapon as he slammed the car door shut. He said not a word.

Seeing the hard cast of his pupil's face, the Master of Sinanju's own expression darkened.

"The beast has escaped," he said.

"Nine lives," Remo said tightly. "You said it yourself. By my calculations she's got seven more left. Smith better have good news on that batch of stuff he's testing."

He started the car.

As they pulled away from the building, Remo

glanced back to the building that housed the offices. He thought of the tiny flecks on the clapboard walls around the back.

Chiun saw his pupil glance down at the wound on his forearm. He noted the look of understanding that seemed to settle on Remo's face as they drove across the parking lot and out onto the wooded road.

Remo sensed his teacher watching him.

"I get it, Little Father," he said without turning.

And it was clear by the cast of his face that this time he truly understood. The old man's lips thinned in quiet relief.

"Be grateful it is only a scratch," the Master of Sinanju said simply, returning his gaze to the road. "Some lessons come at a much higher cost."

Remo nodded. "I guess becoming Reigning Master does give you a bit of a swelled head."

"Perish the thought," Chiun said, aghast. "Your features are already swollen to comedic proportions as it is. With that nose and those ears if your head got any bigger you would have to push it around in a wagon."

In the back seat, Mark Howard purred. Remo shot the assistant CURE director a glance in the rearview mirror.

Although sound asleep, there was a curl of a smile on Howard's lips. As if he were dreaming of happier days.

It was the last peaceful moment Howard was likely to have for some time. The days to come as his own genetic code reemerged would be a nightmare.

A further gift from Judith White.

"You think the kid will pull through?" Remo asked.

Chiun nodded. "In that, as well, Howard is like Smith. Both are stubborn."

Remo thought of Mark Howard and Harold Smith. He had never been a big fan of either, but at the moment the younger man was winning Remo's personal popularity contest.

"Good," he muttered.

Grip tight on the steering wheel, he steered a steady path through the deep forest. Back toward civilization.

37

The San Diego Police Department captain was grateful when the FBI showed up unexpectedly at Genetic Futures, Inc. After all, he hadn't a clue how to handle this bizarre case.

"Employees found the place a shambles when they came in this morning," the detective explained to the two FBI men as they walked along the hall. There were police everywhere. "A lot of equipment's been stolen. They'll be inventorying later. But that's the least of the problems."

The window beside them looked out over an enclosed courtyard. On the well-tended grounds, men and women jumped and cavorted happily. Two bounced up and down on an overturned bench. Some screeched angrily at others, baring gums and pounding their chests. A few swung from trees.

One woman had defecated in her hand. Standing under a tree, she cupped the waste in one hand while waving a fist at the leaves and shouting "ahn-ahn" over and over.

"We tried to talk to them when we first got here, but they're way too far gone. They threw sticks and dirt at us. We finally shut off all the doors and sealed them out there. It's like they're not even human any-more."

The older FBI agent was probably some sort of consultant. He was too old to be an active agent. As they observed the strange behavior of the men and women who had, until the previous day, been the most brilliant minds of Genetic Futures, Inc., the older man offered a troubled nod.

"Whatever they were working on is lost."

The younger one said nothing.

"According to the rest of the staff, the labs had shifts on around the clock waiting for something," the detective said. "It got delivered the other night, I guess, 'cause that's when they kicked into high gear. But just what, the higher-ups don't know. The records seem to be lost, along with the stolen computers. The geneticist in charge might have been able to tell us, but..."

The detective led them from the window. They walked a little farther down the hall.

"Only one body," he said as they walked. "But it's a big mess, so prepare yourselves."

They came to an open door.

Inside the small office, one of the scientists had been butchered like a cow. His mauled body lay sprawled across his desk. The silver name tag on his blood-soaked lab coat identified the deceased as Dr. Emil Kowalski. For some reason a bale of fresh-cut hay stood upright in the corner near a file cabinet.

"So what do you think?" the detective said wor-riedly. "Maybe we got an epidemic on our hands. You think something dangerous got loose?"

The young FBI man didn't say a word. He turned away from the office, heading back down the hall. The older man followed close behind him, deep in thought.

"Wait," the cop said. "What do we do about the ones outside?"

"Fill a paddy wagon with bananas and drive them to the monkey house," called back the FBI agent, who in the end wasn't really quite as helpful as the SDPD captain had originally hoped.

38

Mark Howard switched on the light in his small office in Folcroft's administrative wing.

It was his first day back in three weeks.

After Remo had brought him back from Maine, Mark had spent nearly two weeks in the special security corridor in the basement. The effects of Judith White's genetic tampering had worn off near the twelve-day mark. Then came the chills, sweats, vomiting. And the nightmares.

Once he had regained enough strength and was able to keep down solid foods, he'd been released.

Mark ordinarily came to work earlier than nine o'clock. But Dr. Smith had insisted that he take it easy at first. Half days only for the next few days.

He still felt weak. Thanks to heavy sedatives and an intravenous diet, Mark had lost sixteen pounds in the past twenty-two days. He had always been thin, with a broad face. But his face had now lost its fleshiness. A strong jaw and angular cheekbones had emerged from the lost layer of fat.

Setting his briefcase to the floor, he took his seat at his desk. The chair felt strange. As did the desk, the office, Folcroft. All of it. Everything felt wrong.

He didn't turn on his computer. He just sat in his chair. Staring.

When he heard the sound of a clearing throat nearby, Mark didn't know how long he had been sitting there. He looked to the door.

Harold Smith stood in the doorway. There was a hint of concern on his face.

"How are you feeling, Mark?" the CURE director asked.

"Fine," Mark said. "Good morning, Dr. Smith. I was going to check in with you in a little— I'm fine."

Smith nodded. "I made an appointment for you this afternoon with one of our staff physicians. Just a routine physical. They'll be taking some blood just to be sure. According to your last tests, everything is normal."

At another time in his life Mark might have laughed at Smith's ludicrous use of the word *normal*. But the world had become so strange and wrong. He merely nodded.

"How's Mrs. Mikulka doing?" Mark asked.

"Very well," Smith said. "Given her age and physical condition, her recovery has been slower than yours. As you might know, she has a son who lives with her who is looking after her. I spoke with him yesterday, and he told me she hopes to return to work next week. Until then I've rotated in a woman, Kathleen Purvish, from the regular sanitarium staff to fill in. She used to work as my secretary years ago and has sometimes filled in during Mrs. Mikulka's vacations, so things should run smoothly."

"Good," Mark Howard said. "That's all…good."

Smith hesitated. For an awkward moment, he seemed to be wrestling with some inner dilemma. He finally seemed to reach a decision.

"Mark, what was done to you was horrific," he said. "But it was not your fault. None of it."

He pursed his lips thoughtfully. Checking the hallway, the CURE director shut the door with a quiet click.

He spoke without preamble and without inflection.

"Back during the Second World War, I was captured by German forces on the island of Usedom," Smith began. "There was a Gestapo officer there, one Josef Menk. I'm not sure why he tortured me. I think he was insane, but then so many were in those days. The war was coming to an end. There wasn't much information that any one OSS agent could have had to turn the tide. Yet, for days—day after day—he had his man beat me, cut me, whip me. They hung me from a rafter. No food, no water. It was unspeakably brutal. To this day when the weather changes I feel the results of what they did to me in my joints and bones. Except for my superiors in the OSS, I never told anyone this before. Not my wife, not Remo or Chiun. It is of a personal nature and not something that I feel is appropriate to share."

Smith took a deep breath before continuing.

"Years later, an enemy here in America learned of CURE. I was kidnapped and tortured then, as well. I'll spare you the details, but suffice it to say I was older then and felt the effects far more severely."

Before Smith had begun to speak, Mark Howard had gone back to staring blankly at the wall. But now the older man could see that he had drawn his young assistant out.

"I have heard of others who revolve their lives around the worst things that have ever happened to them. I don't see the use. These things that happened to me were merely days out of my life—they were not my whole life. For the most part I put those events out of my mind. But I am glad at other times to have those memories. You should be, too. Don't forget what happened to you, Mark. Use it. Use it when you need focus or in those moments of doubt. Remember what was done to you. Remember the evil that it represents and use it to understand why it is we do what we do."

Mark absorbed the CURE director's words. Slowly his head began to nod. When he looked up, his eyes were moist.

"Thanks, Dr. Smith." His voice was soft.

Smith gave a crisp nod. "There is one other thing," he said. He reached into his pocket.

When his hand reappeared, he was holding a small, flat tin case. It was smaller around than a half dollar and less than a quarter-inch thick. He handed the container to Mark.

"I told you of Conrad MacCleary, my old associate who died not long after Remo came aboard CURE," Smith said. "After his death, his personal effects were sent here. He had no family and this was his last known address. He had a cover as a former Folcroft patient. There are only a few small items in a strongbox in the records room downstairs. That was included in the items returned by the hospital."

Mark had examined the container for a moment, rolling it over in his palm. It had a tiny hasp on one side. When he popped it, it opened like a locket. Inside was a small white object. When he saw it, Mark looked up at Smith.

The CURE director's face was unreadable. "Because of the nature of his injuries, MacCleary was not able to use it. Keep it with you at all times."

Smith checked his watch.

"I have work to do," the CURE director said. "Don't forget your appointment this afternoon."

With that, Smith left the office.

Alone, Mark Howard looked back at the pill that sat inside the small container. It was identical to the pill Harold Smith carried in his vest pocket. Unlike Smith's, the skull-and-crossbones symbol was not worn with age.

With a click, Mark closed the locket and slipped it in his pocket. For some reason it gave him strange comfort.

Mark found the recessed switch that turned on his computer. When the monitor and keyboard rose up from their hiding spot beneath the desk's smooth surface, he was grateful for the distraction.

With grim resolve, the assistant CURE director threw himself back into his work.

39

"You haven't been able to find her?" Remo asked.

He was on the kitchen phone of his Connecticut town house. Beyond the breakfast bar, the patio doors off the small dining room were open wide. Summer had finally arrived. The Master of Sinanju sat in the small garden outside, parchment face turned up to the warming rays of the midmorning sun.

"No," Smith's voice replied. "She is either lying low or has changed her pattern of behavior. In either case she has slipped back below our radar. But now that we know she is out there, I have set the mainframes on a continuous search using the data Mark assembled. It is only a matter of time before she reveals herself."

"I hope you're right, Smitty. Any luck with the people from that lab she was using?"

"Unfortunately, no," Smith replied somberly. "She did not use the temporary version of the formula on the scientists of Genetic Futures. They are being cared for, but they are human in physical appearance only. They are incapable of speech and will not change back. We can safely assume that she was covering her tracks. I assume, as well, that the simian

DNA was her sick attempt at humor. Reversing the human evolutionary course, as it were.''

"Yeah, she was a regular Ruth Buzzi," Remo said. "Whatever she was up to, at least we know she didn't get what she was after from me.''

Smith had gotten the test results on the second liquid-nitrogen sample the day after Remo and Chiun had returned from Maine. The specimens had been dead. The same was true of the first vial, which had turned up in a search of the San Diego lab.

"That is good news only to a degree, Remo," Smith cautioned. "The fact that she wishes to procreate will likely not change because of her failure with you. She will no doubt move on to another candidate.''

"Just so long as it's not me," Remo said. "She can go back to Maine. She probably still has a hundred of those things stomping around in the woods up there.''

"Not any longer. Most have turned up, bedraggled and malnourished. The rest have probably died by now. You frightened them away from inhabited areas, so the death toll in the ensuing weeks was low. And it seems the majority survived the ordeal without any lasting physical harm.''

"Shh." Remo held the phone out. "Hear that, Smitty?" he said in a stage whisper. "That's the sound of a hundred shrinks revving up their notebooks and pens.''

He hung up the phone.

Remo went out to the patio to where the Master of Sinanju sat cross-legged on the flagstones. The old

Korean still wore his robes of black, gathered up around his ankles.

"I've been thinking, Little Father," Remo announced.

"If I give you a shiny nickel, will you think with your mouth closed?" the Master of Sinanju replied.

His eyes were closed as he faced the sun.

"No, listen," Remo said. "That prophecy you told me the first time we met these tiger things. 'Even Shiva must walk with care when he passes the jungle where lurk other night tigers.' I'm not sure it meant what we thought it meant."

At this did Chiun open his eyes. "Yes?" he asked.

"We were thinking physical harm. Like I'd get killed or something. But maybe I had to walk with care for another reason. Maybe when the Great Wang uttered that prophecy he meant I should look out for horny tigresses."

"Perhaps," Chiun said. It was evident by his tone that he had been considering the same possibility.

"Well, at least it's over now. We passed through the jungle where they lurked and came out more or less intact."

Remo sank cross-legged to the ground. He looked at the spot on his bare forearm nicked by Judith White's fingernail.

It had been such a tiny thing. It had long since healed, leaving no trace of a scar.

"You were right, Little Father," he said all at once.

"Of course," Chiun replied. "What about?"

"About my invulnerability. You kept thinking it was just because of my becoming Reigning Master, but it wasn't only that. When we were in Sinanju a few months back, I had that Shiva moment. It was like...I don't know. I was *connected*. To the past, present and future. Then I became Reigning Master and everything came together. It sort of made me feel like I didn't really have anything to worry about. I guess I was stupid.''

"Do not guess," the Master of Sinanju said, "for I am here to tell you when you are. You were."

"On the other hand, if I hadn't been so worried about how pissed you'd get at me for killing Bugget, I wouldn't have hesitated at all," Remo pointed out.

"Excuses, excuses," Chiun said. "And do not think I forgive you for eliminating the troubadour who was to compose the hymn of glorious me for the beauteous Wylander. Of course, you could make some of it up to me if you were to wear the appropriate garments of celebration, sparing me from traipsing around in these rags for the next year of my life. Which, I might add, at my age could be my last."

"Guilt me no guilt, Little Father. I am not wearing black pajamas for six months. Smitty would have a fit. Assuming, that is, we haven't quit before then," he muttered.

Chiun raised an eyebrow. "Why would we do that?"

"I'm not going to easily forget what he did to me, Chiun," Remo warned. "He froze my wigglies for thirty years. If he'd just kept the temperature a few degrees colder, maybe he'd have given Judith White exactly what she wanted."

The old Korean waved a bony hand, erasing

Remo's complaints from the air. "Whatever wrongs you think Smith committed against you in those days, they predate your becoming Sinanju and therefore have no bearing on Sinanju contracts. However, if this is a grievance you feel you must pursue, you may bring it up at our next contract negotiations."

Remo shook his head. "Ah, it's probably just as well. One year is a long way off. I'll be over all this by then."

"Actually, our current contract is slightly longer than the standard one year."

Remo noted his teacher's sly tone.

"How much longer?" he asked, suddenly worried.

Chiun stroked his thread of beard thoughtfully. "Five years," he admitted. "Give or take."

"You signed on with Smith for five more years?"

"It was during our time in Sinanju. My last official act as Reigning Master was to negotiate our contract."

"Five freaking years?" Remo demanded.

"You said yourself in one year you would forget what Smith had done. Knowing your wandering mind, one month would probably suffice. Think of how much more you will have forgotten it in five years." He held up a hand, halting Remo's protests. "Best of all, our current contract gives us our loophole."

"I keep telling you there is no loophole," Remo groused. "Sinanju tradition forbids a Master from serving his Emperor's successor. According to that rule, we can't work for Howard if Smith goes belly up. End of story."

"*I* may not work for his successor," Chiun said craftily. "You, on the other hand, are another story. I signed a long-term contract with Smith as my final official act as Reigning Master. Until the moment you assumed Reigning Masterhood, you were technically my apprentice. That is how you are referred to in our current contract, which remains in force as long as I live. Tradition says nothing about a Master's successor signing an all-new contract with the successor of his Master's Emperor. When Smith passes, you may sign with Howard without having defied tradition."

Remo opened his mouth to argue, but stopped.

He started again, but again he said nothing.

Finally he tipped his head, nodding. "Dammit, you old shyster, you found a loophole." Remo sighed loudly. "Still, I don't like to be nailed down for that long. But it's been six months since we were in Sinanju, so that leaves just over four years. I guess I can put up with four more years."

"Bearing in mind that there are option years built into the contract," Chiun warned.

"Sweet mother of mercy," Remo said.

"But when the option runs out, you will get to negotiate the next contract all by yourself."

"Swell. I'm really looking forward to the year 3000," Remo said.

"Of course, as Reigning Master Emeritus, I may intervene in the event that you plan to sign something stupid," Chiun warned.

Remo wanted to laugh. Instead, he sat in silence, staring at his hands. Chiun sensed the disharmony in his pupil.

"What is wrong, my son?" the old man asked.

"I don't know," Remo said. "It's kind of odd. It's like for the moment we're right back to where we always are, with contracts and arguing and you telling me I'm stupid. But things are going to be different now. I'm Reigning Master, you've got an eye on that retirement cave back in Sinanju, Smitty's got that kid helping him out. Everything's changing. I kind of don't want it to end."

At this, a smile cracked the aged face of the Reigning Master of Sinanju Emeritus.

"End?" Chiun scoffed. "You are worried about endings? So many years have we been together, so many things have we seen. You have had so many days of running hither and yon for your Emperor, so many nights of adventure that you have become jaded, Remo Williams. You think because you have seen much that you have seen *everything?* You think this is the end? I tell you this. It is only the beginning."

Remo wasn't convinced. "I guess you're right, Little Father," he said with an uncertain shrug.

"Of course I am," the Master of Sinanju insisted. Leaning forward, he smiled knowingly. "Stay tuned."

And with a sadness touched with hope, Remo turned his face to the morning sun.

EPILOGUE

Dr. Jésus Avalos of the Los Angeles Women's Crisis Health Center would have known something was different about this patient even without reading her chart.

The woman lying on the table in the examining room didn't seem like the usual WCHC patient. Sadly, most who came through the front doors of the free clinic had not achieved much in life, financially or in the way of education. But this particular patient seemed intelligent and articulate. According to the form she'd filled out in the waiting room, she didn't smoke, drink or do drugs and—from what Dr. Avalos could tell—she had no visible tattoos.

That last one was the biggest miracle these days. As he applied the gel to her exposed belly, he tried to remember his last patient who hadn't risked HIV and hepatitis by taking a dozen trips to the tattoo parlor. In his less politically correct moments, he wondered how it was that people who relied on federal handouts for their daily bread could afford to get permanent ink disfigurements on their ankles and asses. Maybe tattoo parlors had started taking food stamps.

"You're not from the neighborhood," Dr. Avalos said as rolled the sonogram to the side of the table.

"No," the woman replied.

Her voice was deep, rolling and soft all at once. There was something very feminine and just a little dangerous about her. Dr. Avalos felt drawn to her for some reason.

He tried to keep his mind on work.

"What brings you to us?" he asked. "Besides the obvious, of course."

"I'm leaving the country tomorrow and I want to make sure it's safe to fly."

Dr. Avalos nodded understanding. He pressed the probe to her belly and turned his attention to the monitor.

"Oh, my," he said after a moment. "This wasn't natural."

She didn't say a word. Just smiled a knowing smile.

Dr. Avalos turned his attention away from the monitor. He wore a deeply concerned expression.

"Is your partner here today?" he asked. These days it wasn't safe to assume a husband or even a gender. "There are some important issues you should consider."

"No," she said. "Luckily, he thinks he gave me a cupful of duds, so he won't come snooping around. Most humans have no idea the miracles you can achieve with just a few drops of frozen blood and skin from under a fingernail." Again the knowing smile.

Dr. Avalos wasn't sure what she meant. Nor did he

know why he seemed drawn to this woman. There was something about her. Like perfume, but without odor.

The doctor cleared his throat. "I'll be blunt, even though you've probably heard this before. It would be safer to reduce the number of babies. Two or three would be better to insure healthy births."

His patient looked at him coldly. "No," she said.

He directed her attention to the sonogram. "There's at least six heartbeats." With a pen he pointed to a tiny smudge on the monitor. "Maybe seven. I think that one up there might be another one. Multiple births are risky."

"They'll all be fine," she assured him. "I was designed to carry more than one at a time." She took his hand. "I'm not like other women."

He knew he should pull away. This wasn't proper. He could lose his job, his license. But the odor that couldn't be smelled filled his head with indecent thoughts. There was something beguiling about this woman. Almost as if pregnancy were releasing pheromones he was finding impossible to resist. Of course that couldn't be the case.

The woman stroked his hand.

"We can discuss it over dinner tonight," she said.

Dr. Avalos glanced at the examining-room door, making certain it was closed.

"I'm not sure it would be appropriate to have dinner with a clinic patient," he whispered. In his head he was already making the reservations.

His patient smiled.

"I didn't say *you'd* be eating," purred Judith White.

James Axler
Outlanders®

TALON
AND FANG

Kane finds himself thrown twenty-five years into a parallel future, a world where the mysterious Imperator has seemingly restored civilization to America. In this alternate reality, only Kane and Grant have survived, and the spilled blood has left them estranged. Yet Kane is certain that somewhere in time lies a different path to tomorrow's reality—and his obsession may give humanity their last chance to battle past and future as a sinister madman controls the secret heart of the world.

In the Outlands, the shocking truth is humanity's last hope.

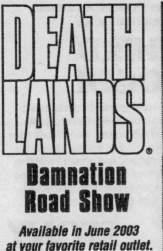